E.F Benson

The Relentless City

E.F Benson

The Relentless City

1st Edition | ISBN: 978-3-75234-130-0

Place of Publication: Frankfurt am Main, Germany

Year of Publication: 2020

Outlook Verlag GmbH, Germany.

Reproduction of the original.

The Relentless City

By

E. F. Benson

CHAPTER I

The big pink and white dining-room at the Carlton was full to suffocation of people, mixed odours of dinner, the blare of the band just outside, and a babel of voices. In the hall theatre-goers were having their coffee and cigarettes after dinner, while others were still waiting, their patience fortified by bitters, for their parties to assemble. The day had been very hot, and, as is the manner of days in London when June is coming to an end, the hours for most people here assembled had been pretty fully occupied, but with a courage worthy of the cause they seemed to behave as if nothing of a fatiguing nature had occurred since breakfast. The band played loud because it would otherwise have been inaudible above the din of conversation, and people talked loud because otherwise nobody could have heard what anybody else said. To-night everybody had a good deal to say, for a case of the kind that always attracts a good deal of attention had just been given that lengthy and head-lined publicity which is always considered in England to be inseparable from the true and indifferent administration of justice, and the vultures of London life found the banquet extremely to their taste. So they ate their dinner with a sense of special gaiety, pecked ravenously at the aforesaid affair, and all talked loudly together. But nobody talked so loud as Mrs. Lewis S. Palmer.

It was said of her, indeed, that, staying for a week-end not long ago with some friend in the country, rain had been expected because one day after lunch a peacock was heard screaming so loud, but investigation showed that it was only Mrs. Palmer, at a considerable distance away on the terrace, laughing. Like the peacock, it is true, she had been making *la pluie et le beau temps* in London this year, so the mistake was accountable. At present, she was entertaining two young men at an ante-opera dinner. A casual observer might have had the impression that she was clothed lightly but exclusively in diamonds. She talked, not fast, but without pause. She was in fact what may be called a long-distance talker: in an hour she would get through much more than most people.

'Yes, London is just too lovely,' she was saying; 'and how I shall tear myself away on Monday is more than I can imagine. I shall cry my eyes out all the way to Liverpool. Mr. Brancepeth, you naughty man, you were thinking to yourself that you would pick them up and carry them home with you to remind you of me. I should advise you not to say so, or I shall get Lord Keynes to call you out. I always tell everyone that he takes as much care of me as if he were my father. Yes, Lord Keynes, you are what I call faithful. I say to everyone, Lord Keynes is *the* most faithful friend I ever had. Don't you think you are faithful, now? Well, as I was saying when Mr. Brancepeth interrupted me with his wicked inquiries, I shall cry my eyes out. Indeed, if it wasn't that Lord Keynes had faithfully promised to come over in the fall, I think I should get a divorce from Lewis S. and remain here right along.'

'On what grounds?' asked Bertie Keynes.

'Why, on the grounds of his incompatibility of residence. Just now I feel as if the sight of Fifth Avenue would make me feel so homesick for London that I guess I should rupture something. When I am homesick I feel just like that, and Lewis S. he notices it at once, and sends to Tiffany's for the most expensive diamond they've got. That helps some, because a new diamond is one of the solemnest things I know. It just sits there and winks at me, and I just sit there and wink at it. We know a thing or two, a big diamond and I. But I conjecture it will have to be a big one to make me feel better this time, for just now London seems to me the only compatible residence. I guess I'll make Lewis buy it.'

Mrs. Palmer's tact had been one of the standing dishes of the season, and it appeared that there was plenty of it still in stock. It was distributed by her with strict impartiality to anyone present, and had a firm flavour.

Bertie Keynes laughed, and drew from his pocket a small printed card.

'I don't know if you have seen this,' he said. '"Admit bearer to see the world. Signed, Lewis S. Palmer."' And he handed it to her.

Mrs. Palmer opened her mouth very wide, and screamed so loud that for a radius of three tables round all conversation ceased for a moment. The scream began on about the note selected by express trains when they dash at full speed through a station, rose an octave or two with an upward swoop like a steam siron, came slowly down in a chromatic scale, broken off for a moment as she made a hissing intake of her breath, and repeated itself. This year it had

3

been one of the recognised cries of London.'

'Why, if that isn't the cutest thing in the world,' she screamed. 'I never saw anything so cunning. Why, I never! Admit bearer to see the world! How can I get one for Lewis? It would just tickle him to death.'

'Pray take this,' said Bertie. 'I brought it on purpose for you.'

'Well, if that isn't too nice of you! I shall just hand that to Lewis without a word the moment I set eyes on him. I guess that'll make him want to buy the world in earnest. Why, he'll go crazy about buying it now that it has been suggested. Well, I'm sure, Lord Keynes, it's just too nice of you to give me that. I shall laugh myself sick over it. I always tell everyone that you are the kindest man I ever saw. Gracious, it's half after nine! We must go at once. I'll be down with you in a moment, but I must give this to my maid to be packed in my jewel-case.'

Mrs. Palmer looked at it again as she rose, gave another shrill scream, and vanished, leaving her two guests alone.

Charlie Brancepeth moved his chair a little sideways to the table as he sat down again, crossed his legs, and took a cigarette from his case.

'If you had asked her a hundred pounds for it, she would have given it you, Bertie,' he remarked.

Bertie Keynes raised his eyebrows a shade.

'A hundred pounds is always welcome, Charlie,' he said, without a shadow or hint of comment in his voice. In fact, the neutrality of his tone was too marked to be in the least degree natural.

Charlie did not reply for a moment, but blew thoughtfully on the lighted end of his cigarette.

'Why this sudden—this sudden suppression of the mercantile spirit?' he asked.

Bertie laughed.

'Don't trouble to be more offensive than is necessary to your reasonable comfort,' he remarked with some finish.

'I am not; I should have been in considerable pain if I hadn't said that. But why this suppression?'

Bertie delayed answering long enough to upset the salt with his elbow, and look reproachfully at the waiter for having done so.

'There isn't any suppression,' he said at length. 'The mercantile spirit is going strong. Stronger than ever. Damn!'

'Is it the salt you asked a blessing on?' said Charlie.

'No; the non-suppression.'

'Then you really are going to America in the autumn?' asked he. 'I beg its pardon, the fall.'

'Yes. Fall is just as good a word as autumn, by the way.'

'Oh, quite. Over there they think it better, and they have quite as good a right to judge as we. If they called it the pump-handle it wouldn't make any difference.'

'Not the slightest. Yes, I am going.'

Charlie smiled.

'Oh, I suddenly understand about the mercantile spirit,' he said. 'It was stupid of me not to have guessed at once.'

'It was rather. Charlie, I should like to talk to you about it. The governor has been making some uncommonly sensible remarks to me on the subject.'

'He would. Your father has an immense quantity of dry common-sense. Yes, come round after the opera, and we'll talk it out lengthways. Here's Mrs. Palmer. I hope Pagani will sing extremely loud to-night, otherwise we shan't hear a note.'

Two electric broughams were waiting at the Pall Mall entrance as Mrs. Palmer rustled out between rows of liveried men, whose sole office appeared to be to look reverential as she passed, as if to have just seen her was the Mecca of their aspirations. Then, after a momentary hesitation between the two young men, Bertie followed her dazzling opera-cloak into the first brougham, and, amid loud and voluble regrets on her part that there was not room for three, and the exaction of a solemn promise that Charlie would not quarrel with his friend for having monopolized her, they started. Charlie gave a little sigh, whether of disappointment or not is debatable, and followed them alone in the second brougham.

The motor went swiftly and noiselessly up Haymarket, and into the roaring whirlpool of the Circus. It was a fine warm evening, and over pavement and roadway the season of the streets, which lasts not for a few months only, after the manner of the enfeebled upper class, but all the year round, was in full swing. Hansom cabs, newsboys shouting the latest details of all the dirty linen which had been washed that week, omnibuses nodding ten feet high above the road, and life-guardsmen nodding six, women plain and coloured, men in dress-clothes hurrying late to the theatres, shabby skulkers in shadow, obscure persons of prey, glittering glass signs about the music-halls, flower-sellers round the fountain, swinging-doors of restaurants swallowing in and vomiting out all sorts and conditions of men, winking sky—signs, policemen controlling the traffic—all contributed their essential but infinitesimal quota to the huge hodge-podge of life, bent as the great majority of life always is on the seizure of the present vivid moment, the only thing which is certainly existent. For the past is already to everyone but of the texture of a dream; the future is a dream also, but lying in impenetrable shadow. But the moment is real.

To Charlie it appeared to-night that the festival of the pavements was certainly gayer than the festival of the Carlton. His own world schemed more, it might be, and substituted innuendo for a bolder and more direct manner of talk, but it really had less capacity for enjoyment. Ten weeks of London broke its wind somewhat, and it retired into the country to graze, to digest, to recoup. But here on the pavements a lustier spirit reigned, the spirit of the people, pressing upwards and upwards like buried bulbs striving towards the light through the good, moist earth, whereas, to continue the metaphor that was in his mind, the folk among whom he moved, whose doings he continually observed with an absorbed but kindly cynicism, were like plants tended in a greenhouse, and potted out when the weather became assured.

And what if the whole of England was becoming every year more like a tended greenhouse plant, compared to the blind thrust of forces from the earth in other countries? For all the old landmarks, as the great wheel of human life whirled down the road of the centuries, seemed to be passing out of sight; the world was racing westwards, where America sat high on the seas, grown like some portentous mushroom in a single night. There, at the present moment, the inexorable, relentless logic of nature was working out its everlasting proposition that the one force in the material world was wealth. England had had her turn, even as Rome had had her turn, and even as the hordes of barbarians had swept over the countries that had been hers till they reached and took the capital itself, even so—well, had he not himself dined with Mrs. Palmer that evening? It was not in his nature to hate anything, so it cannot be said that he hated her screaming, her insensate conversation, her lack of all that is summed up in the words breeding and culture, but he saw these loud defects, and knew of their existence. On the other hand, he saw and knew also of her intense good-nature, her true kindliness of heart, and believed in the integrity of her life; so, if it was fair to consider her presence in London typically as of the nature of a barbarian invasion, it must be confessed that England had fallen into the hands of very kindly foes. They did not even actively resent culture, they were simply not aware of it, and cut it when they met. In any case they were irresistible, for the power that moved them was wealth more gigantic than any which heretofore had furthered the arts of war and peace, and that wealth was grasped by men who only yesterday had toiled with their hands in factories and workshops. Like stars reeling upwards from below the horizon, they swarmed into the sky, and looked down, not cruelly, but merely calmly, into the world which they owned.

Of such was Mrs. Palmer's husband; he had been a railway porter, now he was railways and steamships and anything else of which he chose to say 'This is mine.' Occasionally men like these watered the English greenhouse plants, and an heiress propped up the unstable fortunes of some five-hundred-years-old English name. But such gift of refreshment was but a spoonful out of the great wells; also, in a manner of speaking, having thus watered the plants, they picked them.

His motor got caught in a block at the entrance to Leicester Square, and he arrived at the Opera House some few minutes after the others had got there. A commanding white label with Mrs. Lewis S. Palmer's name printed on it was on the door of the omnibus box on the grand tier, and he found her, with her resplendent back firmly turned towards the stage, discoursing in shrill whispers to Bertie Keynes, and sighing more than audibly for the end of the act. It was the last representation for the year of 'Tristan und Isolde,' and the house was crowded. Royalty was there: a galaxy of tiaras sparkled in the boxes, and a galaxy of stars sang together on the stage. For London had suddenly conceived the almost incredible delusion that it was musical, and flocked to the opera with all the fervour of a newly-born passion. It was not, it never had been, and it never would be musical, but this particular form of the game 'Let's pretend' was in fashion, and the syndicate rejoiced. Soon London would get tired of the game, and the syndicate would be sad again.

But the longest act comes to an end at last, and even as the curtain fell, Mrs. Palmer began screaming again. She screamed when she was amused because she was amused, and she screamed when she was bored in order that it might appear that she was not. Just now she was amusing herself very tolerably, for as soon as the lights were up, the world in general flocked into her box, supplementing the very desirable company already assembled there.

'Why, of course I am coming back next year,' she was explaining. 'And if Lewis doesn't come with me, and take Seaton House for me, so as to be able to have more than one person to dinner at a time, I guess I'll have a word or two to say to him which he won't forget; and if you, Mrs. Massington, don't come over to us in the fall with Lord Keynes, I shall cry my eyes out; and if that monster, Mr. Brancepeth, is as impudent again as he was at dinner, saying that he would pick them up and take them home to remind him of me, I'll ask him to leave my box, and call him back the moment afterwards, because I can't help forgiving him.'

There was a laugh at this brilliant effort of imagination, and Mrs. Massington leaned back in her chair towards Charlie, while Mrs. Palmer continued her voluble remarks.

'You are getting quite polished, Charlie,' she said. 'I should not have suspected you of so much gallantry.'

'I hope you never suspect me of anything,' he said.

'Oh, I do—of lots of things. Chiefly of a disapproving attitude. You are always disapproving. Now, you probably disapprove of my going to America.'

'You have not gone yet,' he said.

'No, but I shall. Mrs. Palmer has asked me to stay with them, and I am going. And Bertie is really going too.'

'So he told me to-night.'

'Who suggested it? His father?'

'Yes. As usual, he has shown his immensely good sense.'

Mrs. Massington laughed.

'You are extremely old-fashioned,' she said. 'I wonder at your dining with Mrs. Palmer at all, and coming to her box.'

'I often wonder at it myself,' said he. 'Never mind that. I haven't seen you for an age. What have you been doing with yourself?'

'I haven't been doing anything with myself. It is other people who have been doing all sorts of things with me. I have been taken by the scruff of the neck and dragged—literally dragged—from place to place. All this week there's been the Serington case, you see. I was in the court for three mornings, getting up at unheard-of hours to be there. Really it was very amusing. Topsie in the witness-box was the funniest thing you can possibly imagine. He jumped every time anybody asked him a question. They seem to have had the most extraordinary manage, and the servants appear to have spent their entire time in looking through keyholes. I wonder how the house-work got done at all. Charlie, you don't appear in the least amused.'

He looked at her a moment gravely.

'Am I really so awfully old-fashioned?' he asked.

'Yes, you old darling, I think you are. Are you shocked at my calling you an old darling? It's quite true, you know.'

'Delighted to hear it. But am I old-fashioned, then?'

'Certainly. Antique, out of date, obsolete. Of course, that sort of thing, all the Serington affair, is extremely shocking, and they are done for, quite done for; nobody will ever speak to them again—at least, except abroad. But because it is shocking, I don't see why I should pretend not to be amused at the really ridiculous figure Topsie cut in the witness-box. It would argue a very imperfect sense of humour if I was not amused, and great hypocrisy if I pretended not to be. I was amused, I roared; I was afraid they would turn me out.'

He laughed.

'Somehow, whatever you do, I can't disapprove,' he said; 'though the notion of all Topsie's friends sitting there and looking at him, and talking it over afterwards, makes me feel ill. But you——'

'Dear Charlie, it is too nice of you. But break those rose-coloured spectacles through which you so kindly observe me. It is no use. I have told you before it was no use, and I don't like telling you again.'

'Why?' he asked.

'Oh, that is so like a man, and especially an Englishman. You know why. Because it hurts you.'

'You dislike hurting me? That is something,' said he.

'But that is all,' she said.

The orchestra had taken their places, and a silence began to spread over the theatre as the lights were lowered. Then suddenly he leaned towards her so that he could smell the faint, warm fragrance of her presence.

'You mean that?' he asked.

She nodded her head in reply, and the curtain rose.

CHAPTER II

Mrs. Palmer, when the opera was over, had many voluble good-byes to say to her friends, for she was leaving London next day, and sailing for her native shores in the middle of the week. Consequently, it was some time before the two young men could get off from Covent Garden, but eventually they strolled away together to pick up a hansom rather than wait for one, Charlie

Brancepeth's rooms were in Half Moon Street, and it was thus nearer one than twelve when they got home. He threw himself into a long easy-chair with an air of fatigue, while the other strolled about somewhat aimlessly and nervously, smoking a cigarette, sipping whisky-and-soda, with the indolent carriage of a man who is at home with himself and his surroundings. In person he was of the fair, blue-eyed type of his family, small-featured, and thin, and looking taller, in consequence, than he really was. His eyebrows, darker than his hair, had the line of determination and self-reliance; but one felt somehow that his appearance had less to do with the essential man beneath than with the ancestors from whom he had inherited it. But his aimless, undetermined strolling one felt was more truly his own.

At last he went to the window and threw it open, letting in the great *bourdon* hum of London, coming somewhat muffled through the heavy air. Only the gentlest draught drew into the room from outside, barely stirring the flowers in the window-boxes, but spreading slowly over the room the warm, drowsy scent of them. Then, taking himself by the shoulders, as it were, he sat down.

'Charlie, I am going to America,' he said, 'in order, if possible, to find an extremely wealthy girl who is willing to marry me.'

'So I understood when you said the mercantile spirit was not suppressed. Well, you are frank, anyhow. Will you tell her that? Will you ask how much she expects to have as a dowry?'

'No, it will be unnecessary to tell her anything; she will know. You don't suppose the Americans really think that lots of us go there to find wives because we prefer them to English girls? They know the true state of the case perfectly well. They only don't choose to recognise it, just as one doesn't choose to recognise a man one doesn't want to meet. They look it in the face, and cut it—cut it dead.'

'I dare say you are perfectly right,' said Charlie with marked neutrality.

'I suppose you disapprove; you have a habit of disapproving, as I heard Sybil Massington say to you to-night. By the way, she is going to America, too, she told me.'

Charlie's face remained perfectly expressionless.

'Yes,' he said slowly. 'You might arrange to travel together. Never mind that now, though. You told me your father had some very sensible things to say about mercenary marriages. Do tell me what they were; he is always worth listening to.'

Bertie Keynes hailed this with obvious relief. It was easier to him to put up his father's ideas for his friend, if he chose, to box with, than receive the attack on his own person. He did not care in the least how much Charlie attacked his father's opinions on matrimony; nor, on the other hand, would the Marquis of Bolton care either, because the fact of his never caring for anything was so widely known as to have been abbreviated like a sort of hall-mark into his nick-name of Gallio.

'Yes, the governor talked to me about it yesterday,' he said to the other. 'He was very convincing, I thought. He put it like this: It is impossible for royalty to marry commoners; therefore, when royalty goes a-wooing, it goes a-wooing in its own class. It is equally impossible for me to marry a poor woman, because I can't afford it. Everything is mortgaged up to the hilt, as you probably know, and, indeed, if I don't marry a rich woman, we go smash. Therefore, I must go a-wooing, like royalty, among the class into which alone it is possible for me to marry. I see the force of that reasoning, so I am going to America. See?'

'Gallio might have gone on to say that it appeared that the English aristocracy is the only possible class for extremely rich American girls to marry into,' remarked Charlie.

'Yes, I'll tell him that,' said the other; 'he would be pleased with that. Then he went on to say that every country necessarily sends abroad for barter or exchange what it doesn't want or has too great a supply of. America has more money than it knows what to do with, so it is willing to let some of it come here, while we have just found out that titles are no longer of the slightest value to us. Nobody cares about them now, so we send them for distribution abroad too.'

'Labelled,' said Charlie. 'Ducal coronet so much, countess's coronet much cheaper, baroness's coronet for an annuity merely. You will be a marquis, won't you? Marquises come rather high. Brush up the coronet, Bertie, and put a fancy price on it.'

Charlie rose with some impatience as he spoke, and squirted some soda-water into a glass.

'Doesn't the governor's view seem to you very sensible?' asked the other.

'Yes, very sensible; that is why I find it so damnable. Sense is overrunning us like some horrid weed. Nobody thinks of anything except what will pay. That is what sense means. A sensible, well-balanced view—a sensible, bank-balanced view! That is what it comes to.'

Bertie Keynes whistled gently to himself a minute.

'I don't think I'll tell Gallio that,' he said; 'I don't think he would like that so much.'

Charlie laughed.

'Oh yes, he would; but you needn't tell him, since he knows it already. Well, in soda-water, I drink success to your wooing. Don't make yourself cheap.'

Bertie lit another cigarette from the stump of the one he had been smoking previously.

'If anybody else had said that, I should have been rather annoyed,' he remarked.

'You are annoyed as it is; at least, I meant you to be. It's no use arguing about it, because we really differ, and you cannot argue unless you fundamentally agree, which we do not. I'm in the minority, I know; almost everybody agrees with you. But I am old-fashioned; I have been told so this evening.'

'By——'

'Yes, by Sybil Massington. She, too, agrees with you.'

There was silence for a minute or two.

'It's two years since her husband died, is it not?' asked Bertie.

'Yes, two years and one month. I know what you are thinking about. I asked her—at least, she saw what I meant—again this evening, but I have asked her for the last time. I suppose it is that—my feeling for her—that to-night makes me think what a horrible cold-blooded proceeding you are going to embark on. I can't help it; I do feel like that. So there's an end of it.'

Bertie did not reply, and a clock on the chimney-piece chimed two.

'There's one more thing,' he said at length. 'You advised me to brush up the coronet. Did you mean anything?'

Charlie took out his watch, and began winding it up. Mechanically, Bertie took his coat on his arm.

'Yes, I meant exactly what you think I meant.'

'It's rather awkward,' said Bertie. 'She's going out to America in the autumn to act. I am certain to meet her in New York; at any rate, she is certain to know I am there.'

'Will that really be awkward?' asked Charlie. 'Is she—is she?'

'I haven't seen her for nearly two years,' said the other.

'I don't know whether she hates me or the other thing. In either case, I am rather afraid.'

Mrs. Massington also had spent the hour after she had got home in midnight conference. Since her husband's death, two years ago, she had lived with an unmarried sister of her own, a woman some ten years older than herself, yet still on the intelligent side of forty, and if she herself had rightly earned the title of the prettiest widow in London, to Judy, even more unquestionably, belonged the reputation of the wisest spinster in the same village. She was charmingly ugly, and relished the great distinction that real ugliness, as opposed to plainness, confers on its possessor. She was, moreover, far too wise ever to care about saying clever things, and thus there were numbers of people who could never imagine why she was so widely considered a gifted woman. To Sybil Massington she was a sort of reference in all questions that troubled her—a referee always to be listened to with respect, generally to be agreed with, but in all cases to be treated with entire frankness, for the very simple reason that Judy invariably found you out, if you concealed any part of the truth, or had been in any degree, when consulting her, what Mrs. Massington preferred to call diplomatic.

Sybil Massington herself, though now a two-years-old widow, with weeds which, as we have seen, others considered quite outworn, was still barely twenty-five. She was one of those fortunate beings who invariably through life see more smiles than frowns, more laughter than tears, for the two excellent reasons that she was always, even when herself tired or bored past the general freezing-point of politeness, alert to amuse and to be interested in other people; the second because she studiously avoided all people and places where frowns and tears were likely to be of the party. K She deliberately took the view that life is a very charming 'business at the best, but full in its very woof—inseparably from existence—of many sombre-tinted threads. It was therefore futile to darken the web of existence by serious or solemn thoughts on the sadness of life and the responsibilities which she did not really think were binding on her. She preferred dancing in the sun to reading tracts in the shade; she wished primarily to be happy herself, and, in a scarcely secondary degree, she wished all her friends to be happy too. In this way her essential selfishness yet had the great merit of giving much pleasure as it went on its pleasant course; and though she had not, to state the fact quite baldly, the slightest desire that anybody should be good, it gave her the greatest pleasure to see that they were happy, and she really spent an enormous amount of trouble and force in advancing this object. Such a nature, whatever may be its final reward or punishment, certainly reaps a rich harvest here; for strenuous and continued efforts to be agreeable, especially when made by a young and pretty woman, yield their sixtyfold and a hundredfold in immediate returns.

It must be confessed that she had immense natural advantages for the rôle she so studiously played. She was rather above the ordinary height of women, and had that smooth, lithe gracefulness which one associates with boyhood rather than womanhood. Her head, small for her height, was set on to her neck with that exquisite pose one sees in the Greek *figurines* from Tanagra; and her face, with its long, almond-shaped eyes, straight features, and small mouth, expressed admirably the Pagan attitude towards life that was hers. It was a face to be loved for its fresh dewy loveliness, a face as of a spring morning, to be enjoyed with a sense of unreasoning delight that such beauty exists. It gave the beholder the same quality of pleasure that is given by the sight of some young animal, simply because it is so graceful, so vital, so made for and capable of enjoyment. And behind her beauty lay a brain of the same order, subtle because she was a woman, but in other respects even as her face, a minister and pastor of the religion of innocent mirth and pleasure. In pursuance of this creed, however, she was capable of subtle and intricate thought, and just now, in her talk with her sister, it was getting abundant exercise.

'Ah, that is no use, dear Judy,' she was saying. 'I do not say to you, "Make me different, then tell me what to do," but "Take me as I am, and tell me what to do."' Judy's shrewd face broadened into a smile, and a pleasant soul looked out of her intelligent eyes—eyes that were bright and quick like a bird's.

'I don't in the least want to make you different,' she said, 'because I think you are a unique survival.'

Sybil's eyes expressed surprise.

'Survival!' she said.

'Yes, dear; you came straight out of Pagan mythology; you were a nymph in the woods by the Ilyssus, and Apollo saw you and ran after you.'

'Did he catch me?' asked Sybil, with an air of dewy innocence.

'Don't be risky; it doesn't suit you. Really, Sybil, considering what—what great natural advantages you have, you should study yourself more closely. Just as a fault of manner committed by a woman who wears a beautiful dress is worse than a fault of manner committed by a char-woman, so you, with your appearance, should be doubly careful not to say anything out of character.'

'Dear Judy, you are charming, but do keep to the point.'

'I thought you were the point; I am sure I have talked about nothing else.'

'I know: it is charming of you; and you have yawned so frightfully doing it that it is cruel to bring you back to it. But I really want your advice now at once.'

Judy poured out some hot water from a blanketed jug, and sipped it. Having an admirable digestion, she was determined to keep it. 'Take care of your health, if it is good,' was a maxim of hers. 'If it is inferior, try to think about something better.'

'State your case, then, in a very few words,' she said, looking at the clock.

'It is fast,' said Sybil, laughing, 'though not so fast as I should wish. Well, it is this: I am twenty-five years old, and I don't believe I have the faculty of what is known as falling in love. It always seems to me I haven't time, to begin with. I was married, as you know, at eighteen, but I can't imagine I was ever in love with John. Otherwise that horror couldn't have happened.'

Judy looked up, forgetting the time and the hot water.

'What horror?' she asked.

The light died out of Sybil's face; she looked like a troubled child.

'I have never told anyone,' she said, 'because I was ashamed, but I will tell you to make you understand me. He was ill, as you know, for months before he died; every day I used to grow sick at the thought of having to sit by him, to talk to him. He got more and more emaciated and awful to look at. One night I did not kiss him as usual. He asked me to, and I refused; I could not— simply I could not. I loathed the thought of the days that were coming; I longed for the end, and when the end came I was glad. I tried to persuade myself that I was glad his sufferings were over. It was not so; I was glad that mine were over. So I think I never loved him, though I liked him very much. Then he got ill and awful, and I was very sorry for him. But that was all. Ah ____ '

She got up, and walked up and down the room once or twice, as if to waken herself from the clutch of some horrid dream. Then she stopped behind Judy's chair, and leaned over her sister, stroking her hair.

'Yes, that was the horror, Judy,' she said; 'and I am that horror. Now, to-night again Charlie would have asked me to marry him, if I had not; "smiling put the question by." I like him very much; I think I should like to have him always in the house. I like everything about him.'

'Don't marry him,' said Judy quickly.

'Judy, when you speak like that, you are saying to yourself, "If only she was different." Well, I am not; I am as I am. I couldn't make my eyes blue by wanting, or make myself an inch taller. Well, it must surely be far more difficult to change one's nature in so radical a way.'

'I think you did not run very fast when Apollo began Judy.

'That does not suit you, either, dear,' remarked Sybil. 'Well, then, I am not to marry Charlie. Am I to marry anybody? That is the point. Or am I to consider that marriage is not for me?'

'How can I tell you, Sybil?' asked Judy, rather perplexed. 'I dare say there are men who regard marriage like you. You can calmly contemplate marrying a man whom you just like. I don't see why, if you can find a man like you, you shouldn't be far happier together than you would be single. I don't see what law, human or Divine, prevents your marrying. You promise to love, honour, and obey—well, fifty people mean exactly fifty different things by love. Because A doesn't attach the same meaning to it as B, B has no right to say that A doesn't love. And perhaps your "liking very much" will do. But don't marry a man who loves you very much. John did.'

'Yes, John did,' said Sybil, and paused a moment. 'Then I think I shall go to America,' she said.

'America?' said Judy.

'Yes; Mrs. Palmer has asked me to go, and I think I shall accept.'

'Do you mean the steam-siren?' asked Judy.

'Yes, the steam-siren. You see, I like steam, go, energy, so much that I don't really mind about the siren.'

'She has the manners,' said Judy, 'of a barmaid, and the mind of a—a barmaid.'

'I know. But I don't mind. In fact—don't howl—I like her; she is extremely good-natured.'

Judy yawned.

'Dear Sybil, she is extremely rich.'

'Certainly. If she lived in a back fourth-floor flat in New York, I shouldn't go to stay with her. You see, I like rich people; I like the quality of riches just as you like the quality of generosity. By the way, you must be rather rich to be generous to any extent, so the two are really synonymous; I'm glad I thought of that. Anyhow, I am going to stay with her.'

Judy got up.

'You are going to stay with her in order to meet other people who are rich,' she said.

'Why not?' asked Sybil. 'Other things being equal, I should prefer to marry a rich man than a poor one. Or shall I cultivate acquaintances in Seven Dials?'

Judy laughed.

'I think they would appreciate you in Seven Dials,' said she, 'and I am sure they will in America. You can make yourself very pleasant, Sybil.'

'Yes, dear, and you can make yourself most unpleasant, and I adore you for it. Judy dear, it's after two. How you keep one up talking!'

CHAPTER III

Mrs. Massington was lying on an extremely comfortable and elaborately padded wicker couch under a conveniently shady tree. The time was after lunch, the day an excessively hot Sunday in July, and the place the lawn of Lord Bolton's present residence on the hills above Winchester. His big country place at Molesworth was let, and had been for some years, since he could not afford to live in it; but in the interval he made himself fairly at home in the houses of other people in equally impecunious circumstances. As he truly said, one must live somewhere, and he very much preferred not to live at Molesworth. The plan partook of the nature of that of those ingenious islanders who lived entirely by taking in each other's washing, but, though theoretically unsound, it seemed to succeed well enough in practice.

For himself he really preferred Haworth, the place he had taken for the last four years; for Molesworth was unmanageably immense, remote from London, and really lonely, except when there was a regiment of guests in the house. Haworth, on the other hand, was small, exquisite in its way, and within an hour or so of London.

From the lawn the ground sloped sharply down to the water-meadows of the Itchen, where in the driest summer the grass was green, and streams of a translucent excellence wove their ropes of living crystal from bank to bank of their courses. A few admirable trees grew on the lawn, and all down the south front of the Tudor house a deep riband of flower-bed, all colour, gleamed and glowed in the summer sun. Sweet-peas were there in huge fragrant groups, stately hollyhocks, with flowers looking as if they had been cut out of thin paper by a master hand, played chaperon from the back; carnations were in a swoon of languid fragrance, love-lies-bleeding drooped its velvety spires, and a border of pansies wagged their silly faces as the wind passed over them. Behind, round the windows of the lower story, great clusters of clematis, like large purple sponges, blossomed, miraculously fed through their thin, dry stalks. At some distance off, in Winmester probably, which pricked the blue haze of heat with dim spires, a church bell came muffled and languid, and at the sound Mrs. Massington smiled.

'That is what I like,' she said. 'I like hearing a railway-whistle when I am not going in the train; I like hearing a church bell when I am not going to church; I like seeing somebody looking very hot when I am quite cool; I like hearing somebody sneeze when I haven't got a cold; I like—oh, I like almost everything,' she concluded broadly.

'I wonder if you, I, we shall like America,' said a voice, which apparently came from two shins and a knee in a basket-chair.

'America?' said Sybil. 'Of course you, I, we will. It is absurd to go there unless one means to like it, and it is simply weak not to like it, if one means to. Bertie, sit up!'

'I don't see why,' said Bertie.

'Because I want to talk to you, and I can't talk to a tennis-shoe.'

The tennis-shoe descended, and the chair creaked.

'Well,' said he.

'You and I are going on business,' she said. 'That makes one feel so like a commercial traveller. The worst of it is neither you nor I have got any wares to offer except ourselves. Dear me! I'm glad Judy can't hear me. Oh, there's Ginger! Ginger, come here!'

Ginger came (probably because he had red hair). He wore a Panama hat, and looked tired. He might have been eighteen or thirty, and was twenty-four, and Bertie's younger brother, his less-used name being Lord Henry Scarton. He sat down suddenly on the grass, took off the Panama hat, and prepared himself to be agreeable.

'There is a Sabbath peace about,' said he; 'that always makes me feel energetic. The feeling of energy passes completely away on Monday morning, and it and I are strangers till the ensuing Sunday. Then we meet. But now it is here, I think I shall go to church. There is a church, isn't there? Come to church, Bertie.'

'No,' said Bertie.

'That is always the way,' remarked Ginger; 'and it is the same with me. I never want to do what anybody else proposes; so don't propose to me, Sybil.'

'Ginger, why don't you do something?' asked Sybil.

'I will go to church,' said Ginger.

'No, you won't. I want you to tell Bertie and me about America. You haven't been there, have you?'

'No. The capital is New York,' said Ginger; 'and you are sick before you get there. When you get there, you are sick again. Then you come back. That is why I haven't been. Next question, please.'

'Why is Bertie going, then?' she asked.

'Because—because he is Bertie instead of me.'

'And why am I going, then?'

'Because you are not Judy. And you are both going there because you are both progressive English people.'

Ginger got up, and stood in front of them.

'All people who on earth do dwell,' said he, 'go to America if they want to dwell—really dwell—on earth. If you want to have all material things at your command, you will, if you are going to get them at all, get them quicker there than anywhere else. But if you attain your ambition, you will come back like cast iron. Everything that was a pleasure to you will be a business; you will play bridge with a cast-iron face, and ask for your winnings; you will study the nature of your soil before you plant a daisy in it; you will always get your money's worth out of everybody. You will be cast iron.'

'No, I won't,' said Sybil. 'You are quite wrong. I will come back in nature as I went.'

'You can't. If you were strong enough for that, you wouldn't go; your going is a sign of weakness.'

Sybil laughed, and stretched herself more at ease on her couch.

'I am not weak,' she said.

Ginger sat down again.

'I am not sure that to do anything is not a sign of weakness,' he said. 'It isn't so easy to loaf as you imagine. Lots of people try to loaf, and take to sheer hard work as a rest from it. I don't suppose anybody in America loafs, and that I expect you will find is the vital and essential difference between them and us. It implies a lot.'

'Go on, Ginger,' said Sybil, as he paused.

'Yes, I think I will. Now, take Mrs. Palmer. She works at pleasure in a way few people in this island work at business. It is her life's work to be gay. She doesn't like gaiety really; it isn't natural to her. But she, by the laws of her nature, which prevent her loafing, works at gaiety just as her husband works at amassing millions. They can neither of them stop. They don't enjoy it any more than a person with St. Vitus's dance enjoys twitching; simply they have

19

lost control of their power to sit still. Now, in England we have lost a good deal; we are falling behind, I am told, in most things, but we still have that power—the power of tranquillity. I am inclined to think it is worth something. But you will go to America, and come back and tell me.'

Ginger lay back on the grass and tilted his straw hat over his eyes after this address.

'Ginger, I've never heard you say so much on end,' remarked Sybil; 'have you been getting it up?'

'I never get things up, but I scent danger,' replied Ginger. 'I am afraid you and Bertie will come back quite different. You will always be wanting to do something; that is a weakness.'

'I don't agree with you,' said Sybil.

'That's all right. If people say they agree with me, I always think I must have said something stupid. What don't you agree with me about?'

'About our power of sitting still. Look at the season in London. All the time we are doing exactly what you say Americans, as opposed to us, do. We make a business of pleasure; we rush about after gaiety, when we are not naturally gay; we——'

'Sybil, you are talking about three or four thousand people among whom you live. I hope you don't think that a few hundred people like that mean England.'

'They include almost all well-known English people.'

'Well known to whom? To themselves. No, that sleepy little misty town down there is just as important a part of England as the parish of St. James's. The parish of St. James's is the office of the company. The people there do the talking, and see after the affairs of the shareholders, and play a very foolish game called politics. They are mere clerks and officials.'

'Well, but as regards the pursuit of gaiety,' said Sybil, 'nobody can be more senseless than you or I, Ginger.'

'Oh, I know we are absurd; you are more absurd than I, though, because you are going to America.'

'You seem to resent it.'

'Not in the least. It is ridiculous to resent what anybody else chooses to do, so long as it is not a personal attack on one's self. That is the first maxim in my philosophy of life.'

'Published? I shall get it.'

'No; it will be some day. It begins with a short history of the world from the days of Adam, and then the bulk of the book draws lessons from the survey. But that is the first lesson. Let everybody go to the devil in his own way. Your way is by the White Star Line.'

'I don't think you know what you are talking about, Ginger,' said his brother.

'I'm sure I don't,' said Ginger cheerfully.

'Why desecrate the Sabbath stillness, then?'

Ginger was silent a moment.

'That is a personal assault,' he said at length, 'and I resent it. It is unjust, too, because meaningless conversation is utterly in harmony with Sabbath stillness. It completes the sense of repose. It is no tax on the brain. Besides, I do really know what I was talking about; I said I didn't because I don't like arguing.'

'You have been doing nothing else.'

'No. I have been reeling out strings of assertions, which Sybil has languidly contradicted from time to time. You can't call that argument. Look! there's Charlie. Why didn't you marry him, Sybil, and stop in England? Who is that with him? Oh, Judy, isn't it? Are they coming here? What a bore!'

Charlie and Judy strolled across the lawn towards them with extreme slowness. To walk across a lawn for tea and walk back again afterwards was the utmost exercise that Judy ever took.

'I am taking my walk,' she observed as she got near them. 'I am now exactly half way, so I shall rest. Sybil, you look as if you were resting too.'

'We are all resting, and we are making the most of it, because Ginger tells us we shall never rest again.'

'Do you want a chair, Judy?' asked Ginger.

Bertie got up.

'Sit there,' he said.

'I am rather tired,' said Judy; 'but pray don't let me turn you out.' And she sat down.

'I'm so glad your father's party broke down,' she went on to Bertie. 'It is so very much nicer to have nobody here, except just ourselves, who needn't make any efforts.'

Ginger gently applauded, his face still hidden by his straw hat.

'The voice of my country,' he remarked.

'Ah, somebody agrees with you,' said Sybil; 'so you are wrong. I am glad; I was beginning to be afraid you were right.'

'Has Ginger been sparkling?' asked Judy.

'Yes, sparkling Ginger-beer. Very tasty,' remarked Ginger fatuously. 'They swallowed it all. If you only talk enough, some of it is sure to be swallowed—not to stick. But it's finished now.'

Charlie had sat down on the bank beside Sybil's couch.

'This is the last Sunday, then,' he said; 'you go to Scotland next week, don't you?'

'Yes,' said she—' just for a fortnight. Then Aix with Judy, and I sail on September 1st.'

'That is earlier than you planned originally.'

'I know; but we get a big boat instead of a small one. I thought it worth while.'

'Do you feel inclined to stroll a bit till tea?'

'By all means.'

'They are going to desecrate the Sabbath stillness by strolling,' remarked Ginger. 'It ought not to be allowed, like public-houses.'

'Ah, we are genuine travellers,' said Sybil. 'Come, too, Ginger.'

'Do I look like it?'

'No; but one never knows with you. Judy dear, would not a good brisk walk do you good?'

'I shouldn't wonder,' said Judy; 'but I shall never know.'

Sybil put up her parasol.

'Come, Charlie,' she said.

They walked off together in the shadow of the big elm avenue that led down to the village. The huge boskage of the trees allowed no inter-penetrating ray of sun to reach them, and in the silence and sleep of the hot summer afternoon they seemed to Charlie to be very specially alone. This feeling was emphasized, no doubt, to his mind by the refusal of the others to accompany them.

'Really, Gallio always succeeds in making himself comfortable,' said she.

'What more can anyone want than a charming house like this? It is so absurd to desire more than you can use. It is a mistake the whole world makes, except, perhaps, Judy.'

'I don't think Ginger does,' said Charlie.

'Oh yes; he desires, at least, to say more than he means. Consequently people attach no importance to what he says.'

Charlie laughed.

'Which, being interpreted, means that Ginger has been saying something which you are afraid is correct.'

Sybil Massington stopped.

'Charlie, for a man you have a good deal of intuition. That is partly what makes me never think of you as a man. You are so like a woman in many ways.'

'I am wanting to have a last word.'

'Last word! What last word?'

'A last word with you, Sybil,' he said; 'I shall never bother you again.'

'Dear Charlie, it is no use. Please don't!' she said.

'I am sorry to disobey you,' said he; 'but I mean to. It is quite short—just this: if ever you change your mind, you will find me waiting for you. That is all.'

Sybil frowned.

'I can't accept that,' she said. 'You have no business to put the responsibility on me like that.'

'There is no responsibility.'

'Yes, there is; you practically threaten me. It is like writing a letter to say you will commit suicide unless I do something. You threaten, anyhow, to commit celibacy unless I marry you.'

'No, I don't threaten,' said he; 'so far from threatening, I only leave the door open in case of Hope wanting to come in. That is badly expressed; a woman would have said it better.'

Sybil was suddenly touched by his gentleness.

'No one could have said it better,' she said. 'Charlie, believe me, I am sorry, but—here is the truth of it: I don't believe I can love anybody. This also: if I did not like you so much, I think I would marry you.'

'Ah, spare me that,' he said.

'I do spare it you. I will not willingly make you very unhappy. Do you believe that?'

He stopped, and came close to her.

'Sybil, if you pointed to the sky and said it was night, I should believe you,' he said.

She made no reply to that, and they walked on in silence. Everywhere over the broad expanse of swelling downs, looking huge behind the heat-haze, and over the green restfulness of the water-meadows beneath them, even over the blue immensity of the sky, there was spread a sense of quiet and leisure. To Sybil, thinking of the after-lunch conversation, it seemed of value; to her at the moment this contented security was a big factor in life. Economically, no doubt, she was wrong; a score of dynamos utilizing the waste power of the streams below that so hurryingly sought the sea would have contributed much to the utility of the scene, and the noble timber which surrounded them could certainly have been far better employed in some factory than to have merely formed a most wasteful handle, as it were, for the great parasol of leaves which screened them and the idle, cud-chewing cattle. Here, as always, there was that silent deadly war going on between utility and beauty; soon, without a doubt, in a score of years, or a score of days, or a score of centuries, principles of economy would prevail, and the world of men would live in cast-iron mood in extremely sanitary cast-iron dwellings. Already, it seemed to her, the death-knell of beauty was vibrating in the air. The rural heart of the country was bleeding into the towns; instead of beating the swords into sickles, the way of the world now was to beat the elm-trees into faggots and the rivers into electric light. For the faggots would give warmth and the electricity would give light; these things were useful. And in the distance, like a cuttle-fish with tentacles waving and growing every moment nearer, New York, and all that New York stood for, was sucking in whatever came within its reach. She was already sucked in.

All this passed very quickly through her mind, for it seemed to her that there had been no appreciable pause when Charlie spoke again.

'Yes, the world is going westwards,' he said. 'I heard a few days ago that Mrs. Emsworth was going to act in New York this autumn. Is it true?'

'I believe so. Why?'

'Mere curiosity. Is she going on her own?'

Sybil laughed.

'Her own! There isn't any. I don't suppose she could pay for a steerage passage for her company. Bilton is taking her,' She paused a moment. 'Do you know Bilton?' she asked.

'The impresario? No,'

'He is a splendid type,' she said, 'of what we are coming to.'

'Cad, I should think,' said Charlie.

'Cad—oh yes. Why not? But a cad with a head. So many cads haven't one. I met him the other night.'

'Where?' asked Charlie, with the vague jealousy of everybody characteristic of a man in love.

'I forget. At the house of some other cad. It is rather odd, Charlie; he is the image of you to look at. When I first saw him, I thought it was you. He is just about the same height, he has the same—don't blush—the same extremely handsome face. Also he moves like you, rather slowly; but he gets there.'

'You mean I don't,' said Charlie.

'I didn't mean it that moment. Your remark again was exactly like an Englishman. But I liked him; he has force. I respect that enormously.'

On the top of Charlie's tongue was 'You mean I have none,' but he was not English enough for that.

'Is he going with her?' he asked.

'No; he has gone. He has three theatres in New York, and he is going to instal Dorothy Emsworth in one of them. Is it true, by the way——'

She stopped in the middle of her sentence.

'Probably not,' said Charlie, rather too quickly.

'You mean it is,' she said—'about Bertie.'

Charlie made the noise usually written 'Pshaw!'

'Oh, my dear Sybil,' he said, 'Queen Anne is dead, the prophets are dead. There are heaps of old histories.'

Sybil Massington stopped.

'Now, I am going to ask you a question,' she said. 'You inquired a few minutes ago whether Dorothy Emsworth was going to act in New York. Why did you ask? You said it was from mere curiosity; is that true? You can say yes again, if you wish.'

'I don't wish,' said he. 'It wasn't true then, and I don't suppose it will be by now. You mean that Bertie saw a good deal of her at one time, but how much neither you nor I know.'

Sybil turned, and began walking home again rather quickly.

'How disgusting!' she said.

'Your fault,' he said—' entirely your fault.'

'But won't it be rather awkward for him?' she asked, walking rather more slowly.

'I asked him that the other night,' said Charlie; 'he said he didn't know.'

Again for a time they walked in silence. But the alertness of Mrs. Massington's face went bail for the fact that she was not silent because she had nothing to say. Then it is to be supposed that she followed out the train of her thought to her own satisfaction.

'How lovely the shadows are!' she remarked; 'shadows are so much more attractive than lights.'

'Searchlights?' asked he.

'No; shadows and searchlights belong to the same plane. I hope it is tea-time; I am so hungry.'

This was irrelevant enough; irrelevance, therefore, was no longer a social crime.

'And I should like to see my double,' said Charlie.

The only drawback to the charming situation of the house was that a curve of a branch railway-line to Winchester passed not far from the garden. Trains were infrequent on it on weekdays, even more infrequent on Sundays. But at this moment the thump of an approaching train was heard, climbing up the incline of the line.

'Brut-al-it-é, brut-al-it-é, brut-al-it-é,' said the labouring engine.

She turned to him.

'Even here,' she said—'even here is an elbow, a sharp elbow. "Utility, utility!" Did you not hear the engine say that?'

'Something of this sort,' said he.

CHAPTER IV

A day of appalling heat and airlessness was drawing to its close, and the unloveliest city in the world was beginning to find it just possible to breathe again. For fourteen hours New York had been grilling beneath a September sun in an anticyclone; and though anticyclone is a word that does not seem to matter much when it occurs in an obscure corner of the *Herald*, under the heading of 'Weather Report,' yet, when it is translated from this fairy-land of print into actual life, it matters a good deal if the place is New York and the month is September. Other papers talked airily of a 'heat wave,' and up in Newport everyone reflected with some gusto how unbearable it must be in town, and went to their balls and dinner-parties and picnics and bridge with the added zest that the sauce of these reflections gave. Even in Newport the heat was almost oppressive, but to think of New York made it seem cooler.

From the corner where Sixth Avenue slices across Broadway and Thirty-fourth Street crosses both, one can see the huge mass of the Waldorf Hotel rising gigantic against the evening sky, and wonder, if one is that way inclined, how many million dollars it has taken to blot out the evening sun. But during the afternoon to-day most people were probably grateful for the shadow which those millions had undesignedly procured them; it was something as one went from Fifth Avenue to Broadway to be shielded a little by that hideous immensity, for the dazzle and glare of the sun had been beyond all telling. And though now the sun was close to its setting, the airlessness and acrid heat of the evening was scarcely more tolerable than the furnace heat of the day, for boiling was not appreciably more pleasant than baking. Yet in the relentless city, where no one may pause for a moment unless he wishes to be left behind in the great universal race for gold, which begins as soon as a child can walk, and ceases not until he is long past walking, the climbings of the thermometer into the nineties is an acrobatic feat which concerns the thermometer only, and at the junction of Sixth Avenue and Broadway there was no slackening in the tides of the affairs of men. The electric street cars which ran up and down both these streets, and the cars that crossed them, running east and west up Thirty-fourth Street, were all full to overflowing, and passengers hung on to straps and steps as swarming bees cluster around their queen. Those in the centre of the car were unable to get out where they wanted, while those at the ends who could get out did not want to. A mass of damp human heat, patient, tired, nasal-voiced, and busy, made ingress and egress impossible, and that on which serene philosophers would gaze, saying, 'How beautiful is democracy!' appeared to those who took part in it to be merely mis-management. Incessant ringings of the conductor's bell, the sudden jerks of stoppages and startings, joltings over points where the lights were suddenly extinguished, punctuated the passage of the cars up and down the street, and still the swarming crowds clustered and hung on to straps and backs of seats wherever they could find foot-hold and standing room. But all alike, in payment for this demoniacal means of locomotion, put their five cents into the hot and grimy hands of the conductor, from which, by occult and subtle processes, they were gradually transformed into the decorations of the yachts and palaces of the owners of the line.

Democracy and discomfort, too, held equal sway in the crowded trams of the elevated railway which roared by overhead down Sixth Avenue, in the carriages of which tired millionaires and tired milliners sat stewing side by side, with screeching whistles, grinding brakes, and the vomiting forth of the foul smoke from soft coal; for a strike of some kind was in progress in Pennsylvania, and the men who had stored coal and also engineered the strike were reaping a million dollars a day in increased prices and slight inconvenience to a hundred million people, for the thick pungent smoke poured in wreaths into the first-floor windows of the dingy, dirty habitations of the street. But the train passed by on the trembling and jarring trestles, and the inconvenience passed also, till the next train came.

Thunder of the passing trains above; rumbling of the electric cars; roar of heavy, iron-shod wheels of drays on the uneven, ill-paved cobbles of the street; jostling of the foot passengers on the side-walks, as they streamed in and out from the rickety wooden staircases of the elevated railway, from the crammed, perspiring cars, from dingy, sour-smelling restaurants; shouts of the newsboys with sheaves of ill-printed newspapers under their arms, giving horrible details of the latest murder, and abominable prints of the victim's false teeth, shoes, and the dress she had last been seen in; the thump-thump of the engines in the *Herald* office; the sickening stew of the streets; the sickening heat of the skies—Democracy, or 'Everyone for himself.'

As an antidote or warning—though it did not seem to have the least effect on the dogged, unending bustle—the note of 'Impermanence' was everywhere sounded loudly. A block or two further up, for instance, the street was torn up for some new underground enterprise (Lewis S. Palmer, as a matter of fact, had floated a company to run a new subterranean line across New York, and had been paid a million and a half dollars for the loan of his credit); and while the cars, which will certainly not cease running till the last trump has been sounded several times, passed over spindle-shanked iron girders and supports, shaken every now and again by the blasting of the rock below, thousands of workmen were toiling day and night deep down in the earth, loading the baskets of the cranes with the splinters of the riven rocks, or giving the larger pieces into the embrace of huge iron pincers that tackled them as a spider tackles a fat fly, and, rising aloft with them above street level, took them along the ropes of their iron web, over the heads of passengers and vehicles, for the carts which waited for them. Elsewhere, half a block of building had vanished almost as the night to make way for something taller, and where yesterday a five-storied building had stood, the site to-day was vacant but for a dozen pistons half buried in the ground, which puffed and shook in a sort of hellish ecstasy of glee at the work, while a gang of men with axe and pick dug out the foundations for the steel house-frames. Yet though to-morrow almost would see the newly completed building again filling up the gap in the street, the exposed walls of the adjacent houses were just for to-day only covered with advertisements, and a notice informed the bewildered shopper that business was going on as usual. That in New York might be taken for granted, but the notice omitted to say where it was going on. But for the crowd in general it was sufficient that work was to be done, and money to be made. That was the whole business and duty of each unit there, and as far as each unit was concerned, the devil might take the rest. Everyone looked tired, worn out, but indefatigable, and extraordinarily patient. One man pushed roughly by another, and where in England the one would look aggrieved, and the other probably, however insincerely, mutter an apology, here neither grievance nor apology was felt, desired, or expressed, for it is a waste of time to feel aggrieved and a waste of energy to express or feel regret. To-morrow the crowd would, on the average, be a little richer than to-day; that was all they wanted. To-morrow the world in general would be a day richer.

Sybil Massington and Bertie Keynes had arrived that morning by the *Celtic*, after a voyage of complete uneventfulness. The sea had been rough, but the *Celtic* had not been aware of it. Bertie had seen a whale blow, or so he said, and Sybil had seen three fisher boats off the banks. There had been six hours' fog, and they had got in that morning in this day of frightful heat. They had been on deck like honest tourists to see the immense green, mean statue of Liberty, or whatever that female represents, and had found the huge sky-scrapers by the docks, the bustling paddle-steamers of the ferries, the hooting sirens, the general hideousness, exactly what they had expected. They were, in fact, neither disappointed nor pleased, and when a small, tired young man with a note-book had met them on the moment of their landing, and asked Bertie his first impressions of America, they had felt that they were indeed in the authentic place. Nor had the impression been in any way dimmed all day, and now, as they sat together in the darkened sitting-room at the Waldorf, just before going to dress for dinner, they felt like old inhabitants. Bertie had bought a paper containing the account of his interview, headed, 'Marquis Bolton's eldest son lands: Lord Keynes' first impressions,' and had just finished reading to Sybil, half a column of verbose illiteracy of which, to do him justice, he had not been in any way guilty.

'You're getting on, Bertie,' said she; 'that interview shows you have struck the right note. And where have you been this afternoon?'

'Like Satan, walking up and down the earth,' said he. 'I went by an overhead railway and an underground railway. There are swing gates into the stations of the overhead railway. As I passed in, I naturally held the gate for the next man, so as not to let it bang in his face. He did not take it from me, but passed through, leaving me still holding it. I might have stood there all day, and they would have all passed through. Then I learned better, and let it slam in other people's faces. It saves time. Somehow I thought the incident was characteristic of the country.'

Sybil lit a cigarette.

'I like it,' she said. 'The air, or the people, or something, makes me feel alert. Now, when I feel alert in England it is mere waste of energy. There is nothing to expend one's alertness on; besides, one is out of tone. But here, somehow, it is suitable. I like the utter hideousness of it, too. Look from that window at the line of houses. They are like a row of jagged, broken teeth. Well, it is no worse than Park Lane, and, somehow, there is an efficiency about them here. One is ninety-five stories high for a definite reason—because land is valuable; the next is three stories high because it belongs to a millionaire who doesn't want to walk upstairs. By the way, Mrs. Palmer came in while you were out. We are going to dine with her this evening, and go to Mrs. Emsworth's first night.'

She looked at him rather closely as she said this.

'That will be charming,' he said quite naturally. 'And to-morrow we go down to Mrs. Palmer's on Long Island, don't we?'

'Yes. Really, Bertie, their idea of hospitality is very amazing. She came up here to-day to this blazing gridiron of a place simply in order not to let us be dull on our first evening here. It seemed to her quite natural. And she has put a motor-car at my disposal. I like that sort of thing.'

Bertie thought a moment.

'I know,' he said. 'But though it sounds horrid to say it, a motor-car doesn't mean anything to Mrs. Palmer.'

'It means the kindliness of thinking of it,' said Sybil.

'It was the same kindliness which brought her up from Long Island. Would you and I, if we were in the country, come up to town to entertain someone who was going to stay with us next day? You know we shouldn't.'

'That is true,' said he. 'Is Mrs. Palmer alone here?'

'Yes. Her husband and daughter are both down in Long Island. She is making a sort of rival Newport, you know. You and I plunge into it all to-morrow. I think I am rather frightened, but I am not sure. No, I don't think I am frightened. I am merely trembling with determination to enjoy it all immensely.'

'Trembling?' he asked.

'Yes; just as when you hold something as tight as you can your hand trembles. You must go and dress—at least, I must. Bertie, I am going to be very English I think they will like it best.'

'Oh, don't pose! You are never so nice when you pose.'

'I'm not going to pose. I am going to be absolutely natural.'

'That is the most difficult pose of all,' said he.

About half-way up Fifth Avenue the two rival restaurants, Sherry's and Delmonico's, glare at each other from opposite sides of the street, each with its row of attendant hansoms and motor-cars. Though New York was technically empty—that is to say, of its millions a few hundred were still at Newport—both restaurants were full, for Mrs. Emsworth's opening night was an occasion not to be missed, and many of those who would naturally have been out of town were there in order to lend their distinguished support to the actress. Furthermore, Mr. Lewis S. Palmer, from his retreat in Long Island, had been operating yesterday on the Stock Exchange in a manner which compelled the attendance of many of the lesser magnates who at this season usually left the money-market to attend to itself. This was very inconsiderate of him, so it was generally thought, but he was not a man who consulted the convenience of others when he saw his own opportunity. But it was extremely characteristic of him that, while nervous brokers, bankers, and financiers rushed back to the furnace of the streets, he remained himself in the coolness of Long Island, and spoke laconically through the telephone.

Mrs. Palmer was waiting in the anteroom at Sherry's when her two English guests arrived, and greeted them with shrill enthusiasm. A rather stout young American, good-looking in a coarse, uncultivated kind of manner, and dressed in a subtly ill-dressed, expensive mode, was with her.

'And here you are!' she cried. 'How are you, Lord Keynes? I'm delighted to see you again. Mrs. Massington, you must let me present to you Mr. Armstrong, who has been so long dying to make your acquaintance that I thought he would be dead before you got here. Mrs. Massington, Mr. Reginald Armstrong. Lord Keynes, Mr. Armstrong.'

The American murmured his national formula about being very pleased, and Mrs. Palmer continued without intermission.

'And I've got no party to meet you,' she said, 'because I thought you would be tired with your journey, and want to have a quiet evening, and we'll go in to dinner at once. Lord Keynes, you look as if America agreed with you, and I see they have been interviewing you already. Well, that's our way here. Why, when Reginald Armstrong gave his equestrian party down at Port Washington last week, I assure you there was a string of our newspaper men a quarter of a mile long waiting to see him.'

The curious shrillness of talk peculiar to America sounded loud in the restaurant as they made their sidling way by crowded tables toward one of the windows looking on the street.

'Equestrian party?' asked Mrs. Massington. 'What is that?'

'Tell them, Reginald,' said Mrs. Palmer. 'Why, it tickled me to death, your equestrian party. Mrs. Massington, those are blue points. You must eat them. Tell them, Reginald.'

'Well, my stable was burned down last fall,' said he, 'and I've been building a new one. So I determined to open it in some kind of characteristic way.'

'His own idea,' said Mrs. Palmer in a loud aside to Bertie. 'He's one of our brightest young men; you'll see a lot of him.'

'So I thought,' continued Mr. Armstrong, 'that I'd give a stable party—make everyone dress as grooms. But then the ladies objected to dressing as grooms. I'm sure I don't know why. I should have thought they'd have liked to show their figures. But some objected. Mrs. Palmer objected. I don't know why she objected—looking at her—but she did object.'

Mrs. Palmer smiled.

'Isn't he lovely?' she said loudly across the table to Mrs. Massington.

'Well, she objected,' again continued Mr. Armstrong; 'and when Mrs. Palmer objects, she objects. She said she wouldn't come. So I had to think of something else. And it occurred to me that the best thing we could do was to have dinner on horseback in the stables.'

He paused a moment.

'Well, that dinner was a success,' he said. 'I say it was a success, and I'm modest too. I had fifty tables made, fitting on to the horses' shoulders, and we all sat on horseback, and ate our dinners in the new stables. Fifty of us in a big circle with the horses' heads pointing inwards, and simultaneously the horses ate their dinner out of a big circular manger. And that dinner has been talked about for a week, and it 'll be talked about till next week. Next week Mrs. Palmer gives a party, and my dinner will be as forgotten as what Adam and Eve had for tea when they were turned out of Paradise.'

'No, don't tell them,' screamed Mrs. Palmer. 'Reginald, if you tell them, I shall never forgive you.'

'Please don't, then, Mr. Armstrong,' said Sybil. 'I should hate it if you were never forgiven. Besides, I like surprises. I should have loved your dinner; I think it was too unkind of you to have given it before I came. Or else it is unkind of you to have told me about it now that it is over.'

33

She laughed with genuine amusement.

'Bertie, is it not heavenly?' she said. 'We think of that sort of thing sometimes in England. Do you remember the paper ball? But we so seldom do it. And did it all go beautifully? Did not half fall off their horses?'

'Well, Mrs. Palmer's husband, Lewis S., he wouldn't get on a real horse,' he said. 'He said that he was endangering too many shareholders. So I got a wooden horse for him, and had it covered with gold-leaf.'

'Lewis on a rocking-horse!' screamed his wife. 'I died—I just died!'

'Luckily, she had a resurrection,' said Mr. Armstrong; 'otherwise I should never have forgiven myself. But you did laugh, you did laugh,' he said.

Mrs. Palmer probably did. Certainly she did now.

The dinner went on its way. Everything was admirable: what was designed to be cold was iced; what was designed to be hot was molten. Round them the shrill-toned diners grew a little shriller; outside the crisp noise of horses' hoofs on asphalt grew more frequent. Mrs. Emsworth's first night was the feature of the evening; and even the harassed financiers, to whom to-morrow, as dictated by the voice of the telephone from Long Island, might mean ruin or redoubled fortunes, had with closing hours laid all ideas of dollars aside, and, like sensible men, proposed to distract themselves till the opening of business next morning distracted them. For Mrs. Emsworth was something of a personality; her friends, who were many, said she could act; her enemies, who were legion, allowed she was beautiful, and New York, which sets the time in so many things, takes its time very obediently in matters of artistic import from unbusiness-like England and France. In this conviction, it was flocking there to-night. Besides the great impresario, Bilton, had let her the Dominion Theatre, and was known to have given her *carte blanche* in the matter of mounting and dresses. This meant, since he was a shrewd man, a belief in her success, for into the value of business he never allowed any other consideration to enter. Furthermore, there had been from time to time a good deal of interest in England over Mrs. Emsworth's career, the sort of interest which does more for a time in filling a theatre than would acting of a finer quality than hers have done. The piece she was to appear in was a *petit saleté* of no importance whatever. That always suited her best; she liked her audience to be quite undistracted by any interest in the plot, so that they might devote themselves to the contemplation of her dresses and herself. Of her dresses the quality was admirable, the quantity small; of herself there was abundance, both of quality and quantity, for she was a tall woman, and, as we have said, even her enemies conceded her good looks.

The piece had already begun when the little *partie carrée* from Sherry's entered, and rustled to the large stage-box which Bilton had reserved for them. Mrs. Emsworth, in fact, was at the moment making her first entrance, and, as they took their places, was acknowledging the applause with which she was greeted. Naturally enough, her eye, as she bowed to the house, travelled over its occupants, and she saw the party arriving. This was made easy for her by Mrs. Palmer's voluble enthusiasm, which really for the moment divided the attention of the house between the stage and her box.

'I adore her, I just adore her!' she cried; 'and she promised to come down from Saturday till Monday to Long Island. You know her, of course, Lord Keynes? There's something magnetic to me about her. I told her so this afternoon. I think it's her neck. Look at her bending her head, Mrs. Massington. I really think that Mrs. Emsworth's neck is the most magnetic thing I ever saw. Reginald, isn't it magnetic?'

The magnetic lady proceeded. She acted with immense and frolicsome enjoyment, like some great good-humoured child bursting with animal spirits. To the rather tired and heated occupants of the stalls she came like a sudden breeze on a hot day, so infectious was her enjoyment, so natural and unaffected her pleasure in exhibiting her beauty and buoyant vitality. The critical element in the audience—in any case there was not much—she simply took by the scruff of the neck and turned out of the theatre. 'We are here to enjoy ourselves,' she seemed to say. 'Laugh, then; look at me, and you will.' And they looked and laughed. Whether she was an actress or not was really beside the point; there was in her, anyhow, something of the irrepressible *gamin* of the streets, and the *gamin* that there is in everybody hailed its glorious cousin. Long before the act was over her success was assured, and when Mr. Bilton came in to see them in the interval, it was no wonder that his mercantile delight was apparent in his face. Once more, for the fiftieth or the hundredth time, he had staked heavily and won heavily.

'I knew she would take,' he said. 'We Americans, Mrs. Massington, are the most serious people on the face of the earth, and there is nothing we adore so much as the entire absence of seriousness. Mrs. Emsworth is like Puck in the "Midsummer Night's Dream." They'll be calling her Mrs. Puck before the week's out. And she's playing up well. There is a crowd of a hundred reporters behind the scenes now, and she's interviewing them ten at a time, and making her dog give audience to those she hasn't time for. Do you know her dog? I thought it would knock the scenery down when it wagged its tail.'

Armstrong in the meantime was regaling Bertie with more details of the equestrian party, and the justice of Bilton's remarks about seriousness was evident from his conversation.

'It was all most carefully thought out,' he was saying, 'for one mustn't have any weak point in an idea of that sort. I don't think you go in for that sort of social entertainments in London, do you?'

'No; we are much more haphazard, I think,' said Bertie.

'Well, it's not so here—anyhow, in our set. If you want to keep in the swim you must entertain people now and then in some novel and highly original manner. Mrs. Lewis S. Palmer there is the centre, the very centre, of our American social life. You'll see things at her home done just properly. Last year she gave a farm-party that we talked about, I assure you, for a month. You probably heard of it.'

'I don't remember it, I'm afraid.'

'Well, you surprise me. All the men wore real smock-frocks and carried shepherd's crooks or cart-whips or flails, and all the women were dressed as milkmaids. It was the drollest thing you ever saw. And not a detail was wrong. All the grounds down at Mon Repos—that's her house, you know— were covered with cattle-sheds and poultry-houses and pig-sties, and the cows and sheep were driven around and milked and shorn just as they do on real farms. And inside the walls of her ballroom were even boarded up, and it was turned into a dairy. She's one of our very brightest women.'

'And next week there is to be a new surprise, is there not?' asked Bertie.

'Yes, indeed, and I think it will top everything she has done yet. What she has spent on it I couldn't tell you. Why, even Lewis S. Palmer got a bit restive about it, and when Lewis S. gets restive about what Mrs. Palmer is spending, you may bet that anyone else would have been broke over it. Why, she spent nearly thirty thousand dollars the other day over the funeral of her dog.'

'Did Mr. Palmer get restive over that?' asked Bertie.

'Well, I guess it would have been pretty mean of him if he had, and Lewis, he isn't mean. He's a strenuous man, you know, and he likes to see his wife strenuous as a leader of society. He'd be terribly mortified if she didn't give the time to American society. And he knows perfectly well that she has to keep firing away if she's to keep her place, just as he's got to in his. Why, what would happen to American finance if Lewis realized all his fortune, and put it in a box and sat on the top twiddling his thumbs? Why, it would just crumble—go to pieces. Same with American society, if Mrs. Palmer didn't keep on. She's just got to.'

'Then what happened to you all when she came to London?' asked Bertie, rather pertinently.

'Why, that was in the nature of extending her business. That was all right,' said Armstrong. 'And here's some of the returns coming in right along,' he added felicitously—' Mrs. Massington and you have come to America.' At this point Bilton interrupted.

'Mrs. Emsworth saw you to-night, Lord Keynes,' he said, 6 and hopes you will go to see her to-morrow morning. No. 127, West Twenty-sixth Street. Easier than your Park Squares and Park Places and Park Streets? isn't it?'

'Much easier,' said Bertie. 'Pray give my compliments to Mrs. Emsworth, and say I regret so much I am leaving New York to-morrow with Mrs. Palmer.'

'Ah, you couldn't have a better excuse,' said Bilton; 'but no excuse does for Mrs. Emsworth. You'd better find half an hour, Lord Keynes.'

CHAPTER V

Mrs. Emsworth's little flat in Twenty-sixth Street certainly reflected great credit on its furnisher, who was her impresario. She had explained her requirements to him briefly but completely before she signed her contract.

'I want a room to eat my chop in,' she said; 'I want a room to digest my chop in; I want a room to sleep in; and I want somebody to cook my chop, and somebody to make my bed. All that I leave to you; you know my taste. If the room doesn't suit me, I shall fly into a violent rage, and probably refuse to act at all. You will take all the trouble of furnishing and engaging servants off my hands, won't you? How dear of you! Now, please go away; I'm busy. *Au revoir*, till New York.'

Now, Bilton, as has been mentioned, was an excellent man of business, and, knowing perfectly well that Mrs. Emsworth was not only capable of carrying her threat into action, but was extremely likely to do so—a course which would have seriously embarrassed his plans—he really had taken considerable pains with her flat. Consequently, on her arrival, after she had thrown a sham Empire clock out of the window, which in its fall narrowly missed braining a passing millionaire, she expressed herself much pleased with what he had done, and gave a standing order to a very expensive florist to supply her with large quantities of fresh flowers every day, and send the account to Bilton.

The room in which she digested her chop especially pleased her. Carpet, curtains, and upholstery were rose-coloured, the walls were green satin, with half a dozen excellent prints on them, and by the window was an immense

Louis XV. couch covered in brocade, with a mass of pillows on it. Here, the morning after her opening night in New York, she was lying and basking like a cat in the heat, smoking tiny rose-scented Russian cigarettes, and expecting with some anticipation of amusement the arrival of Bertie Keynes. Round her lay piles of press notices, which stripped the American variety of the English language bare of epithets. She was deeply absorbed in these, and immense smiles of amusement from time to time crossed her face. On the floor lay her huge mastiff, which, with the true time-serving spirit, rightly calculated to be thoroughly popular, she had rechristened Teddy Roosevelt. Her great coils of auburn hair were loosely done up, and her face, a full, sensuous oval, was of that brilliant warm-blooded colouring which testified to the authenticity of the smouldering gold of her hair. Lying there in the hot room, brilliant with colour and fragrant with the scent of innumerable flowers (the account for which was sent in to Mr. Bilton), she seemed the embodiment of vitality and serene Paganism. Not even her friends—and they were many—ever accused her of morality, but, on the other hand, all children adored her. That is an item not to be disregarded when the moralist adds up the balance-sheet.

In spite of his excuse of the night before, Bertie Keynes had taken Bilton's advice, and before long he was announced.

'Bertie, Bertie!' she cried as he came in, 'I wake up to find myself famous. I am magnetic, it appears, beyond all powers of comprehension. I am vimmy— am I really vimmy, do you think, and what does it mean? I am a soulful incarnation of adorable——Oh no; it's Teddy Roosevelt who is the adorable incarnation. Yes, that dear angel lying there is Teddy Roosevelt and an adorable incarnation, which would never have happened if we hadn't come to America, would it, darling? Not you, Bertie. I christened him on the way over, and you shall be godfather, because he wants a new collar. Let me see, where was I? Bertie, I was a success last night. Enormous. I knew I should be. Now sit down, and try to get a word in edge-ways, if you can.'

'I congratulate you, Dorothy,' he said—'I congratulate you most heartily.'

'Thanks. I say, Teddy Roosevelt, the kind young gentleman congratulates us. Now, what are you doing on these opulent shores? Looking out for opulence, I guess. Going to be married, are we? Well, Teddy is too, if we can find a suitable young lady; and so am I. Oh, such fun! and we'll tear up all our past histories, and put them in the fire.'

She sat half up on her couch, and looked at him.

'It's two years since we met last, Bertie,' she said; 'and you—why, you've become a man. You always were a pretty boy, and you don't make a bad-looking man. And I'm vimmy. I used not to be vimmy, did I? But we are all changing as time goes on. Really, I'm very glad to see you again.'

Bertie felt unaccountably relieved at her manner. His relief was of short duration. Dorothy Emsworth arranged her pillows more comfortably, and lit another cigarette.

'I wanted to see you before you left New York,' she said, 'because I am coming down to stay with Mrs. Palmer next Saturday, and we had better know how we stand. So, what are you over here for? Did you come here to get married? And if so, why not?'

She lay back as she spoke, stretching her arms out with a gesture that somehow reminded him of a cat stretching its forelegs and unsheathing the claws of its silent, padded feet. His feeling of relief was ebbing a little.

'Why not, indeed?' he said.

'Dear Bertie, echo-conversation is so tedious,' she said.

'You always used to be rather given to it. So you have come out to get married. That is settled, then. Do ask me to the wedding. The "Voice that Breathed"; wedding march from "Lohengrin"; ring dropping and running down the aisle like a hoop; orange-flowers; tears; sudden unexplained hysterics of the notorious Mrs. Emsworth; deportment of the bride; wedding-cake; puff-puff. And the curtain drops with extreme rapidity. O lor', Teddy R.! what devils we all are, to be sure!'

Bertie's feeling of relief had quite gone, but his nervousness had gone also. He felt he knew the facts now.

'I see,' he said: 'you propose to make trouble. I'm glad you told me.'

'I told you?' she asked, laughing lazily. 'Little vimmy me? I say, I'm brainy too.'

'What do you propose to do?' he asked.

'Well, wait first of all till you are engaged. I say, Bertie, I like teasing you. When you wrinkle your forehead as you are doing now, you look adorable. I don't mean a word I say, you know, any more than you meant a word of that very, very funny letter you once wrote me, which is now,' she said with histrionic utterance, 'one of my most cherished possessions.'

'You told me you had burned it,' said he.

'I know; I meant to burn it, but I couldn't. When I told you I had burnt it, I really meant to have burnt it, and so I didn't tell you a lie, because for all practical purposes it was burned. But then I found I couldn't; it was too funny for words. Really, there are so few humorous things in the world that it would be murder to destroy it. Of course, you didn't mean it. But I can't burn it. It is here somewhere.'

Bertie did not smile. He sat up straight in his chair, and put the tips of his fingers together.

'And don't look like Gallio,' remarked Mrs. Emsworth.

'Look here, Dorothy,' he said, 'you can make things rather unpleasant for me, if you choose. Now, why do you choose? You know perfectly well that at one time the world said things about you and me; you also know perfectly well that—well, that there was no truth in them. You encouraged me to fall madly in love with you because—I don't know why. I thought you liked me, anyhow. Then there appeared somebody else. I wrote you a letter expressing my illimitable adoration. That was all—all. You have got that letter. Is not what I have said true?'

'Yes—slightly edited. You see, I am a *very* improper person.'

'What do you mean?'

'Well, if you choose to write a very fervent letter to a very improper person, people will say—it is no use denying it—they will say What a fine day it is, but hot.'

Bertie got up.

'That is all I have to say,' he said.

'People are so ill-natured,' said Mrs. Emsworth.

The catlike laziness had left her, though her attitude was the same; instead of looking sensuously lazy, she looked very alert.

'Good-bye, then,' said Bertie; 'we meet next week at Long Island.'

'Yes; it will be very pleasant,' said she.

He left the room without more words, and for five minutes she remained where she was. But slowly, as she lay there, the enjoyment and the purring content faded completely out of her face. Then it grew hard and sad; eventually, with a long-drawn sigh, half sob, she got up and called to her dog. He rose limb by massive limb, and laid his head on her lap.

'Teddy R.,' she said, 'we are devils. But there are two worse devils than you and I. One has just gone away; one is just coming. Worse-devil one is worse because he thinks—he thinks that of me. Worse-devil two is worse because he —he did that to me. So—so you and I will think nothing more about it at all, but keep our spirits up.'

She fondled the great dog's head a moment, then got up suddenly, and drew the blind down to shut out the glare of the sun, which was beginning to lay a hot yellow patch on the floor.

'He thought that,' she said to herself—'he really thought that.'

She walked up and down the room for a moment or two, then went to a table on which stood her despatch-box, opened it, and looked through a pile of letters that lay inside. One of these she took out and read through. At moments it seemed to amuse her, at moments her smile was struck from her face. When she had finished reading it, she paused a few seconds with it in her hands, as if weighing it. Then, with a sudden gesture of impatience, she tore it in half, and threw the pieces into the grate. Then, with the quick relief of a decision made and acted upon, she whistled to her dog, and went into her bedroom to make her toilet. Resplendency was part of her programme, and with the consciousness of a busy hour before her, she told her butler— Bilton's liberal interpretation of her requirements had included a manservant —that if Mr. Harold Bilton called, he was to be asked to wait.

The 'room to sleep in' was, if anything, more satisfactory than the 'room to digest her chop in.' Like all proper bedrooms, there was a bed in it, a large table, winking with silver, in the window, and very little else. By the bedside there was a bearskin; in front of the dressing-table in the window there was a rug; otherwise the room was carpetless and parquetted, and devoid of furniture and dust. Dark-green curtains hung by the window, dark-green blinds could be drawn across the window. The bathroom beyond held the hopeless but necessary accessories of dressing. Her maid was waiting for her —Parkinson by name—and it was not Dorothy who came to be dressed, but Puck.

'Parkinson,' she said, 'once upon a time there was a very fascinating woman called X.'

'Lor'm!' said Parkinson.

'Quite so. And there was a very fascinating young man called Y. He wanted to marry her, and wrote to say so. But meantime another man called Z also wanted to—to marry her. So she said "Yes," because he gave her a great deal of money. But she kept Y's proposal—I don't know why, except because it was so funny. And so now I suppose she is Mrs. Z. That's all.'

'Lor'm!' said Parkinson. 'Will you wear your shiffong and lace dress?'

'Yes, shiffong. Parkinson, supposing I suddenly burst into tears, what would you think?'

'I should think you wasn't quite well'm.'

'Quite right; also there isn't time.'

Mrs. Emsworth had not been gone more than ten minutes or so before Bilton was shown up. He appeared to be in a particularly well-satisfied humour this morning, and as he moved about the room, noting with his quick eye the stamp of femininity which Mrs. Emsworth had already impressed into the garnishing of the place, he whistled softly to himself. In his hand he carried a small jewel-case with her initials in gold upon the top. As always, in the relaxed mood the true man came to the surface; for a man is most truly himself, not at great moments of emergency or when a sudden call is made on him, but when his ambitions for the time being are gratified, when he is pleased with himself and his circumstances—above all, when he is alone. Thus, though just now the hard eagerness of his face was a little softened, yet its alertness hardly dozed; and though he had made, he felt sure, a great success in bringing Dorothy Emsworth to America, he hardly allowed himself even this momentary pause of achievement, but had called this morning to talk over with her the details of a protracted tour through the principal cities of the States. True son of his country, he realized that to pause spelled to be left behind.

As his manner was, Bilton did not sit down, but kept walking about, as if not to be caught idle either in mind or body. As in many of his countrymen, the habit of perpetually being ready and eager to snap up an opportunity had become a second nature to him, so that it was far more an effort to him to rest than to work. Working was as natural to him as breathing; to cease to work required the same sort of effort as to hold the breath. To him in his profession as impresario any movement, any glimpse at a room or a picture, could perhaps suggest what in the fertile alchemy of his mind might be transformed into a 'tip,' and he looked with special attention at two Watteau prints which hung on the walls; for in the second piece which Mrs. Emsworth was to produce under his direction a certain scene was laid in the gardens at Versailles, and the note of artificial naturalness had to be struck in the scenery as Watteau and no one else had struck it. Big trees cut formally and square in their lower branches, but with the topmost boughs left unpollarded; fountain in the centre, quite so, and a glimpse, just a glimpse, of the terrace of the palace with the two bronze fountains beneath the trees.

He stood a moment before the fireplace with eyes half closed, conjuring up the scene, and in particular seeing it with his mind's eye as a setting to that incomparable woman in whom, professionally, at this juncture, he was so deeply interested, to whom he was so managerially devoted, but of whom in other respects he was so profoundly weary. For a year he had been wildly in love with her, for another year he had slowly cooled towards her, and now it required all his steadiness of head and incessantly watchful will not to betray his tedium. Also in years he was now, though still only half way through the thirties, old enough in mind to wish to settle down. His capabilities for passionate attachments were a little cooling, and, with a cynical amusement at himself, he was beginning to realize that married domesticity, even as morals taught, was, though for other reasons, the placid river-bed into which the babbling mountain-streams of youth must eventually empty themselves. Rather bathos, perhaps, but he realized fully that everyone gets in life what they themselves bring to it. The only limitations imposed on a man are those which his own nature makes.

But these unedifying moralities did not occupy him long. They were the background to his thoughts, just as the terrace of Versailles was the background for the picture he was forming. In the foreground of the picture stood Mrs. Emsworth; on the terrace stood another figure, Sybil Massington.

He had let his cigar go out as he revolved these things in front of the two Watteau pictures, and then rose to drop it in the fireplace. A letter in an envelope torn once in half lay there, and he stooped and picked it up, laid the two pieces side by side on the table, and read it through. Then he put the pieces in his pocket, and, with that praiseworthy attention to detail which throughout his life had contributed so largely to his success, he took from the table a sheet of paper, folded it inside an envelope, tore it in half, and replaced the pieces in the grate where he had found the others. The whole thing was quickly and naturally done; it was merely one among a thousand million other cases in which his mind was ready to take advantage of any possible opportunity that Fate might cast in his way. The torn letter might conceivably at some future date be useful to him. Therefore he kept it. It is no use to guard against certainties—such was his gospel—for certainties in this life are so few as to be practically negligible. But he who guarded against contingencies and provided for possibilities was the winner in the long-run.

This done, he dismissed the matter from his mind, and, in order not to let the moments pass without seed, sketched out in some detail the plan of the stage as suggested by the two Watteau prints. He was deep in this when Mrs. Emsworth entered. The 'shiffong' suited her admirably.

'You have been waiting,' she said; 'I am sorry for keeping you. Oh, Harold, they love me over here; they just love me!'

His part was at his finger-tips.

'That doesn't seem to me in the least remarkable,' he said. 'You are a success; no one can be more. I want to be allowed to commemorate it.' And he handed her the jewel-case.

He was no niggard when business was involved; his business now was to keep her in a good temper, and the opal and diamond brooch he had chosen at Tiffany's was really admirable. Even Mrs. Palmer might have found it brought consolation to a wounded spirit.

'That is dear of you, Harold,' she said; 'I adore opals. Is it really for me? Thank you ever so much. It goes on now. Is it rather big for the morning? I think it is. A reason the more for wearing it.'

She pinned it into her dress, and sat down.

'Well?' she said.

'I came really to congratulate you,' said he; 'but as I am here, I suppose we may as well talk over some business that must be talked over. About your tour: are you willing to stop over here till April at least?'

'Yes; I don't see why not. I want to appear in London early in May.'

'Very well. I will draft an agreement, and send it you. Now, you may consider that with your extraordinary success of last night the theatre will be full for some weeks ahead. I propose your giving an evening performance on Saturdays as well as the matinee.'

'Terms?'

'Royalty. Twenty per cent, on total takings. It is worth your while.'

'Is it not more worth my while to be seen from Saturday till Monday at Mrs. Palmer's?'

'It would be if the theatre was not full. But you could fill it—for the present, anyhow—if you had a matinee every day. Besides, you can get down to Long Island with the utmost ease on Sunday morning.'

'I go to Mass on Sunday morning; you forget that!'

He smiled.

'I suggest, then, that you should omit that ceremony, if you want to go to Mrs. Palmer's. However, there is no hurry. Weigh the three things in your mind— eighty or ninety pounds by acting on Saturday evening, or Mass on Sunday morning, or Mrs. Palmer's on Sunday morning. There is another thing: I want to talk over the scenes in "Paris" with you. I am going to Mrs. Palmer's the Sunday after next. I will bring the models down with me, if you will promise to give me an hour. 'They will not be ready till then.'

'Yes. I am going there next Sunday and the Sunday after. They have a theatre there; she wants me to do something in the evening.'

Bilton thought a moment.

'What do I get?' he asked.

'The pleasure of seeing me act, silly.'

He shook his head.

'I'm afraid I must forget that pleasure,' he said. 'Your contract binds you to give no theatrical representations of any sort except under my direction.'

The *gamin* element rose to the surface in her.

'What a beast you are!' she said. 'It is for a charity!'

'And a cheque,' he observed.

'The cheque is purely informal. Besides, we shall be there together.'

He took a cigar out of his case, bit the end off with his long teeth, that gleamed extremely white between the very remarkable red of his lips.

'Look here, Dolly,' he said; 'there are two sides to the relations in which we are placed. One is purely businesslike; the other is purely sentimental. It is a pity to let them overlap. It spoils my devotion to you to feel that it is in a way mixed up with business, and it offends my instincts as a business man to let sentiment have a word to say in our bargains. Briefly, then, I forbid your acting for Mrs. Palmer unless you make it worth my while. After all, I didn't bring you out here for sentimental reasons; I brought you out because, from a financial point of view, I thought it would be good for both of us.'

'What do you want?' she asked.

'Half your cheque.'

'For something you haven't arranged, and which won't cost you a penny?'

'Yes. I am talking business. You can close with that offer any time to-day; to-morrow it will be two-thirds. I'm quite square with you.'

'Americans are Jews,' observed Mrs. Emsworth.

'Possibly; it would be an advantage if everyone was; it would simplify bargaining immensely. The Gentile mind is often highly unreasonable, and, instead of allowing both sides to make profits, it simply refuses to part with its goods. And a fine opportunity goes to—well, to damnation. You won't score if you don't act for her, nor will I. If you do, we both shall. Don't be a Gentile, Dolly.'

She did not answer for a moment. Her eyes saw the torn fragments of the letter in the grate, and she remembered that she had definitely and for ever torn up what Bertie had written to her. Then she got up, crossed the room to where he was standing by the fireplace, and put her hands on his shoulders.

'Are you tired of me?' she asked.

His brown eyes grew black at the fragrance and seductiveness of her close presence; for the blood is stirred long after the imagination has ceased to be fired.

'You witch! you witch!' he said.

But in the background on the terrace there still stood the other figure.

CHAPTER VI

Long Island is separated from New York by a narrow sound, across which ferry-boats ply in both directions with extreme punctuality. From any part of New York city a couple of electric cars or an electric railway will take you to the threshold of the ferry-boat, and trains await you at the back-door, so to speak, of the ferry-boats, to convey you down the length of Long Island. On board the ferry-boat you can buy a variety of badly-printed and sensational daily papers for the sum of one cent; you can get your boots blacked for very little more; and no doubt, if there was sufficient demand, the directors would enable you to have your teeth brushed or your hair combed. No part of the equipment, however, is at all lovely. It answers the purpose of conveying you cheaply and expeditiously from one point to another, and enables you to finish your toilet in transit, which is an invaluable boon to those who want to save time. As a matter of fact, everyone wants to save time, but it has been reserved for Americans to invent such methods of doing it. The rest of the world, therefore, is in their debt. The debt is acknowledged, but the rest of the world, quite inscrutably, does not choose to follow their example. All may raise the flower now all have got the seed, but they do not raise the flower.

There is no 'class' on these boats; there is no 'class' on the elevated railway; there is no 'class' on the electric cars. Millionaires in Long Island, in consequence, have the privilege of enjoying the same discomforts as other people, and even Lewis S., who could have bought up the whole system of electric cars, overhead railway, and ferry-boats (after a little judicious distribution of emoluments to the officials of New York City), habitually went by these unlovely conveyances, because there were no other. During his transit he once sent a cablegram buying, at any price, the whole dinner-service which had been used on the last occasion on which Marie Antoinette dined at

46

Petit Trianon. It was extremely expensive, and, as he wrote, the drippings from the rain fell on to his cablegram form, for the boat was full. Subsequently he argued with the boot-boy who had blacked his boots, but gave in when the boy produced his tariff-card. And Democracy, the spirit of his fellow-passengers, sympathized in the main with him.

Once arrived on Long Island, a walk of a hundred yards or so leads to the ticket-office. Those hundred yards are uncovered, however; but since people who live on Long Island *must* pass them in order to get into the Delectable City, there is no reason why the railroad or the ferry-boat company should offer conveniences in the way of shelter to their passengers. Given competition, any line would vie with the others in mirrors and gilded furniture; but if there is none, why on earth spend a penny? Not a passenger the less will travel because the mode of transit is bestial. Thus, common-sense, as usual, emerges triumphant.

For the purpose of this narrative, the low-lying swamp and companies of jerry-built houses that cluster round the various stations on the line may be disregarded, and after half an hour's travelling the train emerges into a very pleasant land. There are no high uplands to dwarf the immediate landscape, but there are trees of tolerable growth and slim presence to add distinction to it. Underneath these trees, as the train nears Port Washington, grow high clumps of purple Michaelmas daisies, now, in September, full of bursting bud, and the temperate sea-winds give a vividness of colour to the prevailing green, which reminds foreigners of the Devon sea-coast.

Mrs. Palmer's new-built house stood on a charming hill-top some mile or so beyond the station. The site had been occupied till a few years before by a delightful bungalow structure, built of wood, with shingled walls, and surrounded on all sides by deep, shady verandas. The wood in those days came right up to the house on two sides, and was just lopped of its topmost branches on a third, so that where the ground fell away rapidly from the house a charming glimpse of the dim blue sound could be seen framed in sky and tree-tops, while the fourth side was open, the house-front giving on to a broad lawn of velvety turf which changed into rougher meadow-land in the middle distance, while over distant tree-tops and a wash of green country the gray smoke of New York sat on the horizon. The house, in fact, had been like a hundred other houses on Long Island, not perhaps very pretty, still less beautiful, but not without a certain haphazard picturesqueness about it, restful and unpretending, and most eminently adapted for the purpose of affording to the brain-heated business man a draught of coolness and greenness. Moreover, it had expressed somehow the genius of the place; its woods, not huge nor of magnificent trees, but of pleasant growth, always sounded in whispers through the rooms; and even as the greatest heats of summer came tempered by the passage of the winds through the filter of the woodlands, so, one would have thought, the fever of New York was abated here, even as the smoke of the city was but a gray *tache* on the horizon. It had, as all houses should, been in tune with the pleasant, mediocre charm of the island, even as the chateaux on the Loire express the broad grandeur and classical formality of the landscape, as the big houses of England are in the scale of their huge timbered parks, and, for that matter, as the county gaol expresses the security which His Majesty kindly affords to the criminal classes.

But within the last few years the whole place had been completely changed, and it was no longer the genius of Long Island, but the genius of mushroom wealth, that crowned the hill-top. For a quarter of a mile on every side round the house the trees had been felled and their roots dynamited, and huge lawns spread their green carpets in the most ample expanses. Four-square in the centre stood the immense house of gray stone, copied largely from one of the Valois chateaux in the South of France, but with various protuberances, in the shape of a theatre, a swimming-bath, and a tennis-court, grafted on to it. A carriage-drive lay in long curves like a flicked whip-lash, surmounting terrace after terrace set with nugatory nudities, till it reached the lead-roofed portico at the front, where two great Græco-Roman candelabra of Parian marble stood one on each side of the door, pierced for gas, and crowned by large glass globes. To the north lay the Italian garden, all laurels and tessellated pavement, cypresses and statuary, fountains and flower-beds. To the west were the tennis and croquet lawns, and to the south, where the ground in old days had fallen tumbling towards the sea, it had been built up with thousands of tons of earth and faced with masonry, so that from the edge of the terrace one looked down on to the topmost fans of the waving trees. Heavy gilded vanes crowned the lead roofs, and high over the central dome of the building a flag-staff displayed Mrs. Palmer's very original device—Love caught in a rose-bush—to the airs of heaven. Round the extreme edge of the terrace ran the bicycle track, on which Lewis S. Palmer did his ten miles a day, with black hatred in his heart of this extraordinary waste of time.

The estate, which was of great extent, and produced nothing whatever, since, to Mrs. Palmer's way of thinking, to live on an estate which produced anything was of the nature of keeping a shop, was all pressed into the amiable service of providing entertainment for the guests, and of showing the wondering world a specimen of the delectable life. For several miles the road through the woods had been run in artfully contrived gradients, carried on struts over too precipitous ravines, and quarried through cuttings to avoid undesirable steepnesses. The sides of the cuttings were admirably planted, and creepers and ivy covered the balustrades of the bridges. A golf-course, smooth as a billiard-table, and not too heavily bunkered, lay near the house, and Mrs. Palmer had tried a most original experiment last year of stocking the woods with all sorts of game, to provide mixed shooting for a couple of parties in the autumn. This had not been wholly a success, for the deer she had turned out were so tame that they gazed in timid welcome at the shooters, probably expecting to be fed, till they fell riddled with bullets, while the pheasants were so wild that nobody could touch a tail-feather. But the costume of the *chasseurs*—green velvet, very Robin-Hoody—had been most tasteful, and she herself, armed with a tiny pea-rifle and dressed in decent imitation of Atalanta, had shot a roebuck and a beater, the latter happily not fatally.

From the centre of the terrace on the east, which had been brought over entire from a needy Italian palace, a broad flight of steps of rose-coloured marble led down to the sea. A small breakwater was sufficient to provide station and anchorage for the two steam-yachts and smaller pleasure-boats, but otherwise the shore had not been meddled with. There was a charming beach of sand, and a little further on a fringe of seaweed-covered rock-pools. Behind this was a small natural lagoon in a depression in the sandy foreshore, some half-acre in extent, fed by a stream that came down through the woods, but brackish through the infiltration of the salt water. This that highly original woman had chosen to be the scene of the fête which was to astonish society next week; but the secret had been well kept, and no one except Reggie Armstrong knew the precise details of the new surprise. For a fortnight or so, however, it was common knowledge that a great many large pans wrapped in tarpaulin had been arriving, and the shore had been populous with men who plied some sort of bare-legged avocation, which implied wading in the lagoon. But the foreman of the company who was executing Mrs. Palmer's orders had received notice that if any word of what was being done leaked out or reached the papers, at that moment all work would be suspended, and the firm would never have another order from her. She herself, sometimes alone, sometimes with Reggie, inspected the work; otherwise no one was allowed near the place. The yachts of her dearest friends, it is true, constantly passed and repassed up the sound, and many were the opera-glasses levelled at the shore; but what the bare-legged men were doing baffled conjecture and the best glasses.

The house inside was, with the exception of one small suite, of the most sumptuous description. A huge hall, paved with marble, and covered as to its walls with superb wood-work of Grinling Gibbons, occupied the centre of the ground-floor, and *en suite* round it were the rooms for entertaining. Ping-pong being at this moment fashionable, it was to be expected that almost every room had its table, and it was curious to see the hideous little black board on its cheap trestle legs occupying the centre of the great French drawing-room. Old rose-coloured satin was stretched on the walls, an immense Aubusson carpet covered the floor. All the furniture was gems of the early Empire style; the big ormolu clock was by Vernier; great Dresden parrots in gilt mounts held the shaded electric lights, and a statuette by Clodion stood on the Queen's escritoire from the Tuileries. One side of the square block of house was entirely occupied by the picture-gallery, which contained some extremely fine specimens of the great English portrait-school, a few dubious old masters, some good Lancrets, and several very valuable pictures by that very bright young American artist, Sam Wallace. These, as all the world knows, represent scenes from the ballet and such subjects, and he is supposed to have a prodigious eye for colour. Here, too, of course, was an unrivalled place for ping-pong, and Mrs. Palmer had caused to be made a very large court, so that four people could play together. Great grave English footmen, when the game was in progress, were stationed at each end to pick up the balls, and hand them on silver salvers to the server; and they had rather a busy time of it, for the majority of Mrs. Palmer's guests found a difficulty in inducing the ball to go anywhere near the table. But they found it very amusing, and it produced shrieks of senseless laughter.

An observant man might have noticed in a dark corner of the hall a small green baize door. It was in shadow of the staircase, and might easily have escaped him altogether; but if he noticed it, it would have struck him as odd that this plain baize door, with three brass initials on it—L. S. P.—should find a place in this magnificence. If it had only been L. S. D., it would have been quite in place, and might have been taken to be the shrine of the tutelary god of the place. Shrine indeed it was, and the tutelary god sat within; for the initials were those of Mrs. Palmer's husband.

It was a perfectly plain, bare room, with drugget on the floor, an almanac hung near the fireplace, a large table stood in the centre of the room, on which were piles of papers, apparatus for writing, and usually a glass of milk. From the door to the right there came the subdued tickings of telegraph apparatus; near that door sat a young man on a plain wooden chair, and at the table sat a small, gray-haired man, very thin and spare, with bushy eyebrows which frowned over his work. From time to time he would throw on to the floor a scrap of paper. Then the young man would get up noiselessly, pick it up, and go through with it into the room from which came the tickings of the telegraph. Then he would return and sit down again. Occasionally a muffled knock would come at the same door, upon which he would rise and take a paper which was handed him, and lay it quite close to the right hand of the man who sat at the table, who either crumpled it up after reading it or wrote something in reply. These answers and messages were all written on small scraps of paper measuring about three inches by one; there was a pile of them always ready by his left hand. A telephone also stood on this table which rang very constantly. Then the man at the table would, as if automatically, place the receiver at his ear and listen, sometimes not even looking up from his writing, and often replacing the instrument without a word. More rarely he looked up, and he would say a few words—'Yes, yes,' 'No, certainly not,' 'Very well, buy,' or 'Sell at once.'

'Yes, all!' Sometimes, again, it would be he who first used the instrument, and he would ring up his head clerk in New York or a partner, never in a hurry, never apparently impatient. On the other hand, he would not wait idle till the answering bell rang, but go steadily on with his work. At such moments he would raise his eyes sometimes when he was speaking, and if you happened to catch his glance, it is probable you would never forget it, but would understand, though momentarily only and dimly maybe, that at the table in the bare room there sat a Force, a great natural phenomenon, before which all the splendour and magnificence of the house, all the illimitable outpouring of wealth which it implied, became insignificant—a mere shirt-button or a tie-pin to the man from whose brain it had all sprung.

In face, but for those extraordinary eyes, dark gray in colour, but of a vitality so great that it seemed as if each was a separate living entity, his features were somewhat insignificant. He had gray, rather thin whiskers, and iron-gray hair, still thick, and not yet deserting his forehead. His nose was slightly hooked, suggesting that a spoonful, perhaps, of Jewish blood ran in his veins; his mouth was very thin-lipped and compressed. In body, he was short and thin almost to meagreness, and, owing to a nearly total absence of digestive power, he lived practically exclusively on milk, of which he drank some five or six pints a day. And in nothing was his power of control so amazingly shown; for ten years ago he had been both *gourmet* and *gourmand*, and had habitually eaten enormous masses of food with a relish and palate for the curiously delicate and uncultivated sense of taste that Savarin might have envied. Even now, when he sat at the head of the table at his wife's parties, he knew, partly by keenness of nostril, partly by look, whether any dish was not perfectly cooked, and next morning the first of the slips which he dropped on to the floor to be picked up by the young man at the door might run: 'To the *chef*: Not enough asparagus-heads in the sauce Milanaise, Some three weeks ago I told you the same thing.—L. S. P.'

This extraordinary sense of, and attention to, detail, characteristic of the great Napoleon, was also most characteristic of Mr. Palmer. Only the night before his daughter had come down to dinner in a new dress, and found herself the instant target for the piercing gray eye of her father.

'There ought to be two straps on the shoulder, not one,' he said; 'it is copied from the figure of Madame Matignon, in the picture of the last fête of the Empress Eugenie. Pray have it altered.'

'Dear old papa,' remarked Amelie, 'I dare say you know everything, but it wouldn't be so pretty.'

'That is a matter of taste, but it would be right.'

This characteristic, which appeared so strongly even in such branches of human interest as the position of a strap or a bow on a woman's dress, appeared most piercingly of all on questions concerning finance. Figures, indeed, once seen by him, seemed to be indelibly imprinted on his mind, and, without reference, he would embark on enterprises where an accurate knowledge of previous balance-sheets and present prices was essential. It was essential to him; only, instead of referring to books which would give him the required information, he carried it about in his head. To his partners and those who were associated with him in business he was a source of constant wonder. Partners they might be to him in name, and, since they were all well-tried and trusted men, they no doubt were of assistance to him; but as far as executive power was concerned, they might as well have been junior clerks in some other firm, for Palmer went on his way automatically, self-balanced on the topmost crest of the huge wave of prosperity that was flooding America, quicker than the whole of the rest of the New York Market to scent coming trouble or prosperity in the world of money, prompter than any to take advantage of it. Then, when his day's work was done, at whatever hour that might be, it was as if the word 'business' was unknown to him, and there sat at table, dressed in loose and somewhat ill-fitting clothes, a man of very simple and kindly nature, a connoisseur in cookery, art, and millinery, a gentleman at heart, and to the backbone an American—one who, in spite of his gentleness, was without breeding; one who, in spite of his deep and varied knowledge, was without culture.

He and Amelie were seated at lunch alone together on the day following Mrs. Emsworth's triumphant debut. Amelie had only just come in from her ride—the horse she preferred to ride was one which few men could have sat—and she still wore her riding-habit. She was quite obviously the authentic daughter of her father and mother, and, like a clever girl, which she undoubtedly was, she had selected, so it seemed, all the good points possessed by both her parents, rejected all their weaknesses, and embodied the result in the adorable compound known as Amelie Palmer. She had been right, for instance, in possessing herself of her mother's extraordinary vitality and physical health, rejecting her father's digestive apparatus; on the other hand, she had chosen her father's eyes, impressing upon them, however, a certain femininity, and had set them in a complexion of dazzling fairness, which she owed to her mother. And out of the careful selection there had sprung, crowning it all, the quality that more than anything else was *she*—namely, her unrivalled exuberance of enjoyment. Whether it was some new social effort of her mother's to which she brought her glorious presence, whether she rode alone through the flowering woods, or accompanied her father on his hygienic bicycle ride—'papa's treadmill,' as she called it—she brought to all her occupations the great glowing lantern of her joy, the same brilliant smile of welcome for anything that might turn up, the same divine content-She took nothing seriously, but had enthusiasm for everything. Of refinement or intellectual qualities she had none whatever, but he would be a bloodless man who could really deplore their absence when he looked on that brilliant vitality. Surely it would be time enough to think of such gray gifts when the sparkling tide of her life ran less riotously; at present it would be like teaching some clean-limbed young colt of the meadows to sit up and beg or shake a paw.

In a certain way (and it is part of the purpose of this story to draw out the eventual pedigree of the resemblance) her *joie de vivre* was very much akin to that quality which had so captivated the Americans in New York on the occasion of Mrs. Emsworth's first night. In the older woman, since her nature had been longer in the crucible of life, it had necessarily undergone a certain change; but the critical observer, had he hazarded the conjecture that at Amelie's age Mrs. Emsworth had been very like Amelie, would, though he was quite wrong about it, have had the satisfaction of making a really clever mistake. For Mrs. Emsworth at that age had been possessed of a somewhat serious and joyless nature; her present *joie de vivre* was the result of her experience of life, the conviction, thoughtfully arrived at, that joy is the thing worth living for. But Amelie's exuberance was the result, not of philosophy, but of instinct; she laughed like a child merely because she laughed. And the critical observer, if, after making one clever mistake, he had been willing to hazard another, and had guessed that at Mrs. Emsworth's age Amelie would be like Mrs. Emsworth, would have risked a mistake that was not clever. For it is very seldom that experience confirms one's childish instincts; in ninety-nine cases out of a hundred it either eradicates them altogether, or, at any rate, modifies them almost beyond recognition. Mrs. Emsworth had won back to what had not been in her an instinct when she was a child; and it was more unlikely that Amelie, when a woman, would retain the instincts that were now hers.

At the present moment Amelie's enthusiasm was largely taken up with food.

'Papa, you have an angelic nature,' she said; 'and how you can sit there chewing crackers and sipping milk without throwing the table things at me I can't conjecture.'

'Habit of self-control, Amelie,' said he, his eyes smiling at her; 'perhaps you will learn it some day. When does your mother come down?'

'This afternoon, with the two English folk. She's been telephoning all the morning. When mamma gets hold, real tight hold, of the telephone, she doesn't let go under an hour or two. Now, I'm not like that. The moment I ring anyone up, I forget what I was going to say, and have to ask them to dinner instead. I guess you and mamma took all the brains of the family. Papa, I had the heavenliest ride this morning, all through the fir-woods, and Tamburlaine wanted to jump the sound. The daisies are all coming out, and it smelt so good. Oh, it smelt so good, like—like a drug store. There's the telephone again!'

Mr. Palmer considered this a moment.

'When your mother gave her hunting-party last year,' he said, 'she commenced ringing the telephone at half-past ten in the morning, and she was late for lunch because she hadn't finished. Top speed all the time, too. She takes things seriously; that's why she comes out on top every time.'

'Yes, some more,' said Amelie to the footman.

Mr. Palmer looked quickly at the dish as it was handed her.

'What mess is that?' he asked.

'Pigeons once,' said she; 'it won't be anything in a minute or two.'

'There ought to be mushrooms in the stew. It's meant to be *à la Toulon*. I've forgotten more about cookery than our present *chef* ever knew.'

Amelie laughed.

'Poor papá! what a lot you must forget! I guess you're failing. Well, I've regretfully finished my lunch. Are you going treadmilling?'

'Yes. Who comes down with your mother?'

'Mrs. Massington and Lord Keynes. The others come on Saturday—Mrs. Emsworth, Bilton, and that lot. Papa, I've thought of the right name for Reggie Armstrong at last. It's Ping-pong. He's just that.'

Mr. Palmer considered this.

'Yes, Ping-pong is about the size. Small set, though. Come and treadmill, Amelie.'

She got up and stretched herself, then let one arm fall round her father's neck.

'There are schemes in the air,' she said to him, as they walked out. 'But on the day you see me marry Ping-pong you may tie me up by the heels to Tamburlaine's tail.' From which it may be seen that either Amelie was charmingly lacking in the wisdom of the world, or that her mother had more of it than one would have guessed.

CHAPTER VII

Mrs. Palmer's house-party, which was to be with her during the week of the 'Revels,' as they were called, had arrived at Mon Repos the same afternoon. Mon Repos had been taking its rest in its usual relentless manner, and Bertie Keynes and Mrs. Massington were beginning to get into training. It had dawned on them both very soon that they were engaged in the exercise of the most strenuous mental and physical activity that their dawdling English lives had ever known. The whole party breakfasted together in a marquee on the lawn, and from that moment till after the ensuing midnight were engaged *ohne rast* with a prodigious quantity of *hast* in a continuous social effort. Bathing, boating, bridge (the two latter simultaneously) lasted till lunch; these and similar pursuits, all executed in the dazzling light, in the dazzling crowd, and largely to the dazzling sound of a band, went on without pause till dinner, after which was a short one-act play in the theatre, followed by a 'quiet dance.' After one day of it Mrs. Massington's quick perceptions made discoveries which she communicated to Bertie.

'You are here to play up,' she said, 'and not to amuse yourself. Don't drink any wine at lunch, and very little at dinner.'

'Then I shall die,' said Bertie.

'No, you will not; you will feel much less tired. The whole day is a stimulant, so why take more? Besides, alcohol produces a reaction. That doesn't matter in England, because we sit down and react; here you can't. Also don't attempt to sparkle in conversation. Here they sparkle naturally—at least, they open their mouths and let it come—whereas in England we tend rather to shut our mouths unless we want to say something. But you are being a great success. Go away now; I am going to rest for three minutes before I dress for dinner.'

Bertie lingered a moment at the door of her room.

'They are awfully kind,' he said. 'If only I was stronger, I should enjoy it enormously.'

'I am enjoying it,' said she; 'it suits me. You will, too, if you take my advice.'
'I feel more inclined to take to drink,' said he.

But the fact once grasped that life at Mon Repos was not a holiday, but hard, relentless work of a most exacting kind, they began forthwith to settle down to it and grapple with it. At once the difficulty and charm of it absorbed them. It was a continual piece of acting; whatever your mood, you had to assume a species of reckless gaiety, and all day long feverishly and seriously engage in things that were originally designed to be relaxations, but which the ingenuity of social life had turned into instruments of the profession. None of those present particularly cared for bridge, boating, or bathing in themselves; they would not have boated or bathed alone, or played bridge even with a dummy, but they used these relaxations as a means of accomplishing social efforts. Such a life cannot be undertaken frivolously, though it is purely frivolous; twenty years of it ages its devotees more than thirty years of hard and reasonable brain-work, and though they find it intensely fascinating, yet they know they have to pay for their pleasure, and grow quickly old in its service. Indeed, it might almost be classed as a dangerous trade; and if the pursuit of wealth is a relentless task, not less so is its expenditure as a means of social success. Certainly Mrs. Palmer worked quite as hard as her husband.

Three days passed thus, and it was now the afternoon of the first day of the Revels. In consequence, the telegraph and telephone lines down to Port Washington were congested with messages, for the greater part of the evening papers in New York had kept their first page open for them, and nothing could be sent to press until it was known in what manner the first afternoon would be spent. A good deal, of course, was ready to be set up, for the list of the guests was public property, and their dresses could be, even if imagined only, described; but as long as the lagoon on the shore held its secret, the page could not be made up. It was known also that there would be a ball at Mon Repos in the evening, and that the walls of the ball-room were to be covered —literally covered, as a paper covers a wall—with roses. But for the secret of the lagoon the papers had to wait, since it had been inviolably kept. Another event, too, hardly less momentous, hung in the balance, for only two days before the reigning Prince of Saxe-Hochlaben, a dissolute young man of twenty-five, with a limp, a past, and no future, had arrived like a thunderbolt in New York.

Now, to the frivolous and lightminded this does not seem a world-curdling event, but that very enlightened paper, the New York *Gutter Snipe*, was not frivolous, and with extreme rapidity it set the red flame of war ablaze when it announced in huge headlines: 'ARRIVAL OF HIS ROYAL TRANSPARENCY THE PRINCE OF SAXE-HOCHLABEN. MRS. LEWIS S. PALMER'S REVELS DOOMED TO DIRE

FAILURE. FRITZ (that was his name) PROMISES TO FAVOUR MRS. JOHN Z. ADELBODEN AT NEWPORT.'

The editor of the *Gutter Snipe*, it may be remarked, had once been a man of enormous wealth, and had honoured Mr. Palmer by singling him out as an adversary in a certain financial campaign. Mr. Palmer had dropped quite a number of little notes on to the floor over him, and he was now poor but spiteful.

The effect of his announcement was magical, for there was already war to the knife between Mrs. John Z. Adelboden and Mrs. Palmer, the latter of whom had planted her standard at Long Island in direct defiance of Newport; and those headlines brought things to a crisis. The news of his arrival was of course telegraphed to Newport by the *Gutter Snipe*, which did not telegraph it to Mon Repos. Consequently Mrs. John Z. Adelboden knew it by mid-day (the *Germanic* having come in at 11.49), whereas it went down to Long Island in the ordinary issue of the paper. Thus, Mrs. John Z. Adelboden had seven hours' start.

That remarkable woman grasped the event in every aspect in about three minutes and a quarter. She knew—everyone in America knows everything—that Timothy Vandercrup, the editor of the *Gutter Snipe*, was her ally against Mrs. Palmer; she guessed also that the news would not reach Mrs. Palmer for some hours. So, within five minutes of the arrival of the telegram, she had called on Newport to rally round her, and sent out six hundred and fifty invitations for a ball two nights later—that is to say, on the evening of the first day of Mrs. Palmer's Revels. To each invitation she added on the bottom left-hand corner, 'Arrival of Prince of Saxe-Hochlaben.' That was rather clever; she did not actually commit herself to anything. The notes were sent out by a perfect army of special messengers, and the same evening all the answers arrived. There were no refusals. Simultaneously she wrote a rather familiar little note to H. R. T., whom she had met and flirted with in England the year before, saying: 'Pray come up to our little cottage here. We have a ball on Monday night. All Newport will be there.'

At Mon Repos the same evening the papers arrived as usual, and Mrs. Palmer (as usual) picked up the *Gutter Snipe*, since it always contained the manoeuvres of the enemy. And, though at that moment her guests were in the middle of arriving, she left Amelie to do the honours, instantly left the room, went to her boudoir, and read the paragraph through twice. She also, it may be remarked, had met the Prince before; he had tried to flirt with Amelie, who had given him no encouragement whatever. But he had tried to flirt with so many people who had given him a great deal that she thought he might easily have forgotten that.

She sat with the paper in her hands for some five minutes, after she had read it through for the second time, her nimble brain leaping like a squirrel from bough to bough of possible policies, and she paused on each for a moment. The New York *Evening Startler*, for instance, would put in whatever she chose to send it, and she went so far as to seize a pen and write in capital letters: 'Mrs. Lewis S. Palmer refuses to receive Prince Fritz.'

Then she sat still again and thought. That would not do; Newport would only laugh at her—the one thing she dreaded; for to be laughed at drives the nails into the coffin of social failure. Then suddenly all the tension and activity of her leaping brain relaxed, and she smiled to herself at the extreme simplicity of The Plan. She took one of her ordinary Revel invitation-cards out of her desk, on which the word 'Revels' was printed at the bottom left-hand corner. Before this she inserted one word, so that it read 'Indiscriminate Revels.' That was all; she directed it to the Prince's address at the Waldorf, and went back to her guests.

Now, a matter so momentous is best described in the simplest possible manner, and the emotions that for the next day or two swayed two factions—that of Newport and that of Long Island—more bitterly and poignantly than the War of Independence swayed the North and the South cannot be too simply treated.

The plain upshot, then, was as follows:

Mrs. John Z. Adelboden's familiar little note to the Prince arrived the same evening as Mrs. Palmer wrote hers. H. R. T. accepted it in his own hand with some effusion. Mrs. Palmer's card arrived next morning. H. R. T. read it in bed, thought to himself—the 'Indiscriminate' did it-' That will be more amusing.' He had forgotten altogether about his acceptance of the Newport invitation, and if he had remembered it he would not have done differently. So, after a light and wholesome breakfast of a peach, washed down with some hock and soda, he accepted Mrs. Palmer's invitation.

The news was all over Newport (that he was coming there) before evening, and the *Gutter Snipe* gave his portrait and biography (both unrecognisable). The news was all over Long Island (that he was coming there) by evening, and the *Startler* gave the portrait and biography of Mrs. Lewis S. Palmer. Then followed two days of suspense and anxiety which can only be called sickening. Eventually the two announcements were laid before Prince Fritz by his trembling secretary, who asked him what he meant to do. He flew into a violent passion, and exclaimed with a strong German accent: 'Olso, I shall go where I choose, and when I choose, and how I choose.' And suspense continued to reign.

So the momentous afternoon arrived that was to bring the Prince in Mrs. Adelboden's private railway-carriage to Newport or in Mrs. Palmer's motor to Mon Repos, and still no word of enlightenment had come which should pierce the thick clouds of doubt which hid the face of the future. Newport and Long Island were both *en fête*, and at the rail-way-station of the one, and on the lawns of Mon Repos at the other, the rival factions were awaiting the supreme moment in a tense, unnatural calm. Mrs. Palmer alone was absent from her guests, sitting at the telephone. At length it sounded, and with a quivering lip she unhooked the receiver. Then she gave one long sob of relief, and rejoined her guests. The motor-car had started, and the Prince was in it. And the Revels began.

At the supreme moment of his arrival, when all attention was breathlessly concentrated on him, a large signboard, bearing the mystic inscription '*To the Pearl Fishery*,' had been erected at the head of the staircase leading down to the lagoon, and with charming directness the Prince pointed to it, and said: 'What does that mean, Mrs. Adelboden—I should say, Mrs. Palmer?' And Mrs. Palmer replied: 'I guess, sir, we'll go and see.'

The expectant crowd followed them; it was felt that the secret on which so much fruitless curiosity had been wasted was about to be revealed, but, like a good secret, it baffled conjecture up till the very last moment. The crowd screamed and chattered through the woods, following their illustrious leader, and at last emerged on to the beach. There an immense sort of bathing establishment had been erected, containing hundreds of little cabinets; there were two wings—one for men, one for women—and in each cabinet for women was a blue serge skirt and sandals, a leather pouch, and a small fishing-net; in each cabinet for men was the same apparatus minus the skirt. The lagoon itself smelt strongly of rose-water, for thousands of gallons had just been emptied into it, and the surface was covered with floating tables laden with refreshments, and large artificial water-lilies. And scattered over the bottom of the lagoon—scattered, too, with a liberal hand—were hundreds of pearl oysters.

There was no time wasted; as soon as Prince Fritz grasped the situation, and it had been made clear to him that he might keep any pearls he found, he rushed madly to the nearest cabin, rolled his trousers up to the knee, put the sandals on his rather large, ungainly feet, and plunged into the rose-watered lagoon. Nor were the rest slow to follow his example, and in five minutes it was a perfect mob of serge-skirted women and bare-legged men. Mr. Palmer himself did not join in the wading, for, in addition to a slight cold, wading was bad for his chronic indigestion; but he seized a net, and puddled about with it from the shore. Shrieks of ecstasy greeted the finding of the pearls; cries of dismay arose if the shell was found to contain nothing. Faster and more furious grew the efforts of all to secure them; for a time the floating refreshment-tables attracted not the smallest attention. In particular, the Prince was entranced, and, not waiting to open the shells where the oyster was still alive (most, however, had been killed by the rose-water or the journey, and gaped open), he stowed them away in his pockets, in order to examine them afterwards— not waste the precious moments when so many were in competition with him;

and his raucous cries of 'Ach, Himmel! there is a peauty!' resounded like a bass through the shrill din. He paid no attention whatever to the throng round him; for the present he was intent on the entertainment, and paused once only to empty a bottle of Munich beer which had been especially provided for him on a table with a scarlet tablecloth; for the day was hot, and the exertions of grubbing in the sand quite severe.

Bertie Keynes had not entered the water with the first wild scramble, but had stood on the bank a few minutes, divided between amazement and helpless giggling as he observed Mrs. Cyrus F. Bimm, a stout, middle-aged woman, lately widowed, plunge in without even pausing to take her stockings off, and fall flat on her face. But, though soaked, she was utterly undismayed, and, grasping her net, Wasted no time in idle laments or in changing her clothes. Her hat was naturally black, and streams of dye poured down her face and neck. Her dress was black, too, and as wet as her hat. But then the indescribable frolic of the thing—there is no other word for it—seized him, and just as Amelie, looking like a nymph of Grecian waterways, hurried past him, radiant, slim-limbed, an embodiment of joy, and beckoned to him, he delayed no longer, but joined the rest. But, 'Oh, if Judy could see me now!' he said to himself, as he took off his socks.

For an hour or more the pearl-hunting went on, and every oyster had been fished up and the whole lagoon churned into mud long before the Prince could be persuaded to leave it. Twice he made a false start, and came out of the water, only to seize his net again and hurry back on the chance of finding another, his pockets bulging with the shells he had not yet opened. All the time the telegraph was whirring and clicking the news of the huge success of Mrs. Palmer's first afternoon of Revels and the ecstasies of the Prince all over the country; and Mrs. John Z. Adelboden, like Marius, sat and wept among the ruins of Newport.

Bilton and Mrs. Emsworth had driven down together in a motor from New York, but the latter had to get back in time to act that evening, to return late on Saturday night, stop over Sunday, and act at Mon Repos on Sunday evening. Bilton, on the other hand, had taken a rare holiday, and was not returning to town till the next week. Constitutionally, he disliked a holiday; this one, however, he had less objection to, since there was a definite aim he wished to accomplish during it. He was a man to be described as a person of appetites rather than of emotions, and his appetites partook of the nature of the rest of him. They were keen, definite, and orderly—not clamorous or brutal in the least degree, but hard and clear-cut. He was supposed not many years ago to have proposed by telegram to the lady who subsequently became Mrs. John Z. Adelboden, who had replied by the same medium, 'Much regret; am otherwise engaged.' This had tickled Bilton tremendously, and he had the telegram framed and put up in his flat.

During the past summer Mrs. Massington had seen a good deal of him in London, and though she had frankly conceded that, according, anyhow, to Charlie Brancepeth's notions, he was a cad, there was a great deal about him she liked immensely. Just as she liked the clearness of line, absence of 'fluff,' in a room, so she liked—more than liked —precision of mind in a person. He was quick, definite, and reasonable in the sense that he acted, and could always be counted on to act, strictly in accordance with conclusions at which he had arrived, and which would be found to be based on sound reasoning. She liked also his spare, business-like habit of body, his scrupulous tidiness of attire, his quick, firm movements, his extreme efficiency of person. Underlying this, and but dimly present to her consciousness, was the fact that he so much resembled in face and frame Charlie Brancepeth, towards whom she had always felt a good deal of affection—whose devotion to her touched, though at times it irritated, her. Had things been different, she would have married him, but since matrimonially he was impossible, she did not in the least propose to practise celibacy. As she had told Judy, she believed she was incapable of what many other people would call love; but she was a great believer in happiness, and knew that she had a fine appetite for it. Many things might contribute to it, but love was by no means an essential constituent. And more and more, especially since her arrival in America, she liked the quality of mind which may be broadly called sensibleness. Americans—except when they were revelling—seemed to her to have a great deal of it.

The pearl-fishing had been succeeded by bridge, bridge by dinner, and dinner by a ball in the room entirely papered with roses. Sensationally—from the point of view, that is, of cost—it was a great success, but practically the scent was so overpowering that it was impossible to dance there for more than a few minutes at a time without, so to speak, coming up to breathe. Consequently, there was a good deal of sitting-out done, and Bilton firmly and collectedly managed to spend a large part of the evening with Sybil Massington.

'I should so like to know what you really think of us all,' he said on one of these occasions in his quiet, English-sounding voice.

'I adore you,' said she—' collectively, I mean.'

'Ah, that spoils it all,' said he; 'we all want to be adored individually.'

'There are too many of you for me to do that,' she said; 'I should have to cut my heart up into so many little bits. Wherever I go—there's a song about it—I leave my heart behind me. I always do that. People seem to me very nice.'

'You are taking the rest of the stuffing out,' remarked he in a slightly injured voice.

She laughed.

'Well, I find you all charming,' she said again. 'Will that do?'

'I suppose it will have to. And your friend, Lord Keynes?'

'Ah, he finds one person so charming that I don't think he thinks much about the rest,' she said. Look, there they are.'

Bilton did not look; he had already seen them; he usually saw things first.

'Do you think he will marry her?' he asked.

'Yes; certainly, I hope so. If he marries at all, he must marry money.'

'And Nature clearly designed Miss Palmer to be a peeress. In fact, the match was made in heaven.'

'I hope it will be ratified on earth,' she said. 'Why are you cynical about it?'

'I am never cynical; what makes you think that?'

'Well, simple, direct; it comes to the same thing. To tell the truth is often the most cynical thing you can do.'

'Not if it is a pleasant truth. And it will be very pleasant to Miss Palmer to be an English peeress. And, as you said yourself, it is only possible for Lord Keynes to marry money. And he is fortunate in his money-bag,' he added.

She frowned a little; there was something in this speech which, with all her admiration for his countrymen, struck her as both characteristic and disagreeable. He saw it.

'Ah, that offends you,' he said quickly. 'I apologize. I wish you would teach me better. You know there is a something, an inherent coarseness, about us, which I have seen get, ever so slightly, on to your nerves fifty times a day.'

She laughed.

'Teach you!' she said; 'I am learning far too much myself.'

'You learning? What, for instance?'

'Not to be finicking, not to be slack and dawdling. To go ahead and do something. If a person of my nature was in Mr. Palmer's place, do you suppose I should go on working as he does? I would never touch a business question again.'

He shook his head.

'Believe me, you would; you would not be able to help it. Lewis Palmer can't stop; his wife can't stop; I can't stop, in my small way. But you at present have the power of stopping. It is the most exquisite thing in the world. To us, to me, I assure you, it is like a cool breeze on a hot day to see you leisurely English people. In England you have a leisured class; we have none. Our wealthy class is the least leisured of all. If you adore us, as you say, grant us the privilege of seeing you like that.'

There was something in this speech that rather touched her—something also that certainly pleased her, and that was the tone of honest deference in which he spoke.

'In fact, you want to be English,' she said, laughing it off, 'and I want to be American.' And she looked at him, smiling.

But he did not smile at all, only again his brown eyes grew hot and black. That, too, pleased her. Then suddenly she felt vaguely frightened; she had not definitely intended to give him his chance now, and she did not wish him to take it. So she rose.

'Take me back,' she said. 'Take me into a crowd of your people. I want to learn a little more.'

CHAPTER VIII

The Revels ended on Saturday, on which day the wonder-stricken guests for the most part dispersed, their faces probably shining like Moses' at this social revelation, and went back to their humble homes. The success of them had been gigantic. Nobody (except Newport) talked about anything else for days, and to find news of international importance in the papers was almost impossible, for everything else except the Revels was tucked away into odd corners. Newport alone maintained an icy silence, but disaffection was already at work there, and those who were only struggling on the fringe of Newport society said openly that they would go to Long Island next year, since there really seemed to be some gaiety there, whereas Newport was like a wet Sunday afternoon. Mrs. Palmer's two English guests, however, stopped on. So also did Bilton; and Mrs. Emsworth, having decided not to go to Mass on Sunday morning, was coming down with the larger part of her company on Saturday night after her performance in New York. Sunday, however, was going to be a quiet day, with the exception that there was a large dinner-party in the evening and a play in the theatre afterwards. Ping-pong Armstrong also remained, for he was the recognised tame cat without claws about the house. Mrs. Palmer sometimes secretly wished, in her full consciousness of innocence, that people would 'talk' just a little about him and her, but nobody ever did. Even the *Gutter Snipe* never alluded to his constant presence in the house, but this was probably due to the fact that the editor—who knew a good deal about the meaner side of human nature—guessed that it would have pleased Mrs. Palmer. For it is a most extraordinary, though common, phenomenon to find that perfectly virtuous and upright people often like to be thought just a little wicked, whereas bad people are totally indifferent for the most part as to whether anyone thinks them good or not.

During the two or three days that had elapsed since Bilton and Mrs. Massington had their talk together, his conduct had been immensely pleasing to her. He had taken the hint she had given him like a gentleman, and had not allowed himself to drift into intimate conversation with her until she gave him the signal. He had been diplomatic and delicate—above all, he had been intelligent, not blundering, and she could not help contrasting him, much to his advantage, with the average Englishman, who either insists on 'talking the thing out,' or else looks sulky and wears a woebegone aspect. But Bilton had done neither; he had remained brisk, not brusque, and had resisted, apparently without effort, any attempt to bring her to the point, while remaining himself absolutely normal. In the meantime, during the self-imposed pause in her own affairs, Mrs. Massington watched with extreme satisfaction the development of that mission which had brought Bertie Keynes to America. Affairs for him certainly appeared to be running very smooth; she almost wished for some slight *contretemps* to take place in order to put things on the proper proverbial footing. In other words, Amelie and Bertie had made great friends, and owing to the extraordinary freedom which eligible young folk are given in America, with a view to letting them improve their acquaintance, they had got under way with much rapidity. The house being full, they had many opportunities for finding the isolation which exists in crowds, and took advantage of it. Mr. Palmer, however, with a strong sense of paternal duty, thought it well not to let the matter go too far without satisfying himself that he was justified in letting it go to all lengths. With this in his mind he went to his wife's rooms on Sunday morning to have a quiet talk, as was his custom.

'Pleased with your party?' he asked amiably.

'Lewis, I'm just sick with satisfaction,' she said. 'Long Island, I tell you, is made, and Newport will crumble into the sea. But what am I to do next year? Why, I believe that if at this moment I built a house on Sandy Hook, I could make it fashionable.'

'That would be very convenient,' said he. 'We could flag the liners and save half a day. I'm glad you are satisfied. Now, what do you get by it all?'

'Same as what you get when you've made a million dollars,' said Mrs. Palmer with some perspicacity. 'You don't want them. You don't know you've got them. But you like getting them.'

His bright gray eyes gleamed suddenly, and he looked at her approvingly.

'I guess that's true,' he said. 'I guess you've hit the nail on the head, as you do every time. We've got to get, you and I; and when we've got, we've got to get again. It's the getting we go for.'

His eyes wandered round the room a moment, and he went to a cabinet of *bric-à-brac* that stood between the windows.

'Where did you get that Tanagra figure from?' he asked. 'It's a forgery.' And he took it up and threw it into the grate, where it smashed to atoms.

'Well, I suppose you know,' said Mrs. Palmer calmly. 'Bilton sold it me.'

Lewis laughed.

'Spoiled his market,' he remarked. 'That man's very clever, but he lacks—he lacks length of vision.'

'Perhaps he didn't know it was a forgery,' said Mrs. Palmer charitably.

'That's worse. Give him the credit of knowing.'

Mrs. Palmer put down the paper she was reading.

'Lewis, you didn't come here just to break my things,' she said. 'What is it?'

'Lord Keynes. What do you know of him?' he asked, with his usual directness.

Had Mrs. Palmer been in the company of other people, she would have executed her famous scream, because she was amused. But she never wasted it, and it would have been quite wasted on her husband.

'He's charming,' she said. 'He's in excellent style; he's in *the* set in London. And he wants a wife with a competency. That's why I brought him here.'

'But what does he do?' asked her husband. 'Does he just exist?'

'Yes, I guess he exists. Men do exist in England; here they don't. They get.'

'Some exist here. Ping-pong does.'

'And who's Ping-pong?' she asked.

'Why, Armstrong. Amelie thought of it. He is a ping-pong, you know.'

This time Mrs. Palmer gave the scream, for she was so much amused as to forget the absence of an audience.

'Well, I'm sure, if Amelie isn't bright,' she said. 'But you're pretty far out, Lewis, if you think that Lord Keynes is a ping-pong. If he was an American, and did nothing, he would be. But men do nothing in England without being.'

'England's a ping-pong, I think sometimes,' remarked Lewis. 'She just plays about. However, we're not discussing that. Now I see you mean business with Lord Keynes. You'll run it through on your own lines, I suppose. But remember '—he paused a moment—' I guess it's rather difficult for one to say it,' he said, 'but it's just this: When a girl marries a man, if she doesn't hit it off, the best thing she can do is to make believe she does. But I doubt if Amelie can make believe worth a cent.'

'Well, she just adores him,' said Mrs. Palmer.

'That's good as far as it goes.'

'It goes just about to the end of the world,' said she.

Mr. Palmer considered this.

'The end of the world occurs sooner than you think sometimes,' he said. 'I'll get you a genuine Tanagra, if you like,' he added, 'and I'll guy Bilton about the other. I'll pretend he thought it was genuine. That'll make him tender.'

Though Mrs. Palmer had no objection to exaggeration in a good cause, she had not in the least been guilty of it when she said that Amelie adored Bertie Keynes. Most girls have daydreams of some kind, and Amelie, with the vividness that characterized her, had conjured up before now with some completeness her own complement. Unless a woman is celibate by nature (a thing happily rare), she is frequently conscious of the empty place in herself which it is her duty and her constant, though often unconscious, quest to find the tenant for. And Amelie was not in the least of a celibate nature; her warm blood beat generously, and the love of her nature that should one day pour itself on one at present overflowed in runnels of tenderness for all living things. The sprouts of the springing daisies were dear to her—dogs, horses, even the wild riot of the Revels, was worthy of her affectionate interest. But the rather unreasonable attention she bestowed on these numberless objects of affection was only the overflow from the cistern. One day it would be all given in full flood, its waters would bathe one who had chosen her, and whom her heart chose.

This morning she was riding through the woods with Bertie Keynes, the charmingly sensible laws of American etiquette making it possible for her to ride with anyone she wished, alone and unattended. They had just pulled up from a gallop through the flowering wood paths, and the two horses, muscle-stretched and quiet, were willing to walk unfrettingly side by side.

'Oh, it all smells good, it smells very good,' she said. 'And this morning somehow—I suppose it's after mamma's fête—I like the fresh, green out-of-doors more than ever. I think we live altogether too much indoors in America.'

'But the fêtes were entirely out of doors,' said Bertie.

'Yes; but the pearl-party was just the most indoor thing I ever saw,' said she. 'Certainly it was out of doors, but all the time I wanted somebody to open the windows, let in a breath—a breath of——'and she paused for a word.

'I know what you mean,' he said.

'Did you feel it too? I want to know?'

'In that case, I did.'

He looked at her a moment.

'But all the time you were my breath of out-of-doors,' he said.

Amelie was not fool enough to take this as a compliment, or to simper acknowledgments. As he spoke he wondered how she would take it, hoped she would look at him, anyhow, then hoped she would not.

'Ping-pong is indoors enough,' she said. 'Do tell me what you think of him.'

'I don't think of him,' said Bertie. 'If I sat down to think of him I should instantly begin, without meaning to, to think about something else.'

'Do you loathe him?' she asked.

'Good heavens, no! But—but there are people like husks. Just husks.'

She considered this.

'Husky Ping-pong,' she said, half to herself. 'Poor Husky Ping-Pong. Do you grow them in England?'

'Yes, heaps. They grow in London. They are always at every party, and they know everybody, and make themselves immensely agreeable. It is all they do. And you see them in the back seats of motor-cars.'

She looked at him with some mischief in her eyes.

'And what do you do?' she asked.

'No more than they. Anyone is at liberty to call one a ping-pong. Only I'm not.'

'I know. I was wondering what the difference was according to your description.'

'There is none, I suppose. But don't confuse me with ping-pongs.'

She laughed.

'Lord Keynes, you are just adorable,' she said. 'I'll race you to the end of the avenue.'

'Adoring me all the time?'

'Unless you win,' she said.

'Then I will lose on purpose.'

'That will be mean. I never adore meanness. Are you ready?'

And her beautiful horse gathered his legs up under him and whirled her down the grassy ride. Bertie got not so good a start, and rode the gauntlet of the flying turf scattered by his heels, till, a bend of the path favouring him, he drew nearly abreast, pursuing her through sunshine and the flecked shadows on the grass. He had seen her day after day in the Revels, night after night at ball or concert, yet never had her beauty seemed to him so compelling as it did now, as, swaying the rein with dainty finger-tip, her body moving utterly in harmony with the grand swing of her horse's stride, she turned her smiling face to him, all ecstasy at the exhilaration of the gallop, all wide-eyed smile of consternation at the decreasing lead which she had got at the start. And all at once, for the first time, his blood was kindled; he had admired her form as one may admire a perfect piece of sculptured grace, he had admired her splendid vitality, her charming companionship, her intense *joie de vivre*. But now all the separate, isolated admirations were fused and glowed flamelike. Suddenly she laughed aloud, as he had nearly caught her up.

'Ride, ride!' she cried, in a sudden burst of intimate, upwelling joy that came from she knew not where. 'You will win.'

Apollo pursued Daphne in the vale of Tempe, and in the vales of Long Island Bertie Keynes rode hard after Amelie. And she encouraged him to win, she even drew rein a shade—just a shade—though she had wanted to win so much.

All the afternoon motor-cars, bicycles, carts, tandems, brakes, were arriving, for though it was a quiet Sunday, Mrs. Palmer, it was well-known, liked to see a few friends about teatime, who usually stopped for dinner, and before evening it was as if the Revels were extended a day longer. The weather was extremely hot, and in consequence dinner was served in the great marquee on the terrace. Among others, Mrs. Emsworth had come with those of her company who were to act that night in the theatre. The *petit saleté* to be produced had never been presented on any stage before, the Lord-Chamberlain of England, with a fatherly regard for the morals of the nation entrusted to him, having deemed that it was too *sale*; and, as a matter of fact, Mrs. Emsworth rather embraced this opportunity of playing it before a private audience, with a view to seeing whether her public in New York, with their strange mixture of cynical indifference to anything but money, and the even stranger survival of the Puritan spirit, which crops up every now and then as some rare border plant will crop up among the weeds and grasses of a long overgrown garden, would be likely to swallow it. She herself was a little nervous of presenting it there. Bilton, on the other hand, who might be supposed to know the taste of the patrons for whom he catered so successfully, thought it would be an immense success.

'After all, Paris loved it,' he said, as he had a few words with her when they went up to dress for dinner. 'And what is bad enough for Paris is good enough for New York. You may take my word for it that what Paris swallows America will gobble.'

'You mean they are more—more emancipated here?'

'Not at all, but that they are eager to accept anything that has been a success in London or Paris. Why, I produced "Dram-drinking" here. Dead failure. I took it to London, where it ran well, and brought it back here. Tremendous success. We Americans, I mean, are entirely devoid of artistic taste. But we give our decided approbation to what other people say is artistic, which, for your purpose and mine, is the same thing. Left to ourselves, we like David Harum. I produce "Hamlet" here next week. The house is full for the next month. But alter the name and say it is by a new author, and it won't run a week. The papers, to begin with, would all damn it.'

'But the critics. Do you mean they don't *know* "Hamlet"?'

'There are no critics, and they don't know anything. They are violent ignoramuses who write for unreadable papers.'

'Then why do you ever consider them?'

'Because they are not critics, and because in New York everyone reads the unreadable. This is my room—you are next door, I think.'

'I shan't come to dinner,' she said. 'I am rather tired. By the way, is that large, beautiful girl Mrs. Palmer's daughter?'

'Probably. Why?'

'Will she be at the play to-night?'

'Probably. Why?'

Mrs. Emsworth frowned.

'It is not fit,' she said.

Bilton raised his eyebrows. This was indeed a woman of 'infinite variety.'

'You cannot alter your play for fear she will be there,' he said.

'No; I suppose not. I say, what devils we are!'

The play was an enormous success, and Mrs. Emsworth's personality seemed to lift it out of the regions of the equivocal. The part, that of a woman who represented the triumph of mind over morals, fitted her like a glove, and it was as impossible to be shocked as it is when a child uses a coarse or profane expression. Her impropriety was no more improper than is the natural instinct of a bird or animal improper; by a supreme effort of nature rather than art she seemed to roll up like an undecipherable manuscript the whole moral code, and say, 'Now, let's begin again.' Her gaiety covered her sins; more than that it transformed them into something so sunlit that the shadows vanished. Even as we laugh at Fricka when she inveighs against Siegmund and Sieglinde, feeling that condemnation is impossible, because praise or blame is uncalled for and irrelevant, so the ethical question (indeed, there was no question) of whether the person whom Mrs. Emsworth represented behaved quite 'like a lady 'never occurred to anyone. Her vitality dominated the situation.

Of all her audience, there was none so utterly surprised at the performance as Bilton. He knew her fairly well, but he had never seen in her half so clearly the triumph of temperament. Knowing her as he did, he knew it was not art; it was only an effort, unique and unsurpassable, to be herself. Again and again he longed to be a play-wright; he could write her, he felt, could he write at all, a part that would be she. For never before had she so revealed herself a sunlit pagan. And as the play went on, his wonder increased. She was admirable. Then Mrs. Massington, who sat next him, laughed at something he had not seen, and for the moment he was vexed to have been called down from the stage to a woman less vivid, for his sensualism was of a rather high order.

Late that night, after the supper that followed the entertainment, he went upstairs. In Mon Repos there was no barbaric quenching of electric light at puritanical hours, no stranding of belated guests in strange passages, and he walked up from the smoking-room with his hands in his pockets, unimpeded by any guttering bedroom candle. The evening had been a triumph for Dorothy—in the mercantile way it had been as great a triumph for him, for the *cachet* of success at Mrs. Palmer's would certainly float the play in New York. The *Gutter Snipe*, he reflected, would have at least a column of virulent abuse, since it had been performed at Mon Repos. So much the better; he would have a whole procession of sandwich men, London fashion, parading Fifth Avenue, every alternate one bearing the most infamous extracts from that paper. To use abuse as a means of advertisement was a new idea ... it interested him. Certainly, Dorothy had been marvellous. She was a witch ... no one knew all her incantations ... and he paused at his bedroom door. She had gone upstairs only five minutes before him. Since the performance she had been queen bee to the whole party; he himself had not had a word with her. Surely even Puritanical Long Island would not be shocked if he just went to her even now for a minute, and congratulated her. Besides, Puritanical Long Island would never know. So he tapped softly and entered, after the manner of a man whose tap merely means 'I am coming.'

The room was brilliantly lit. Mrs. Emsworth was standing by the bed. By her, having looked in for a go-to-bed chat, was Sybil Massington.

CHAPTER IX

Mrs. Emsworth had a rehearsal early next morning at New York, and in consequence she had to leave by the Stock Exchange train at nine, while most of the inhabitants of Mon Repos were still reposing. She herself was down and out before anyone had appeared, for she had slept but badly, and had awoke, definitely and irrevocably, soon after six. Sleeping, as her custom was, with blinds up and curtains undrawn, the glory of the morning quickly weaned her from her bed, and by soon after seven she was strolling about outside in the perfection of an early September hour. There had been a little thunder during the night, and betwixt waking and sleeping she had heard somewhat heavy rain sluicing on to the shrubberies and thirsty grass, and now, when she went out, the moisture was lying like unthreaded diamonds in the sun, and like a carpet of pearls in the shade. Many gardeners were already at work, some on the grass and flower-beds, others bringing up fruit from the greenhouses, and all looked with wide-eyed yokel amazement at the famous actress as she walked up and down. One of them had brought his small child, a boy of about six years old, with him, and the little lad, with a bunch of Michaelmas daisies in his cap, very gravely pushed at one handle of his father's wheelbarrow.

Now, children and Mrs. Emsworth were mutually irresistible, and the barrow was stopped, and the father stood by in a sort of proud, admiring sheepishness, while Mrs. Emsworth made herself fascinating. She had a story to tell about those particular flowers the child had in his hat. The fairies had made them during the night. One had brought the white silk out of which they were cut, another had brought oil-paints to colour them, a third had brought a watering-pot with a rose to sprinkle them. But the bad fairy had seen them, and had come on her broomstick, surrounded by an army of flying toads and spiders and slugs, to destroy the flowers. And a toad had just begun to eat the top of one of the flowers when the sun said, 'Pop, I'm coming,' and before the bad fairy could get under shelter it had shone on her, so that she instantly curled up like a burnt feather, and died with a pain so awful that stomach-ache was nothing to it.

This was so absorbing both to the narrator and the audience that neither had observed that someone else was listening, and as the boy broke out into childish laughter, crying, 'That was nice!' at the awful fate of the wicked fairy, Mrs. Emsworth looked behind her, half hearing a sudden rustle, and saw Amelie standing there, also absorbed.

She instantly sat down on the other handle of the barrow.

'Yes, Tommy, that was nice,' she echoed. 'And do you think the lady will tell us another story? Ask her.'

The lady was so kind as to oblige them again. This time it was about a real live person, who was always very good in the morning, and sat down and did her work as she should, with the good fairy sitting beside her. But later on the good fairy would sometimes go to sleep, and as soon as she was asleep all the bad fairies who had not curled up like burnt feathers came in. And one of them made her eat peas with her knife, and another made her spill her bread-and-milk down her new dress, and another made her lose her temper, and another made her make mud pies in the middle of her nice room, so that it had to be swept again. And she was very unhappy about this, and used to put pins in the good fairy's seat to prevent her going to sleep, and give her strong coffee to drink for the same purpose. But it was all no good, until one day she noticed that as long as a child was with her the good fairy kept awake. So the poor lady set to work again, and tried to see a child every day, because even if she talked to a child for a little in the morning, and especially if it gave her a kiss, the good fairy was much less sleepy.

Tommy's eyes grew wide.

'Oh, I do love you!' he said, and hoisted himself with his dirty boots into her lap. Then, smitten with a child's sudden shyness, he clambered down again, and the wheelbarrow went on its way.

The two others strolled on in silence for a moment over the grass, Amelie with a strange lump in her throat. Then she put her arm round Mrs.

Emsworth's waist.

'Good-morning,' she said quietly, and they kissed.

'I think I love you too,' she said. 'I came out to tell you that.'

Mrs. Emsworth kissed her again.

'That is nice too,' she said. 'But what makes you?'

'I don't know. I think it was seeing you in that horrid play last night. You were like a sunbeam in—in a cesspool. But why do that sort of thing?'

Mrs. Emsworth shrugged her shoulders.

'Because people are beasts, my dear,' she said—'because they like that sort of thing. And one has to live.'

Amelie thought a moment, with her face growing grave.

'Oh, I am sorry, I am sorry,' she said.

A sudden impatience and ungovernable irritation filled Dorothy. She felt as if she was being hauled back to her ordinary life, when she was so happy in the sweetness of the early morning hour. Why did this stupid, gawky girl come and speak to her like this? But with an effort at self-control stronger than she usually bothered herself to make, she mastered it.

'Oh, never mind, never mind,' she said. 'Walk with me a little further, and let me look at you because you are beautiful, and the trees because they are beautiful, and the grass and the sky. What a heavenly moment! Do not let us waste it. Look, the lawns are empty, where yesterday they were full with all sorts of silly and wicked people. Is that an insult to your mother's guests? I think it is. Anyhow, I was one of the silly, wicked people. But now I am not silly or wicked; I am very good, and very innocent, and I want to take everything into my arms and stroke it. My God! what a beautiful world! I am so glad I did not die in the night.'

Amelie laughed. This mood found in her a ready response.

'Yes, yes,' she cried; 'go on. I know what you mean. You want to be rid of all else, to be just a consciousness in the world. I have felt that. What does it say?'

Dorothy shook her head.

'It never says the same thing for five minutes,' she said. 'Just now you and I feel that. If we sat here for a quarter of an hour we should begin to talk *chiffon*. If we sat here longer we might talk scandal. Only I think these moments are given us as a sort of refreshment. God washes our faces every now and then, and we proceed to soil them instantly.'

She turned to her companion eagerly.

'Don't soil yours,' she said. 'Don't let others soil it. It grows on you; it is like using rouge,' and she broke off suddenly.

There was silence a moment, then Amelie said:

'Look, here is Tommy coming back from the house.'

Mrs. Emsworth rose.

'Let us go in,' she said. 'It is time for me to have breakfast, as I am going by the early train. But remember that I was good for ten minutes—if '—and her voice quavered—' if people, as they are sure to do, tell you things.'

They passed Tommy, who paused as they got near. Mrs. Emsworth seemed not to notice him. Then she looked back.

'Dear little chap,' she said, and, retracing her steps, kissed him again.

It must be allowed that by the time they got to the station there was nothing of the early-morning Mrs. Emsworth left about her. On the platform Bilton approached her with rather an anxious face.

'I particularly want to speak to you, Dorothy,' he said in a low voice. 'You can help me.'

She looked at him with extremely vivid virulence.

'Oh, go away, you beast!' she said. 'I can help you, you say. No doubt I can. But I won't. Go away!'

Bilton had the sense to see that he needed help, for there had been a very awkward moment when he went into Mrs. Emsworth's room the night before. He himself was very good at acting quickly in any emergency he had foreseen, but this one was utterly unforeseen, and had found him helplessly unprepared. Had he had even a moment's preparation, he felt sure that he could have said something which would anyhow have been palliative; but since the thing was done, he did not trouble his head about what the palliative would have been. For he had come in—his knock unheard—and found the two ladies together. Upon which Dorothy laughed, Mrs. Massington turned pink, and he retreated. There was the situation. And the most unpromising feature of it was that Dorothy had laughed. With all his quickness he could see no way out. It was clearly impossible for him to open the subject again to Mrs. Massington; it was equally obvious that she would put a construction on his presence. The only person who could conceivably help him was Dorothy, and now she had called him a beast.

But, apparently, during the journey to New York she relented, for as they boarded the mangy-looking ferry-boat that conveyed them across the river, she threw a word to him over her shoulder.

'I shall be in at lunch,' she said. 'You can come if you like.'

He did not like that either, though it was better than nothing, for he felt that she had in a sense the whip-hand of him, and knew it. And Bilton was not accustomed to let anybody have the whip-hand of him.

Mrs. Emsworth always took her rehearsals herself; she had a stage-manager, it is true, who sat meekly in the wings, and whom she contradicted from time to time, his office being to be contradicted, and to write down stage directions which she gave him. Occasionally Bilton looked in for an hour or two; him she contradicted also at the time, but usually incorporated his suggestions afterwards. Her author, if it was a new play, was also in attendance in the stalls; his office was to cut lines out or put lines in. Though, perhaps, she could not act, she certainly had a strong sense of drama; that was why she had laughed at Bilton's entrance the night before, for the situation struck her as admirably constructed. She had seen, with a woman's sixth sense, as correctly and minutely as in a photograph on what footing he and Mrs. Massington were, and though she was not in the slightest degree in love with the man—or, indeed, ever had been—yet she looked on him as her possession, and while she did not want him, she distinctly did not wish him to change hands. Jealousy of the ordinary green variety had something to do with it. A shrewd eye to business, the knowledge of how much better her career went if the great impresario was her devoted admirer, had about as much. Only, if her devoted admirer was to become the confirmed, settled, and sealed-up admirer of someone else, she did not propose to be the candle at which the sealing was done. To be cat's-paw to an act of treason against herself was a feat of altruism of which she was hopelessly incapable. Then, finally, in this jumble of feelings which had resulted in her calling Bilton a beast, there was something neither sordid nor selfish—namely, the determination, distinct and honest, that Mrs. Massington, a woman whom she both liked and respected, should not, at any rate by any auxiliary help of hers, be deceived as to what Bilton really was. She herself, no doubt, with the aid of liquid eyes and a mouth so beautiful that it looked as if it must be made for the utterance of perfect verity, could persuade Mrs. Massington that she and Bilton had never been in intimate relations, and assure her, even to conviction, that his slightly informal visit last night was only—as was indeed true—a visit for the utterance of a few words of congratulation on her success. But she did not intend—from motives good, bad, and indifferent, all mixed—to do this for him. Only, into the composition of this intention the good and honest and fine motive entered.

It was not wonderful that this *pot-au-feu* of feeling, amounting to positive agitation, did not tend towards the comfort of her company at the rehearsal, nor indeed, on the part of the manageress, toward the calm attitude of the thoughtful critic. In consequence, before the rehearsal was an hour old—it was the first 'without books' rehearsal —the second leading lady was next door to tears, the leading gentleman in sulks, the author in despair, and Mrs. Emsworth in a mood of dangerous suavity that made the aspiring actors heartsick.

'Miss Dayrell,' she was saying, 'would you mind not turning your back completely on the audience when you speak those lines. Mr. Yates'—this was the leading gentleman—' I am *so* sorry to interrupt your conversation, but my throat is rather sore this morning, and I cannot hear myself speak if you talk so loud to your friends. Yes; I think, as you are not on the stage just now, it would be better if you left it. Yes, Miss Dayrell, you see these are perhaps the most important lines in the play which you have to speak, and the audience will have a better chance of understanding it if you let them hear what Mr. Farquar has given you to say. Mr. Farquar, I am afraid the second act is about twice as long as it ought to be. I have cut some of it—at least, with your approval, I propose to cut some of it.'

Mr. Farquar sighed heavily in the stalls. He had spent the greater part of the last three nights in writing more of the second act, because it was not long enough.

'Thank you,' continued Mrs. Emsworth, interpreting the sigh as silence. 'You will see my alterations when we get to them. Would you kindly begin, Miss Dayrell, at "If I had a pitch-fork."'

Suddenly her voice changed to a wheedling tenderness.

'And if my own Teddy Roosevelt hasn't come down of his own delicious accord to see his aunt in her pretty theatre! Teddy, the world is very evil, and my mother bids me bind my hair. I beg your pardon, ladies and gentlemen, but I had to say a word to Popsie Tootsicums. Now, dear Miss Dayrell, let's begin again. You enter. Excellent. You turn. Yes, that's exactly what I want. Now.'

A murmur of relief went round, and the faded actors and actresses raised their drooped heads as when a shower has passed over a drought-dried garden. And Teddy R., the angel in disguise, sat sparsely down in the middle of the stage, and smiled on the spectacle of his beneficent work.

But because the happy appearance of Teddy Roosevelt had made *le beau temps* for the members of Mrs. Emsworth's company, it did not at all follow that Bilton, when he came to lunch, would find the same sunshine awaiting him, even as there is no guarantee that, because at twelve o'clock on an April day pellucid tranquillity flooded the earth, there will not be a smart hail-storm an hour afterwards. On the contrary, it was safe to bet that, whatever mood Mrs. Emsworth was in, she would be in a different one before long. The spring-day temperament of hers was, in fact, the only thing to be reckoned on. Consequently, since Bilton had not witnessed the varied phases exhibited at the theatre, he hoped, somehow sanguinely, that she would not be in a temper that so roundly labelled him 'beast' at Port WashingtonStation.

She seemed to have forgotten he was coming to lunch—as a matter of fact, she had, and welcomed him charmingly.

'Dear man,' she said, 'how nice of you to look in. I'm nearly dead with fatigue; let's have lunch at once. Harold, I've acted every part in 'Telegrams' through from beginning to end this morning. Those people are so hard-working, but they are so stupid. In fact, I know every part but my own. That I have promised them to be word perfect in by five o'clock this afternoon.'

'You don't rehearse again this afternoon?' asked he.

'Oh yes, I do. Three hours more this afternoon, then just time for dinner, then theatre again till half-past eleven, then supper at the Waldorf. To-morrow, rehearsal all morning, matinee, evening performance, every interval filled up with reporters and milliners and lime-light people. Oh, well, thank God, we shall all soon be dead. Time to rest then, and time to lunch now.'

'Don't overdo it, Dolly,' said he, as they sat down.

'Overdo it?' My dear boy, it is rather late in the day to recommend me not to overdo it. Besides, we women, and in special this woman, are so much stronger than men. My company follow me through hours of rehearsal, faint yet pursuing. They drop asleep, and I wake them with a gentle touch on their shoulders, and they say, "Is it morning yet?" And I say, "Kindly wake up for ten minutes, and go through this scene, dear, and then you shall go to sleep again." Then, at the end, when I say, "That is all for to-night, ladies and gentlemen," they all hurry away in desperate fear lest I should ask them to supper. "*Il faut lutter pour l'art*," as Daudet says. I'm so glad I'm not a prig, Harold, who thinks about the exigencies of the artistic temperament. I'm not an artist at all. People come to see me act because I'm (*a*) rather good-looking, (*b*) in rollicking good spirits. What delicious cantaloupe! I like my food.'

'All the same, I wish you would take more care of yourself,' said he, fostering her present temper with a light and, he hoped, skilful hand. 'I'm sure you do too much, and some day you will break down. You are spending more than your income of nervous energy, you are living on the capital.'

'Just what I mean to do. Like Mr. Carnegie, I think it would be a disgrace to die with an ounce of nervous force left in one. What use is it when one is dead? I am living on the capital; I intend to spend it all. I shall die sooner, no doubt—but, oh, Harold, what an awful old person I should be at sixty if I proposed, which I do not, to live as long. Look at the old women who have spent their youth as I have done. Rouge on their raddled cheeks, clinging to life, mortally afraid of dying, trying to get a few more successes, with one bleary eye anxiously fixed on some back door into heaven, the other roaming round to see if they can't have another little flirtation before they die. No; let me die at the height of my success. I don't want to stumble down-hill into my grave. I want to find it on the mountain-top. And I shall lie down in it quite content, for I have had a good time, and ask no further questions. And, Harold, plant a great crimson rambler, and a vine like Omar, and a few daffodils, and some Michaelmas daisies, on my grave, so that I shall flower all the year round. And come, if you like, once a year to it, and think over any occasion when I have pleased or amused you, and say to yourself if you can, "She was rather a good sort." Then go away to the woman who happens at the time to—oh, I forgot. We've got to have a talk. And I've been doing all the talking. Have you finished lunch? Come into the next room.'

The April day was behaving quite characteristically. It had got cold and cloudy, and a bitter wind blew suddenly. Mentally he shivered, and followed her.

She had thrown herself down on the big Louis XV. couch. Teddy Roosevelt was having his dinner. There was no mitigation within the horizon.

'About Sybil Massington,' she said, and shut her mouth again as if it worked on a steel spring.

Bilton lit his cigar, and took his time, wishing to appear not nervous.

'Ah, yes,' he said. 'I remember.'

'That line is no good,' remarked Dorothy critically. 'You must get more sincerity into it, or drop it.'

He dropped it, and sat down.

'I've been wanting to tell you for some time, Dorothy,' he said, 'that I hope to marry Mrs. Massington. I should have done so before, only it's an awkward thing to say.'

'There is always a slight crudeness in that situation,' said she. 'Men always try to explain away what can't be explained at all. So cut it short. I know you must say a few words, but let them be few.'

'Well, it's just this,', said he: 'we've been great friends, we've got along excellently; you have always been charming to me, and I hope I haven't treated you badly.'

'Oh no, first-class time,' said she, the *gamin* coming to the surface.

'Well, now I want to marry,' he said, 'and I come to you for your help. If you had been in my position, I would have helped you.'

'Thanks. Well?'

'You know it was a devilish awkward moment last night. And you made it worse. You laughed. You shouldn't have done that.'

Dorothy's face relaxed.

'I couldn't help it,' she said. 'Dramatically, it was perfect, and so funny. Harold, if you could have seen your own face of blank amazement, I really believe you would have laughed too.'

He frowned.

'A pal ought to help a man out,' he said.

'I'm sure you went out pretty quick,' she interpolated. 'Oh, don't peashoot me,' he said. 'Now, a word from you will help me. I can't offer any explanation to Mrs. Massington, simply because, if I tried, she would be convinced there is something to explain. You can. A half word from you will do it. Represent me as your business manager—very business—with an urgent question to ask, and in my stupid, unconventional American way, it not occurring to me that there was any impropriety——'

'And my laugh? How shall I explain that?'

'Because it did occur to you what construction Mrs. Massington would put on it. Because my face of horror when I saw what I had done was so funny. You said so yourself.'

Dorothy paused.

'In other words,' said she slowly, 'I am to tell Mrs. Massington, either directly or by implication, that you and I are you and I, not we—that—just that.'

'Quite so,' he said, 'and very neatly put.'

She sat up.

'I refuse,' she said.

'Why? For what possible reason?'

'For a reason you couldn't appreciate.'

'Let me try.'

'I can't explain it even. But the outline is this: I respect and like Sybil Massington, therefore I will not assist you to marry her. It is not my business to open her eyes—you may marry her if you can—but neither is it my business to close them. Even if you wished it, I would not marry you myself, because I don't think you would be a—well, a satisfactory husband. So I will not help you.' 'Bilton's face was clearly given him to conceal his thoughts. On this occasion it expressed nothing whatever, though he thought a good deal.

'You want to stand in my light, then,' he said.

'Not at all, only I won't hold the candle for you.'

'You refuse to tell the truth to Mrs. Massington; you refuse to tell her what you know—namely, that I came to your room last night merely to congratulate you on your success?'

'I refuse to tell her a fag-end of the truth like that—a truth that is designed to deceive.'

His eye wandered round the room before he replied, and in its course fell on the grate. To-day also there was a torn letter lying in it. A slight tinge of colour came into his face.

'I can't understand you,' he said. 'As far as I know, you on the whole wish me well; you have assured me that you would not marry me yourself. What do you want, then? Do you want to be paid for doing it? If you are not unreasonable in your demands, I will meet them.' She got up, her eyes blazing.

'That is enough,' she said. 'Not another word, Harold, or I assure you I will throw the heaviest and hardest thing I can lift at you. I mean it.'

A rather ugly light came into his eyes—a stale, unwholesome sort of glow.

'Pray don't,' he said; 'we will leave the subject. I think you are behaving most ungenerously—that is all. I should like a few words with you about your dresses in "Telegrams." I will wait till you are ready to discuss them with me. Take a cigarette.'

She looked at him a moment in silence. In spite of herself, she could not help feeling the infernal mastery he had over her. As always, the more violent she became the more he seemed steeped in a calm compound of indifference and almost boredom. And since it is obviously more exhausting to continue violent than to continue calm, it followed that she had to compose herself, thus changing first, while he merely remained unmoved. It had happened often before, and it happened now.

'What is it you want me to say to Mrs. Massington?' she asked at length.

'Pray do not let us discuss it. You might throw something at me,' said he, smiling inwardly.

'Don't you see my point?' she asked. 'Besides, a word from me would do no good. She saw the terms we were on. It was obvious, blatant.'

'Then no harm would be done by your saying a word. She would not be deceived.'

'No; but she would think I tried to deceive her.'

'Would you mind that?' he asked.

'Very much. I like her.'

Bilton knew well the value of the waiting game in an argument, the futility of trying to persuade a woman to do something, especially if she shows the least sign of persuading herself. So he said nothing whatever, since her re-opening the subject pointed to an already existing indecision. But her final answer, when it came, was not in the least what he expected.

'And I refuse finally to help you,' she said. 'If you wish, I will discuss the dresses.'

Bilton would never have made himself so successful a career as he had had he not possessed to a very high degree the power of concentrating his mind on one thing, to the complete exclusion of other preoccupations, and for the next half-hour no cloud of what had happened crossed in his mind the very clear sky of the new play's prospects. He was able to give his whole and complete attention to it, until between them they had settled what he desired to settle. Then, since, like all other days, it was a busy day with him, he rose.

'Good-bye, Dorothy,' he said, 'and don't overdo it.'

Once again she wavered.

'And do you forgive me?' she asked.

'Not in the least. But I don't imagine you care.'

'But I do care.'

He drew on his gloves with great precision.

'I beg your pardon; if you really cared you would do as I ask,' he said. 'Good-bye. I shall be at the theatre this evening.'

She let him go without further words, and, in spite of the heat, he walked briskly down Fifth Avenue. He was not a forgiving man, and though he would not put himself out to revenge himself on anyone, since he had more lucrative ways of employing his time and energies, he was perfectly ready, even anxious, to do her an ill-turn if he had the opportunity. And certainly it seemed to him that there was a handle ready to his grasping when he remembered the torn note from Bertie Keynes which he had picked up in the grate. How exactly to use it he did not at present see, but it seemed to him an asset.

CHAPTER X

One afternoon late in October Ginger was sitting cross-legged on the hearthrug of Judy's drawing-room. Outside a remarkably fine London fog had sat down on the town during the morning, and, like the frog footman in 'Alice in Wonderland,' proposed to sit there till to-morrow, if not for days and days. But a large fire was burning in the grate, for Judy detested unfired rooms, and the electric light was burning. The windows were not shuttered nor the blinds drawn, because Ginger, a Sybarite in sensations, said it made him so much more comfortable to see how disgusting it was outside. So the jaundiced gloom peered in through the windows, and by contrast gave an added animation to Ginger's conversation. He had usually a good deal to say, whether events of interest had occurred lately or not. But just now events of some importance to him and Judy had been occurring with bewildering rapidity, and in consequence conversation showed even less signs than usual of flagging.

'In fact, the world is like a morning paper, so crammed with news that one can't read any one paragraph without another catching one's eye. And your new paragraph, Judy, is most exciting. What has happened, do you suppose?'

'Nothing—probably nothing; Sybil is just tired of it all. She is like that. She goes on enjoying things enormously till a moment comes; at that moment she finds them instantly and immediately intolerable. I am only surprised that it didn't occur sooner.'

'Well, she had enough of New York pretty soon,' said Ginger. 'She only stopped down at Long Island for ten days. Then she had a month's travelling;

she returns to New York on a Monday, and leaves for England forty-eight hours afterwards. You know, she enjoyed it enormously at first. I think something did happen.'

Judy shook her head.

'No; on her return she found she couldn't endure it for a single moment longer. And I'm sure I don't wonder. The description of the pearl-fishing party made me sick. Besides, what could have happened?'

Ginger handed his cup for some more tea.

'If you want me to guess, I will,' he said; 'but I don't think you'll like it.'

'Pray guess,' said she.

'Well, I guess that Bilton—her own Bilton—suddenly behaved like—like Bilton.'

'Why?' said Judy.

'Because she wrote me a letter full of Bilton one week, since when his name has not occurred.'

Judy nodded.

'The same applies to Mrs. Emsworth,' she said. 'Do you think——?'

'Yes,' said Ginger.

'For a fool, you are rather sharp,' said Judy. 'I wonder if it is so.'

'I don't; I know it,' said Ginger. 'By the way, I saw poor Charlie yesterday.'

'Were you down at Sheringham?'

'No; he has left Sheringham. Apparently you have to get up when a bell rings, and eat all that is given you, and live out of doors till another bell rings. Charlie said he would sooner die like a gentleman than live like a Strasburg goose. So he left. He is down at Brighton in his mother's house, living out of doors.'

Judy stirred her tea thoughtfully.

'Has he told Sybil yet?' she asked. 'You remember he would not let us tell her; he said he wished to tell her himself.'

'I don't know; I know he meant to.'

'Humanly speaking, what chance has he got?' she asked.

'A good one, if he will be sensible; he probably won't. But one person could make him sensible.'

Judy never asked unnecessary questions, and let this pass in silence.

'And have you heard from the millionaire?' she asked.

'Bertie? Yes. Bertie seems uncommonly happy. So should I be if I was going to marry the richest girl in the five continents. Also I think he's in love with her.'

'Isn't Gallio delighted?'

'Yes; for the first time in his life, he really takes an interest in Bertie. He says a man's efficiency is measured by his success. Success means income, you know. Gallio speaks of himself as the most inefficient man of his own acquaintance. But the pictures have to be sold, all the same. Bertie's news came a little too late.'

'Pictures?' asked Judy.

'Hadn't you heard. You see, Gallio, about a month ago, suddenly became aware that he had a genius for speculating on the Stock Exchange. He chose American rails to exercise his genius on. But the American rails went flat, and knocked him flat. So all the Dutch pictures are up at Christie's next week. He doesn't care. As soon as he gets the money for them, he is going to speculate again. He has written to Bertie in case he can get any sort of special information from Palmer. He has stockbrokers to dinner, and lunches with bulls and bears.'

Judy was silent a moment.

'What about Mrs. Emsworth?' she asked suddenly.

Ginger had got hold of a large Persian cat, and was stroking it. The animal was in the full ecstasy of sensuous pleasure, with eyes shut and neck strained to his hand. But, as Judy asked this, he paused a moment, and stroked it the wrong way. It hit at him with its paw, and fled in violent indignation.

'Well, what about Mrs. Emsworth?' he repeated.

'Ginger, don't be ridiculous. It is loyal of you to pretend not to know what I mean, but still ridiculous. How has Bertie managed to do this under her very guns?'

'I suppose he silenced them first,' said Ginger cautiously. 'Or perhaps she has no guns.'

'Why, then, two years ago, did we all talk about nothing else but her and Bertie?'

'Because we are gossips,' said he.

'Do you mean that?'

Ginger examined his injured hand.

'Yes, I mean that,' he said. 'Bertie told me all that happened. He fell desperately in love with her; he wrote her a very foolish letter, which proposed, oh, all sorts of things—marriage among them. Immediately afterwards she—well, we all began talking about her and Bilton.'

'What happened to the letter?' asked Judy.

'Don't know,' said he.

Judy was silent a little.

'Anyhow, it all hangs together with your idea about Sybil and Bilton,' she said at length.

'I wondered if you were going to see that,' said Ginger rather loftily.

Judy went to the window and looked out.

'I like that fog,' she said, 'because it renders all traffic and business of all sorts out of the question. I like the feeling that London, anyhow, has to pause, and just twiddle its thumbs until God makes the wind blow.'

'After all, a fog comes from smoke, and it was man who lit the fires,' remarked Ginger parenthetically.

'You needn't remind one of that,' said she. 'Now, Sybil told me there were no fogs in New York. That is awful. Her letters were awful. The whole of life was a ceaseless grind; if you stopped for a moment, you were left behind. How hopelessly materialistic! Why, the only people who do any good in the world—apart from making Pullman cars and telephones, that is to say—are exactly those who do stop—who sit down and think. All the same, it is possible to stop too much. You are always stopping. Ginger, why don't you ever do something?'

'Because it is so vastly more amusing to observe other people doing things,' said he. 'As a rule, they do them so badly. Besides, Sybil seems to me an awful warning. She deliberately went to seek the strenuous life. Well, something has happened; the strenuous life has been one too many for her. Oh, by the way, I have more news for you -the most important of all, nearly. You have been talking so much that I couldn't get a word in.'

'Slander,' said Judy. 'Get it in now.'

'Gallio, as you know, has been trying to sell Molesworth. Well, advances have been made to him through an agent about it. He wants to know the name of the purchaser, but he can't find out.'

'What does Gallio care as long as the price is a good one?'

'You can't tell about Gallio; he has some charming prejudices. Besides—I don't understand the ins and outs of it—Bertie's consent has to be obtained. But he is offered two hundred thousand for a barrack he never lives in, and some acres of land which nobody will farm. He has telegraphed to Bertie about it to-day.'

'Well, I suppose it's no use being old-fashioned,' said Judy; 'but I think it's horrible to sell what has been yours so long. Probably the buyer is some awful South African Jew.'

'Very likely. But it's nothing new. Money has always possessed its own buying power—it always will. Only there's such a devil of a lot of it now in certain hands that a poor man can't keep anything of his own. And the hands that own it are not English. But they want England. Anyhow, as you say, it is no use being old-fashioned; but it is an immense luxury. You are luxurious, Judy.'

'What do you mean?'

'Well, the greatest luxury of your life was refusing to ask Mrs. Palmer to your house. How you could afford it I don't know.'

'It was delicious,' said Judy with great appreciation.

'Sybil was so sensible about it. She took just your view; she said she couldn't afford it herself, but that I was my own mistress. I wonder—I really wonder—why I find that class of person so intolerable.'

'Because you are old-fashioned; because you do not believe what is undoubtedly true—that wealth will get you anything——'

'Anything material it certainly will get you.'

'Quite so. And this is a materialistic age. I must go, as I'm dining out. Mind you let me know anything fresh in all these events that concern us.'

Ginger went out into the thick, dim-coloured evening with a sense of quickened interest in things. His only passion in life was the observation of other people, but for the last month or two he had found very little to observe. Apart from his work as a clerk in the Foreign Office, which could have been done quite as well in half the time by an ordinary bank clerk at a quarter of his salary, his life was valueless from an economical point of view, while as far as his work went (from the same point of view) he was positively fraudulent. Thus, judged by the relentless standards of America, where work is paid for strictly by the demand which exists for it, and that demand is tested simply and solely by the criterion of whether it adds directly or indirectly to the wealth of the country, Ginger's services would have been dispensed with. For he was—though the wedge was being pulled out, not pushed in—the thin end of that wedge which in the days of George III. had provided so amply for the younger sons, nephews, and connections of the nobility. But the leisured ease in which those fortunate people could live in those days was rapidly passing away, and Ginger, from an economical point of view, was a very small specimen of an interesting survival. For, provided that a thing is done equally well in a cheap way as in an expensive way, it is inexcusable in the public service not to have it done as cheaply as possible. Whether the complete application of this principle will be found wholly successful in its working will be for succeeding generations to determine. But even to-day we have, so to speak, a working model of it in America. The money, once earned, of course becomes the entire property of the individual, and it is perfectly right that beggars should starve for a crust, while on the foreshore of Mon Repos the glutted vulgarocracy gabble and search for pearls.

So the interesting survival made his groping way westwards, in order to dress for dinner. The fog was extremely dense, and the light from the street-lamps was not sufficient to pierce the thickness that lay between them, so that a man following the curb of the pavement had passed out of range of one before he came within range of the next. Dim shadows of people suddenly loomed large and close, and as suddenly vanished into the fog. In the roadway omnibuses and cabs proceeded at a foot-pace, some drivers even leading their horses; here a hansom had gone utterly astray, and was at a standstill on the pavement, being backed slowly off into the road. Through the dense air sound also came muffled and subaqueously; it was like a city in a dream.

At the corner of Bond Street a man, walking faster than is usual in a fog, ran into Ginger just below a gas-lamp, and apologized in a voice that struck him as familiar. The next moment he saw who it was.

'Pray don't mention it,' he said. 'I thought you were in America, Mr. Bilton.'

Bilton peered at him a moment, and recognised him also. 'Really, Lord Henry, if it was necessary for me to run into someone, I should have chosen you. At the present moment I may be in Australia for all I know. Is this London, and if so, what part?'

'Corner of Bond Street,' said Ginger. 'Which way are you going?'

'South Audley Street,' said the other; 'I'm going to see your father, in fact, about the sale of Molesworth.'

'Are you going to buy it?' asked Ginger.

'No; but I have been asked to communicate direct with him about it. The intending purchaser wants me to see about doing it up.'

'I am going that way too,' said Ginger; 'let us go together. Walking is the only way. You know, we don't know who the intending purchaser is.'

'That so?' asked Bilton. 'Well, there's no reason any longer for secrecy; it's Lewis S. Palmer.'

'Lewis Palmer?' asked Ginger.

'Yes; pity your father didn't ask an extra ten thousand.'

'He would have, if he had known who the purchaser was,' said Ginger candidly. 'Do you know if Mr. Palmer means to live there?' he asked.

'No more than he means to live on the new Liverpool and Southampton line.'

'Ah! he hasn't got that through yet,' said Ginger, with a sudden feeling of satisfaction that there had been considerable difficulties in getting the Bill through the House last session. There had really been no reason why it should not have been passed, except that the Commons objected to it merely because the line was practically to belong to a man who was not English.

Bilton laughed a short, rather shoulder-shrugging laugh.

'London is the last place to know what happens in London,' he said. 'The Bill was passed this afternoon. Lewis S. Palmer owns that line as much as I own my walking-stick. He could sit down on the up-track and Mrs. Palmer on the down-track, and stop all traffic if he chose. You don't seem to like it.'

Ginger rather resented this, chiefly because it was true.

'Why should I not like it?' he said.

'Can't say, I'm sure,' said Bilton. 'I guess your country ought to be very grateful. Palmer will show you how to run a line properly. He won't give you engines which are so pretty that they ought to be hung on the wall, and he won't give you cars covered with gilt and mirrors. But he'll run you trains quicker than you ever had them run yet; he'll give you express freight rates that will be as cheap as transport by sea, and he'll pull the two ports together like stringing beads, instead of letting them roll about unconnected. Of course, he'll get his bit out of it, but all the benefit of rapid transport and cheap fares will be yours. I guess your House of Commons was annoyed they didn't think of it themselves.'

They had got to Hyde Park Corner, and the fog had suddenly grown less dense and the darkness was clarified. Across the open square they could see the dark mass of the arch at the top of Constitution Hill, and farther on the dim shapes of the houses in Grosvenor Place. Hansoms no longer passed as if going to a funeral, but jingled merrily by to the cheerful beat of the horses' hoofs on the road. All the traffic was resuscitated; buses swayed and nodded; silent-footed electric broughams made known their advent by their clear metallic bells, and the two turned more briskly up Hamilton Place.

'And what has brought you to England so suddenly?' asked Ginger. 'I thought you intended to stop in America throughout Mrs. Emsworth's tour.'

'Circumstances altered my plan,' said Bilton. 'I had several pieces of business here; for instance, Lewis S. Palmer wished me to conduct the negotiations of Molesworth, as his agent seemed to be a sort of fool-man, and tell him what must be done to make it liveable in.'

'It is going to be lived in?' said Ginger, quite unable to stifle the curiosity he felt.

'Oh, certainly it is going to be lived in. Then I wanted to secure—I have secured—the lease of the Coronation Theatre for next summer.'

'I thought Mrs. Emsworth had taken it,' said Ginger.

'No; she meant to, but she did not complete her contract before leaving for America. In fact, she let an excellent chance slip.'

'You have cut her out?'

'Certainly. Then there was another thing. Now, do you know, Lord Henry, whether Mrs. Massington has arrived in London yet? She sailed the day before I did, but we made a very fast voyage. She was in the *Oceanic*.'

'She arrives this evening,' said Ginger.

'And goes to her sister's, to Miss Farady's?' asked Bilton.

'Yes. Here we are. Won't you come in with me? I will see if my father is at home.'

Gallio was in, and very much at Bilton's service. Personally, he detested the man, but he liked his way of doing business, and he particularly liked the business he had come to do. Bertie's consent had been received by cable that afternoon, and a short half-hour was sufficient to draw up the extremely simple deed by virtue of which Molesworth, the house and park, and all that was within, house and park passed into the possession of Lewis S. Palmer on payment of the sum of two hundred thousand pounds.

'And I'll cable to Lewis right along,' said Bilton at the conclusion, 'and you'll find the sum standing to your credit to-morrow morning. By the way, Lewis expressly told me to ask you whether you had any wishes of any sort with regard to Molesworth—any small thing you wanted out of it, or anything you wanted kept exactly as it is.'

Gallio considered a moment.

'Ah, there's the visitors' book,' he said; 'I should rather like to have that. I don't think it could be of any value to Mrs. Palmer, as it only contains the names of friends of mine who have stayed there.'

'Distinguished names?' asked Bilton.

'I suppose you might call some of them distinguished.'

'I guess Mrs. Palmer might like to keep it on,' said Bilton.

'But I'll ask. Anything else?'

'I should rather like the oak avenue left as it is,' said Gallio. 'It was planted in the reign of Henry VIII., and several what you would call distinguished people—James I. and George I. among them—planted trees there.'

'Mrs. Palmer will have a gold fence put round it,' said Bilton, with a touch of sarcasm.

'That will add very greatly to the beauty of the sylvan scene,' Gallio permitted himself to remark. 'In fact, if I ever have the pleasure of seeing Molesworth again, I shall expect to find it improved out of all recognition.'

'I expect Mrs. Palmer will smarten it up a bit,' said Bilton, quite unmoved.

That excellent man of business went down to Molesworth next day in order to inspect it generally, with a view to estimating what would have to be spent on it to make it habitable. He had sufficient taste to see the extraordinary dignity of the plain Elizabethan house; and though he felt that Mrs. Palmer would probably have called it a mouldy old ruin, he did not propose, even though he got a percentage on the sale and the costs of renovation, to recommend any scheme of gilding and mirrors. The tapestries were admirable, the Sheraton and Chippendale furniture was excellently suited to the thoroughly English character of the place, and the gardens wanted nothing but gardeners. Bilton's extremely quiet and businesslike mind had its perceptive side, and though he did not care for, yet he appreciated, the leisurely solidity, the leisurely beauty of the place, so characteristic of England, so innate with the genius of the Anglo-Saxon. The red, lichen-toned house had grown there as surely as its stately oaks and lithe beeches had grown there out of the English soil— indigenous, not bought and planted. Cedar-trees with broad fans of leaves, and starred by the ripe cones, made a spacious shade on the lawn, and whispered gently to the stirring of the warm autumn wind, as they bathed themselves in the mellow floods of October sunshine. Below the lawn ran a dimpling trout-stream, and within the precincts of the park stood the small Gothic church, grown gray in its patient, unremitting service, gathering slowly round it the sons of the soil. Attached to one aisle was the chapel of the family, and marble effigies of Scartons knelt side by side, or, reclining on their tombs, raised dumb hands of prayer. One had hung up his armour by him; by the feet of another his hunting dogs lay stretched in sleep. One, but a beardless lad, the second of the race, had been killed in the hunting-field; his wife, so ran the inscription, was delivered of a child the same day, and died within twenty-four hours of her lord. And over all was the air of distinction, of race, of culture that could not be bought, though Lewis S. Palmer, by right of purchase, was entitled to it all. Bilton felt this, but dismissed it as an unprofitable emotion, and made a note on his shirt-cuff to inquire whether the right of presentation to the living belonged to the family.

Sybil Massington, in the meantime, had arrived in London, and while Bilton was engaged in appraising the Molesworth estate, was herself in the confessional of the wisest spinster in London. All her life she had been accustomed to knowing what she wanted, and, knowing, to getting it. But now, for the first time in matters of importance, she did not know what she wanted, and was afraid of not getting anything at all. Things in America, in fact, had gone quite stupendously awry; she was upset, angry at herself and others, and, what to her was perhaps most aggravating of all, uncertain of herself. To one usually so lucid, so intensely reasonable as she was, this was of the nature of an idiocy; it was as if she—the essential Sybil—stood by, while a sort of wraith of herself sat feeble and indifferent in a chair, unable to make up its mind about anything. She longed to take this phantom by the shoulders and shake it into briskness and activity again, open its head and dust its brain for it. But perhaps Judy could do it for her; anyhow, the need, not so much of consultation, but of confession, was urgent. She did not in the least want absolution, because she had done nothing wrong; indeed, she wanted to confess because she was incapable of doing anything at all. She had to make up her mind, and she could not; perhaps stating the problem of her indecision very clearly might, even if it did not elicit a suggestion from Judy, help her, at any rate, to see what her difficulties were more clearly. And, though indecisive, she still retained her candour, and told Judy all that had happened, exactly as it had happened.

'Oh, I know it,' she said in answer to some question of Judy's. 'A woman feels in her bones when a man is going to propose to her; only I wasn't quite ready for it, and for two days I kept him from actually asking me. Then, on the night that Mrs. Emsworth was acting there, I went upstairs with her to her room. Two minutes afterwards Bilton came in—strolled in.'

'You mean he didn't knock?' asked Judy.

'Oh, my dear, what does it matter whether he knocked or not? As a matter of fact, I think he did, but he came in on the top of his knock. Anyhow, there was no doubt in my mind as to what their relations were; but, to make sure, I asked Mrs. Emsworth. It was a horrible thing to do, but I did it. I like that woman; she is what she is, but she is extremely *bon enfant*, a nice, straightforward boy. And she told me. I was perfectly right: he had been living with her for the last two years.'

Sybil got up, and began walking up and down the room. 'It hurt me,' she went on; 'it hurt me intolerably. It hurt my self-respect that he should come to me like that. No, he had not broken with her—at any rate, not definitely. She was perfectly straightforward with me, and in a curious sort of way she was sorry for me, as one is sorry for a pain one does not understand. She could not see, I think, that it made any difference.'

Judy's rather short nose went in the air.

'Luckily, it does not matter much what that sort of woman thinks,' she said.

Sybil did not reply for a moment.

'You don't see my difficulty, then,' she said; 'my difficulty, my indecision, is that I am not certain whether she is right or not. Look at it this way: I was attracted by Mr. Bilton; I felt for him that which I believe in me does duty for love. I liked him and I admired him; I liked the fact that he admired me. Now, all the time that I liked and admired him this thing had happened. I liked the man who had done that. What difference, then, can my knowing it make?'

Judy looked at her in surprise.

'If he had happened to be a murderer?' she said.

'I should not ever have liked him.'

'I don't know what to say to you,' said Judy, really perplexed. 'What you tell me is so unlike you.'

'I know it is. I have changed, I suppose. I think America changed me. What has happened? Is it that I have become hard or that I have learned common-sense? What I cannot make out is whether I would sooner have learned this or not. If I had not learned it, I should be now engaged to him; but, knowing it, shall I marry him?'

'Have you seen him since?'

'No. He has behaved very typically, very cleverly. He neither tried to see me again nor wrote to me. He has very quick perceptions, I am sure. I am sure he reasoned it out with himself, and came to the conclusion that it was better not to approach me in any way for a time. He was quite right; if he had tried to explain things away, or had even assured me that there was nothing to explain, I should have had nothing more to say to him. I should have told him that he and all that concerned him was a matter of absolute indifference to me. He has been wise: he simply effaced himself, and he has therefore made me think about him.'

Sybil paused in front of the looking-glass, and smoothed her hair with an absent hand. Then she turned round again.

'You will see,' she said. 'He will follow me to England. I don't think you like him, Judy,' she added.

'My approbation is not necessary to you.'

'Not in the least; but why don't you?'

'Because I am old-fashioned—because we belong to totally different generations, you and I. I don't like motor-cars, either, you see; and a person's feeling for motor-cars is a very good criterion as to the generation to which he belongs.'

Sybil laughed.

'How odd you are!' she said; 'they are fast and convenient. But about Mr. Bilton: he is a very remarkable man. He can do anything he chooses to do, and whatever he chooses to do turns into gold. He owns half the theatres in New York; he has a big publishing business there; he furnishes houses for people; he has made a fortune on the Stock Exchange. Some of those Americans are like spiders sitting in the middle of their webs, which extend in all directions, and whatever wind blows, it blows some fly into their meshes. Just as a great artist like Michael Angelo can write a sonnet, or hew a statue out of the marble, or paint a picture, fitting the artistic sense like a handle to any knife, so with a man like him. He sees money everywhere. He is very efficient.'

'Is he quite unscrupulous?' asked Judy.

'Not unscrupulous exactly, but relentless; that is the spirit of America: it fascinates me, and it repels me. Some of them remind me of destiny—Mr. Palmer does. By the way, he asked me, when I was over there, if Molesworth was for sale. Have you heard anything about it?'

'Yes; Ginger told me that negotiations were going on. He didn't know, nor did Gallio, who the possible purchaser was. No doubt it was Mr. Palmer.'

Sybil put her head on one side, considering.

'What was the price?' she asked.

'Two hundred thousand.'

'Of course, money does not mean anything particular to the Palmers,' she said; 'but I rather wonder why they bought it. Mr. Palmer has been looking out for an English house, I know, but I should have thought Molesworth was too remote.'

'I expect they paid for the spirit of ancestry which clings to the place,' said Judy. 'Molesworth seemed to me, the only time I saw it, to be the most typically English house I had ever seen. Mrs. Palmer can't procure ancestors, but she can procure the frame for them.'

'That is not charitably said, dear Judy,' said her sister; 'besides, I am sure that is not it. Ah, I know! They have bought it to give to Bertie on his marriage; that must be it.'

'If so, there is a large-leaved, coarse sort of delicacy about it,' said Judy.

'There again you are not charitable. Besides, you have not seen Amelie. She is charming, simply charming—a girl, too, a real flesh and blood girl. And she adores him; she adores him with all her splendid vitality.'

'And Bertie?' asked Judy.

'Oh, they will be very happy,' said Sybil. 'It will be a great success. He admires her immensely; he likes her immensely. Dear Judy, there are many ways of love; one way of love is Bertie's and mine. That is all.'

'Did he adore Mrs. Emsworth like that?' asked Judy.

'Well, no, I imagine not; that was the other way of love.'

She took up the morning paper. Then a sudden thought seemed to strike her, and she laid it down again.

'By the way, is Charlie in town?' she asked. 'I heard from him just before I left America; he said he had not been well. His letter made me feel rather anxious. There was an undercurrent of—of keeping something back.'

'Did he tell you no more than that?' asked Judy.

Sybil glanced up, and, seeing Judy's face, knitted her brows into a frown.

'Judy, what is it?' she asked quickly; 'tell me at once.'

'I can't, dear; he wished to tell you himself. I promised him I wouldn't.'

'But is there something wrong—something really wrong?'

Judy nodded.

'Where is he?'

'Down at Brighton with his mother.'

'Judy, you must tell me,' said her sister; 'it is merely saving me a couple of hours of horrid anxiety. I shall go down to see him this afternoon. Now, what is it? Is it lungs? I will tell Charlie I forced you to tell me.'

'There is no use in my not answering you,' said Judy.

'Yes, it is that.'

'Serious?'

'Consumption is always serious.'

Sybil said nothing for a moment.

'I shall go down this afternoon,' she said. 'Why is he at Brighton? Why is he not at some proper place?'

'He went to Sheringham for a time, but he left it.'

'But he has got to get better,' said Sybil quickly. 'He must do what is sensible.'

Judy glanced up at her a moment.

'As things at present stand, he does not much want to get better,' she said.

Sybil turned, and looked at her long and steadily.

'You mean me?' she asked.

There was silence. Sybil went to the writing-table and wrote a telegram, while her sister took up the paper she had dropped and looked at it mechanically. Almost immediately a short paragraph struck her eye, but her mind, dwelling on other things, did not at once take in its significance.

'Yet you advised me yourself not to marry him,' said Sybil, as she rang the bell.

'I know I did; nor have I really changed my mind. But it is in your power to make him want to live.'

Sybil turned on her rather fiercely.

'You have no right to load me with such responsibilities,' she said. 'It is not my fault that he loves me; it is not my fault that I am as I am.'

'I know it is not,' said Judy; 'but, Sybil, be wise—be very wise. I don't know what you can do, but certainly nobody else can do anything. I am very sorry for you.' Sybil gave the telegram, asking Charlie if she could come, to the servant, and stood in silence again by the fire. After a pause Judy took up the paper again.

'There is something here that concerns you,' she said; 'it is that Mr. Bilton arrived in London yesterday.'

Sybil turned, then suddenly threw her arms wide.

'Oh, Judy, Judy,' she cried, 'I am unutterably unhappy! I am perplexed, puzzled; I don't know what I feel.'

And she flung herself down on the sofa by Judy's side, and burst into uncontrollable sobs.

CHAPTER XI

Charlie Brancepeth was sitting in a wooden summer-house on the lawn of his mother's house at Brighton. It was set upon a pivot in the centre of its floor, so that it could be turned with little effort to any point of the compass, so as to face the sun and avoid the wind. In it—so much, at any rate, he practised of the treatment which he had compared to the fattening of a Strasburg goose— he passed the whole day, only sleeping indoors. But this he did because it seemed to him a very rational and sensible mode of life, soothing to the nerves, and producing in him a certain outdoor stagnation of the brain. He did not want to think; he wanted merely to be as quiet and drowsed as he could, and not to live very long; for, since Sybil's final rejection of him, the taste had gone out of life—temporarily it might be only—but while that was still very new and bitter within him had come this fresh blow, the discovery that he was suffering from tubercular disease of the lungs. For some months before he had suspected this; then, soon after the departure of Sybil and Bertie for America, he had had an attack of influenza from which he did not rally well; he had a daily rise of temperature, a daily intolerable lassitude, and his doctor, seeking for the cause of this, had found it. Then, following his advice, he tried a cure on the east coast of England, in which he had to get up at the sound of a bell and proceed out of doors, there to remain all day till a bell summoned him and the other patients in again. At frequent intervals he had to eat large quantities of fattening food; at other hours he had to walk quietly along a road. Work of all sorts, even more than an hour or two's reading, was discouraged, and the days had been to him a succession of nightmares, all presenting the same dull hopelessness. So, after a fortnight of it, he decided to persevere with it no more, and, if he had to die, to die. He had talked the thing out once with his mother, and had promised to go to Davos for the winter, if it was recommended to him, and in the interval to lead a mode of life that was rational for his case without being unbearable. They both agreed finally to dwell on the subject as little as possible in their thoughts, and dismiss it altogether from their conversation.

Just now she was away for a day or two, and he was alone as he waited for Sybil's arrival. That he was alone he had felt himself bound to tell her, but he felt certain that she would come all the same. And though he waited for her in a sort of anguish of expectation, he felt that life, for the first time since the Sunday at Haworth at the end of July, was interesting. What she would say to him, how he would take it, even the vaguest predication of their intercourse, was beyond him to guess. Indeed, it was scarcely worth while, he thought, trying to conjecture what it would be. For Love and Death were near to him, august guests.

The shelter was lit by an electric light, and he had just turned this on when he heard the wheels of her cab drive up. He went in through the garden-door to meet her, his heart beating wildly, found her in the moment of arrival, and advanced to her with outstretched hands.

'Ah, this is charming of you,' he said; 'I am delighted to see you!'

But she had involuntarily paused a moment as she saw him, for, though his disease had made no violent inroads on him, yet the whole manner of his face, his walk, his appearance, was changed. His eyes were always large, they now perhaps looked ever so little larger; his face was always thin, it was perhaps a shade thinner; he always stooped, he stooped perhaps a little more. But, even as one can look at a portrait and say 'I see no point on which it is not like, yet it really has no resemblance to the man,' so, though Charlie was changed so little, yet he was not like him with whom she had walked on the hot Sunday afternoon of July last. Then it was summer, now it was autumn; and, instead of the broad brightness of sun, a little bitter wind stirred among the trees. For the flame of life there was substituted the shadow of death, intangible, indescribable, untranslatable into definite thought, but unmistakable.

But her pause was only momentary; the quick, practical part of her nature leaped instinctively to the surface to do its duty. She was here, if possible, to help, and she came quickly forward to meet him.

'My dear Charlie,' she said, 'it is good to see you again.'

She took both his hands in hers.

'You bad boy,' she said, 'to get ill. Judy told me. It was not her fault; I made her.'

'I meant to tell you myself,' said he; 'but it does not matter. Now, that is enough of that subject; my mother and I never talk of it—we hardly ever think of it. Now, will you take off your things?'

Sybil drew her cloak round her.

'No, certainly not,' said she. 'Judy told me you lived in a summer-house. Well, I did not come down here to see you through the window; lead on to the summer-house.'

'It will be too cold for you,' said he.

'It will be nothing of the kind.'

They talked till dinner on indifferent subjects; she sketched New York for him with a brilliant, if not a very flattering, touch; she did her best for the Revels, but suddenly in the middle broke down.

'It really is awful what a beast one is!' she said. 'But there, somehow, where what I am describing to you is natural, where everyone is so extraordinarily kind and so entirely uncultured, the vulgarity did not strike me. I like the people, and, as you know, I like the sense of wealth. Who is it who talks about moral geography? Burke, I think. Well, that is a very suggestive expression. You can do in New York what you cannot possibly conceive doing in England, just as you can grow plants in the South which will not stand our climate.'

Charlie shook his head.

'I don't think I could stand that anywhere,' he said.

'Oh yes, you could. *Milieu*, environment is everything; but now, as I sit here and look at the big trees in the garden, covered with that wash of moonlight, it is different. You too—you are so very un-American. I always told you you were old-fashioned.'

Charlie looked at her in silence a moment.

'And you,' he said at length—' you yourself? Have you changed, as Ginger prophesied? Do I seem to you more old-fashioned than ever? I am a very good test question, I imagine.'

'Why?'

'Because you have seen, have you not? a good deal of my double, Bilton. The contrast of our natures ought to be all the more apparent for the similarity of our appearance.' She got up.

'I have a great deal to talk to you about, Charlie,' she said; 'but it is after-dinner talk. A good deal is about you; the rest is about myself. I have also made another discovery: I am a more profound egotist than I knew. Did I always strike you as egotistic?'

'Dominant people are always egotistic,' said he.

'Dominant? Am I dominant? You will not think so when you have heard.'

'Have things gone wrong?' he asked.

'Yes—or right; I do not know which. Anyhow, they have gone differently to what I—well, planned. Now, the plans of dominant people go as they expect them to go.'

'Until they meet a more dominant person,'

She shook her head.

'No, if my plans have been upset, anyhow, I have upset others,' she said.

They dined rather silently, for both of them were thinking of the talk which was coming, and Sybil again was conscious of her own indecision. Then, after dinner, since delay only made her more heavily conscious of it, she went straight to the subject.

'Judy told me you had left Sheringham,' she said—'that you had practically taken yourself out of the hands of doctors who, humanly speaking, could probably have cured you. Do you think you have any right to do that?'

'My life is my own,' said he.

'Ah, I dispute that. One does not belong to one's self—at any rate, not wholly. One belongs to one's friends—to those who care for one.'

'Who cares for me? Bertie Keynes, I suppose, cares for me, but I entirely deny his right to any disposal of what I do.'

'Your mother, then.'

'In the main she agrees with me. Supposing I had cancer, she would not urge me for a moment to have an operation which was uncertain of success; and my case is similar.'

Sybil was silent a moment.

'I, then,' she said. 'I entirely disapprove of your action. I care for you; you should consider me as well. It is in that sense your life is not your own; you have made yourself a niche, so to speak, in other people's lives; you have put an image of yourself there—given it them—and you have no right to take it away.'

He took a cigarette from a box near him.

'And you are not allowed to smoke,' she added.

He laughed and lit it.

'We have got to talk,' he said. 'If you convince me I have no right to—well, to commit what will probably be a very lengthy suicide, I will smoke no more. If you don't, I shall continue to smoke, and in the interval I can talk more easily. Now you have spoken so frankly to me, I shall use the same frankness.'

She nodded.

'A man's life,' he said, 'belongs to himself until he has given it to a woman, and she has accepted it. Then it is no longer his, but hers, and she may dispose of it. No woman has accepted mine.'

She made a little movement in her chair, as if wincing, and he saw it.

'Shall I not go on?' he said.

'No, go on; it is this for which I came here.'

'So everybody,' said he, 'has about the same weight with me, and that combined weight is less than my right to do as I choose. Bertie Keynes, you, Judy, Ginger—you all want me to be what you call sensible, and live as long as possible. But my indifference to life is stronger than your desire that I should live. My mother alone wishes me to do as I choose, because she understands.'

He paused, and saw that Sybil was looking, not at him, but into the fire, and that unshed tears stood in her eyes, fighting with some emotion that would not let them fall.

'I understand too,' she said in a whisper; and it looked as if the tears would have their way. Then they were checked again as she continued: 'But you are grossly unfair to me—both you and Judy. You saddle me with this responsibility. You say it is my fault that you are indifferent to life. Indeed it is not fair. I am what I am. You may hate me or love me, but it is me. I am hard, I dare say, without the power to love; that is me too. And you say to me, "Alter that, please, and become exceedingly tender and devoted." And because I don't—ah, there is your mistake; it is because I can't. I could pray and think and agonize, and yet not add an inch to my stature; and do you think, then, it is likely that I could alter what is so vastly more *me* than my height?'

'Ah, I don't blame you,' said he, 'and I don't saddle you with any responsibility.'

'But if I loved you, you would care to live.'

'Yes; but I don't say that it is your fault that you don't. That would be interfering in your life—a thing which I am deprecating in regard to my own.'

She made a hopeless gesture with her hands.

'We are talking in a circle,' she said. 'Leave it for a moment; I have something else to tell you.'

He sat very upright in his chair, grasping the arms in his hands, feeling that he knew for certain what this was.

'You mean you are going to marry Harold Bilton?'

'No, I mean exactly the opposite; I mean that I am not.' He dropped the cigarette he had just lit into the fireplace. With her woman's quickness, she instantly saw the symbolical application of this, and, with her passion for analysis, could not resist casting a fly, as it were, over it. She pointed to the grate.

'You have dropped your cigarette,' she said.

He looked at her for one half-second, and then, with rather slower-moving mind, recalled what he had said about not smoking any more.

'Yes, the doctors told me not to,' he said, feeling again the thrill of even this infinitesimal piece of fencing with her.

'They said it was a bad habit for me.'

She got up.

'Charlie, I don't know if I was right to tell you that,'she said.

'You mean it may lead me to hope that—I assure you it shall not. But it leaves things less utterly hopeless.'

She shook her head.

'You mustn't even think that,' she said.

'I can't help thinking that. While there is life, you know——I was lying'—and his eye brightened with a sudden excitement—' with throat ready for the guillotine. I could see it; they had not bandaged my eyes—but they have taken the knife away. No, I don't ask "What next?" The knife is gone: that is sufficient for the moment.'

She stood close to him by the fire, with eyes that strayed from him to a picture, down to the fire again, and again back to him.

'It is late,' she said at length; 'I must go to bed, and so must you. I have got to go back to-morrow. I shall see you in the morning. Good-night.'

He lit a candle for her, and she went to the foot of the stairs, then paused a moment, with her back to him.

'You will stop to smoke another cigarette before you come up,' she said.

She heard him take a couple of steps inside the room she had just left, and then a vague sort of rustle.

'I have thrown them all into the fire,' said he.

'Oh, Charlie, how wasteful!' she cried, beginning to ascend the stairs; 'and how——' And she paused at the corner.

He appeared in the doorway on the instant.

'How?' he asked.

'Nothing.'

'What were you going to say, Sybil?' said he. 'On oath, mind.'

She leaned over the banisters.

'Premature,' she whispered, and rustled up the remaining steps.

Charlie did not smoke another cigarette after she had gone, for the simplest of all reasons, but he broke another rule of health by sitting up much later than he should. He listened, in the way a man does, for the sound of the closing of her door, hoping, for some hopeless, groundless reason, that she would come back. Then, because the room was hot, and to him, in his open-air sojournings, airless with the closed windows, he opened one and sat by it, looking out into the still, starry night. And even as the coolness and breeze of air refreshed his body, so the thought of the talk he had had with her refreshed and was wine to his soul. At present he hoped for nothing; it was not necessary for him to tell himself not to be sanguine, for she had done nothing for him that she would not have done for a hundred other friends. She had, in fact, told him no more than others when she had said that his life did not belong entirely to himself; and she had told him no more than a penny newspaper might have told him when she had said she was not going to marry Bilton. Yet the imminent knife had gone; whether her mere presence again was tonic to him, or whether it was that there was again for him a loophole for hope—something possibly his to win—he did not stop to inquire. The upshot was that life (his life, that is to say, which is all that the most altruistic philosophers really mean when they talk of life) was again interesting, worthy of smiles or tears, as the case might be. Whether it was to be smiles or tears he did not at this moment care; the fact that it merited emotion was enough. 'The chequer-board of nights and days' was still in movement; he was not yet a taken piece. For the last three months he had thought of himself as exactly that, and simultaneously with that conviction had come the conviction that the chequer-board and the game played thereon was utterly without interest. His part in it was over; he no longer cared. And, as has been said, even the most altruistic and the most philosophical cannot do much better. 'Quelle perte irréparable!' was Comte's exclamation when he was told that he had to die.

'How premature!' Was not that, too, an indication, however veiled, that it was not premature? She would not have said that his holocaust of the cigarettes was premature if it was so; she would merely have thought to herself, 'Poor fellow!' But the hopelessness of the thought was neutralized by its announcement. Not the most matter-of-fact physicians broke news of fatal illness like that.... And again he reminded himself that he must not be sanguine. Anyhow, she had reminded him (like everybody else, no doubt) that his life was not entirely his own. She had told him also (there was nothing secret about it) that she was not going to marry Harold Bilton. But it was she who had told him.

Bilton, meantime, with the speed of his race, had completed his contract for the lease of the Coronation Theatre for the next season, and had finished, on behalf of Lewis S. Palmer, the purchase of the Molesworth property. It was quite characteristic of him that he should postpone for these affairs which were really imminent the piece of private business which had, more than either of them, perhaps more than both, brought him to England. Consequently, it was not till the afternoon of the next day that he called at Judy's and asked to see Mrs. Massington. Sybil had spent the morning at Brighton, and had arrived only some half-hour before he called. But, with the instinct of the autumn perhaps strong in her, she had said she would see him, rejecting Judy's offer to put herself in the way of a *tête-à-tête*.

He was shown into the room where Judy usually sat, a sitting-room off the drawing-room. It had been furnished with her unerring bizarre taste, and looked like nothing whatever except Judy's room. There was a bearskin on the floor because somebody had given it her.' Two execrable water-colours were on the wall for the same reason, and on the same walls were three wonderful prints of Reynolds' engraved by Smith. There was a grand piano there, making locomotion difficult, because Judy played much and badly, and Steinway, so she always said, knew what she meant better than anybody. There was some good French furniture there because it was hers, and some hopeless English armchairs because they were comfortable. Finally, there was Sybil there because she was her sister, and at this moment there had entered Harold Bilton because she had said she would see him.

She got up, and advanced to him.

'This is quite unexpected,' she said. 'I thought you were in America. Pray sit down. What has happened? Has Mrs. Emsworth also come back?'

Bilton sat down. He brought his hat and stick with him, according to the custom of his countrymen, and Sybil, who had never noticed it there, noticed it in London. She noticed it more particularly since the stick fell down from the angle where he had propped it with a loud clatter.

'No; Mrs. Emsworth is still in America,' he said. 'She has left New York, and gone on tour. I think her tour will be very successful.'

'So glad,' said Sybil. 'Tea?'

'I guess I won't, thank you,'said Bilton; 'I don't want anything. I want just to talk to you.'

Sybil pulled herself together. In other words, she tried to remember that a man in New York, if he crosses an insignificant ocean, is the same man who lands at Liverpool. She succeeded moderately well.

'And how is everybody?' she asked. 'How is Mrs. Palmer, and Amelie, and all the Long Island party?'

'They're all right,' said Bilton. 'Mrs. Palmer's giving a woodland fête this week; it will be very complete, and I guess the sea will come and swallow up Newport. But I didn't come here to talk about Mrs. Palmer.'

He finished taking off his gloves, threw them into his hat, and took a chair exactly opposite her, so that they faced each other as in a waggonette, which to Sybil was an odious vehicle for locomotion. His likeness to Charlie was somehow strangely obliterated to-day; she thought of the latter as of something suffering, in need of protection, whereas the same-featured man who sat opposite her looked particularly capable of self-defence, and, if necessary, of aggression. For the first time she rather feared him, and dislike looked hazily out through the tremor of fear.

'You ran away from America in a great hurry,' he said. 'You left us very desolate.'

Something in this quite harmless speech displeased Sybil immensely.

'Ran away?' she asked.

'Yes, ran away; but only incidentally from America. You ran away from me; I came after you.'

Sybil got up.

'Really, Mr. Bilton,' she said, 'you have left your manners the other side of the Atlantic.'

She went half-way across the room with the intention of ringing the bell, but she stopped before she got there; curiosity about the development of this situation conquered, and she sat down again.

He took no notice of her remark about his manners.

'I have come to ask you to marry me,' he said. 'You are the woman I have been looking for all my life. I will try to make you very happy.'

She answered him without pause.

'I am very grateful to you,' she said; 'but I cannot.'

'You led me to suppose you would,' said he.

'I am very sorry for it.'

There was a moment's silence.

'You changed your mind when you saw me come into Dorothy Emsworth's room,' he said. 'Now, I always meant to tell you about that. It is perfectly true that for nearly two years——'

She held up her hand.

'You need not trouble,' she said. 'I know.'

Bilton paused a half-second to arrange his reply in the way he wished.

'I always supposed she would tell you,' he said.

Her silence admitted it, and he had scored a side-point. He wished to know whether Dorothy had told her.

'I think you are hard on me,' he said; 'or perhaps I do not understand. You were, before you knew that, prepared to accept my devotion. Do you reject it now because I have led that sort of life?'

Sybil frowned.

'I can't discuss the question with you,' she said. 'I will just suggest to you this, that you went to see your mistress while I, to whom you had expressed devotion, was staying in the house. If you can't understand my feeling about that, I can't explain it to you.'

'I will promise never to see her again,' said Bilton.

Suddenly and almost with the vividness of actual hallucination the figure of the man who was so like him rose up before Sybil, and she all but saw Charlie taking Bilton's place there, and imagined that it was he who was saying what Bilton said. For a moment she invested him with the grossness of his double, and loathed and shuddered at the picture she had conjured up. Charlie behaving like Bilton was an image so degrading and humiliating that she could not contemplate it. The very thought was to do him dishonour. But Bilton, so she recognised, was acting now up to his very best; it was the best of his nature which promised not to see Mrs. Emsworth again. But Charlie in a corresponding position was unthinkable. Against this grossness all Sybil's fineness, all her taste, ran up like a wave against a stone sea-jetty, and was broken against it, and the jetty did not know what it had done. She rose, conscious that she was trembling.

'It is a matter of entire indifference to me,' she said, 'when or where or how soon you see her again. I want you to understand that.'

Bilton sat quite unmoved.

'If you were quite certain of yourself, you would not be so violent,' he said. 'You are overstating your feelings; that is because you are rather perplexed as to what they are.'

Sybil turned quickly round to him. She could not help showing her appreciation of this.

'Ah, you are frightfully clever,' she said; 'I do you that justice.'

He rose.

'I shall not give up hope,' he said.

'That is as you please,' she said. 'I have stated as clearly as I can that I can give you none.'

'It is not your fault that you don't convince me,' said he; 'it is the fault of my own determination. Good-bye.'

Sybil shook hands with him.

'What are your movements?' she asked.

'I return to America almost immediately to collect my company for the Coronation Theatre.'

'Ah, you are going to have an American company, then?' she asked.

'Certainly—two companies, rather. I shall have two pieces running simultaneously, with two performances a day. No one has yet thought of producing entertainments to last from about five till eight in the evening.'

When he had gone, she sat down without book, paper, or work, simply to think. Despite herself, and despite the disgust for him which, sown by that moment in Mrs. Emsworth's room, had grown up fungus-like in her mind, this unhurrying, relentless activity, so typical of him and of the nation to which he belonged, which had so stirred her in America, stirred her again. The practical side of her nature responded to it, as an exhausted man responds to alcohol. It woke in her the need to do something definite with her life; it reminded her that the mere observation of other people was not to her, as it was to Ginger, a sufficient excuse for her existence. She felt that her quick brain, her sure analytic grasp, could not find its permanent fruition in mere quickness or in mere analysis. Something of the passion for deeds, for accomplishment, that instinct which blindly spurs on bees to labour and men to work, had got hold of her. But what was she to do? She refused to marry Bilton, for, apart from the fungus of disgust, this very need for activity rejected him. That niche for herself, in front of which should burn in her honour the thick incense of wealth, no longer attracted her. She wanted to accomplish, to make; to be, in however small a degree, an active, creating force. So strong at the present moment was the impulse that she wondered, probably correctly, whether her refusal of Bilton did not dip some root-fibre into this soil.

The thought stirred within her till sitting still became impossible, and she rose and walked up and down the room. Soon her eye fell on the great nosegay of Michaelmas daisies which she had gathered in Charlie's garden that morning before leaving, and, with her keen dislike of waste, her unwillingness that anything should perish without having got the best out of itself, she busied herself for a few moments in filling a tall Venetian vase with water to place them in. The stalks were a little dry and sapless at the ends, and she made another journey to her room in order to get some scissors to cut off the dry pieces. Even a flower should be made to do its best, to look its best, and last as long as possible. Even flowers should be strenuous, and here was she and nine-tenths of her nation drifting like thistledown on a moor wherever the wind happened to carry it. To work—that was the impulse she had brought back with her from America—not to scheme merely with her busy brain, to intrigue, to find, as she always had found, endless amusement and entertainment in watching others, even though she exerted her intellect to its fullest in intelligently watching them; but to make some plan, and carry it out —to find some work to do, and do it.

Suddenly, in the middle of her neat, decisive clipping of the flower-stalks, she stopped and laid the scissors down. Surely there was a piece of work that lay very ready to her hand, though twice in the last day or two she had resented the responsibility being laid on her. But if she took it on herself—if she led Charlie back to interest in life, if she coaxed from him his apathy—was not that worth doing?

There were difficulties in the way sufficient to rouse enthusiasm in one who was much less on fire with the desire for production than she. She would be quite honest with him; she would not hold out any hope of which the fulfilment was not sure; she would not let him think for a moment that she would ever marry him. If the thing was to be done at all, she would do it by inciting him to live for the sake of life, by making him feel the unworthiness of giving in—the unworthiness, too, of the only condition on which he at present cared to live. She was not in love with him, but even if she had been, that would have made but a poor motive. The vitality that was hers was so abundant that surely she could impart some of it to him—make something of it bubble in his veins. His nature, his perception, were of a fine order, and though disappointment first and then disease might have dulled their sensibilities for the time, yet surely their numbness was only temporary—a passing anaesthesia. Anyhow, here lay a work worth doing.

CHAPTER XII

Mr. Lewis S. Palmer was sitting at his table in the sitting-room of the quiet, modest little suite he had taken at the Carlton Hotel, and was studying with some minuteness a large ordnance map of Worcestershire. He had some dozen of the sheets arranged in front of him, and the Molesworth estate, which he had been down to see only the day before, occupied a considerable portion of the central one of them. By him was seated Bilton, who answered, usually monosyllabically, the questions which Mr. Palmer asked him from time to time. 'Yes' or 'No' was generally sufficient; occasionally he thought a moment and then said, 'I don't remember.' Of the answers he received, Lewis Palmer sometimes made a short note.

Finally, he studied the map for a considerable time in silence, and then folded up each sheet separately, and replaced them in the bookstand that stood on the table. Then he read his notes through twice and tore them up.

'Complete the purchase of the Wyfold estate as soon as possible, literally as soon as possible,' he said. 'If you can do it by half-past four this afternoon, let it be done by then, not by five.'

'It's a huge price,' remarked Bilton, 'for half a dozen unproductive farms.'

'It is a necessity,' said the other, 'and a necessity is cheap at any price. But the fact that they ask so much leads me to think they have some kind of inkling as to what I am going to do. That's why I want you to do it at once.'

He rose, and sipped the glass of milk that stood on the side-table.

'There is one more thing,' he said. 'I want someone who will give a general supervision to my affairs here, which are growing important to me. I offer you the place because I like your way of doing business.'

'How much time do you want me to give to it?' he asked.

'Roughly, two days a week, anything of emergency to be dealt with separately.'

Bilton smiled.

'You chiefly deal in emergencies,' he said.

Mr. Palmer tapped the table rather impatiently.

'What do you make a year?' he asked.

'Round about two hundred thousand dollars.'

'I guarantee you a hundred thousand,' he said, 'on the two days a week basis. If it takes you longer than that, let me know. Only my affairs come first.'

Bilton considered this a moment without the slightest trace of exultation or pleasure.

'That's right, then,' he said. 'I guess I'll go off over the Wyfold business.'

'Yes, do. I'm going to look at Seaton House. I shall be in by two. Will you lunch with me?'

'Can't say,' said Bilton. 'I'm rather busy to-day.'

Lewis Palmer continued sipping his milk in a regular, methodical manner till he had finished it, and then put on some rather shabby dogskin gloves, an extremely shiny and obviously perfectly new tall hat, and rang his hand-bell. Almost before it sounded his bedroom door opened noiselessly, and his valet stood there.

'Lunch at two,' he said. 'If Lord Keynes gets here before me, ask him to wait.'

'Lunch for how many, sir?' asked his servant.

'I don't know.'

Mr. Palmer's progress out of the Carlton was made easy for him. Doors flew open as he neared them, and by the time he had reached the pavement his motor had drawn up exactly opposite the entrance, and the door was being held open for him.

Mrs. Palmer had had her eye—or part of an eye—on Seaton House for some time. Quite a year ago her husband had given her to understand that London might very possibly be the headquarters of his business for a considerable time, and when she spent her season there last summer she had considered London as a residence. On general principles, it was highly attractive— Americans, as she knew from experience, could command all that was worth having there, with, on the whole, a less expenditure than was necessary to keep up the same position in New York. Prince Fritz, for instance, in the autumn, had been a very heavy item, and though Prince Fritz had yielded high social dividends in America, yet it was easily possible to 'run' a royalty of the same class in England at a far lower figure. On the other hand, Prince Fritz in London would not be worth exploiting at all—that she recognised—but her conclusions had been that social success of a first-rate order in London could be done on less than the same article in New York. In both towns it was necessary to stand up among the ruck of ordinary hostesses like a mountain-peak; you had in any case to spend much more than most other people. Since, therefore, most other people spent less in London than in New York, the mountain-peak need not be so high. She saw also, with her very clear-sighted eye, that England, the professedly aristocratic, was far more democratic than the professedly democratic America. Lady A——, Duchess B——, Countess C——, she saw, as regards their titles alone, were quite valueless socially in England except among suburban and provincial people. That was natural— the prophet has no honour in his own country. Again, England, or rather that small section of English society which, in her mind, was equivalent to England, was rapidly conforming to the American ideal. It no longer cared for birth or breeding; it wanted to be greatly and continuously amused; a hostess was worth her power of entertainment. Nobody cared here in the least whether her grandfather was a butcher or a boot-black; all they cared was whether they were sufficiently lavishly entertained.

So far she had seen clearly and correctly enough; dimly, she had seen a little farther, and knew that for a reason she could not grasp there were in England some few families who had a *cachet* altogether independent of wealth. She could have named some half-dozen who floated on the very tip-top of everything, to whose houses Kings and Queens drove up, so to speak, in hansoms, and played about in the garden. They might be poor, they might apparently have no particular power or accomplishment which could account for it, but it was into that circle that Mrs. Palmer now desired to get. To one of these families Bertie Keynes belonged. Anyhow, she had secured him as a son-in-law, she had cut a step on the steep ice-wall. Furthermore, it could not be a disadvantage to have one of the few really fine houses in London for one's own. That was why Mr. Palmer had bought Seaton House.

He drove there now in his noiseless motor-brougham, looking out with his piercing gray eyes on to the grimy splendour of Pall Mall. It was a brilliant winter day, and primrose-coloured sunshine flooded the town, giving an almost Southern gaiety to the streets. As usual, a large extent of the pavement was up for repairs, and it vexed his sense of speed and efficiency to see the leisurely manner in which the work was done. Frankly, England seemed to him in a very bad way; her railways, her trade, her shipping, all the apparatus of her commerce, was haphazard, unconcentrated, uneconomical, just like her mode of making repairs to her streets. Personally, except that at this moment his motor was stopped, he did not at all object to it, since it gave him the opportunity which he had been preparing for of stepping in in the matter of her railways, and introducing American methods. He had, now three months ago, got through his Bill for a direct railway between Liverpool and Southampton, and the work of construction was going on with a speed that fairly took away the breath of contractors who were accustomed to think that slowness was essential to solidity. That boast of solidity, so characteristic of the English, had long amused Lewis Palmer.

'What they call solid,' he had once said to Bilton, 'I call stodgy. They make a brick wall three feet thick, that would bear the weight of the world, when all they want is a two-inch steel girder riveted to an upright. And when they have spent a couple of months in building it, they think they have done better than the man who puts up the steel girder. It is false economy to put up what is not necessary, just as it is false economy not to put up what is. And they think that to paper their railroad cars with looking-glasses in gold frames will console the shareholders for an absence of dividends. No, before we financed the Liverpool and Southampton we made certain of getting the line built the proper way.'

But this line was by no means all the control he meant to get in English railways. Its success, his financial knowledge told him, was certain; it was as sure that the traffic between the ports would come by a directer and faster route than that which already existed as that the sun would rise to-morrow; it was equally sure that facility of communication would lead to increased traffic. What followed?

Cardiff would be forced to get direct communication with his line instead of letting her trade 'walk about in country lanes,' as he expressed it. To do that, a new line from there must join the Liverpool and Southampton at the nearest possible point. That point lay, allowing ample margin, somewhere within the borders of the Molesworth estate, which he had purchased in the autumn, and the Wyfold estate, which he had given orders to Bilton to purchase that day. There was another thing as well. Geologically, it seemed most probable that there was coal on the Molesworth estate. It had been suspected half a dozen years ago, but Gallio, out of a mixture of reasons, partly indifference, partly want of cash, partly repugnance to turn the park into a colliery, had never made so much as a boring for it. But Lewis Palmer was neither indifferent nor bankrupt. He also had no particular feeling about parks. And his gray eyes brightened, and the momentary stoppage of his motor, owing to the slovenly and dilatory way in which the street was being repaired, irritated him no longer. One could not say he was lost in reverie. He was rather picking his way through his reverie with very firm and decisive steps, directing his course to a well-defined goal.

An assemblage of upholsterers, paperers, carpenters, plumbers, furniture dealers, and painters, were awaiting his arrival, for he had promised his wife to get the house into habitable shape before Easter, and, to save time to himself, he took them all round in his inspection and gave orders to each as they went along.

'I shall want a large brocade screen to stand straight in front of the door of the inner hall,' he said. 'Let it be at least seven feet high. Send me the patterns first. Don't put much furniture into the hall; a big plain mahogany table there for cards and small things. A long line of hat-racks there with an umbrella rack below it. Don't think you can make a hat-rack pretty, so make it plain. Half a dozen Chippendale chairs, and an old English steel fender with dogs. I will choose the rugs and stair carpet myself, but polish the whole of the staircase. Put a big *vitrine* for china in that corner. Cut a circular *louvre* window above the front—door, and copy the mouldings round it from the north door of the Erechtheum. You will find the drawings in Schultz's book. Big candelabra will stand at the bottom of the stairs. I will send them here. Fit them with electric light, but do not pierce them. There will be six lamps in each of eight candle-power.'

It was extremely characteristic of Mr. Palmer that he went thus into everything himself. Nothing escaped him; he grasped at once the difficulty of bringing the dining-room into directer communication with the kitchen, a problem that had puzzled his architect, and solved it in five minutes by a lift and shutter arrangement so simple that it seemed mere idiocy not to have thought of it. He went into every servant's bedroom, every bathroom, into the sculleries, the coal-hole, the wine-cellar, and knew immediately what was wanted. And the more he saw of the house the better it pleased him; the big oak staircase to the reception-rooms was admirable, and more than admirable was the circular dining-room, with its walls panelled in excellent Italian *boiseries*, and its cupola-shaped roof, with carved converging wreaths of fruit and flowers. With his amazing knowledge of furniture and decoration, he had in an hour's time chosen the scheme for every room in the house, and provided the dealers, the paperers, the painters, with a week's work in looking out and bringing for his inspection the kind of thing he wanted. But it was not his way to allow a week for a week's work, and these gentleman were appointed to meet him there again in three days' time to submit for his approval carpets, papers, rugs, tables, chairs, kitchen ranges, refrigerators, wardrobes, and specimens of carving. Then, at exactly three minutes to two, he again stepped into his motor to go back to the Carlton, where Bertie

Keynes was to lunch with him.

There were other people there as well, he found, waiting for him when he got back, and it was not possible for him to talk privately, as he intended to do, to his future son-in-law. He had observed him once or twice during lunch, not eating much, and apparently rather silent and abstracted, and wondered vaguely if anything was the matter. He guessed indeed that some money difficulty or accumulation of debts might be bothering him, but as his talk with him was to be partly on that subject, he considered that if that was the cause, Bertie's evident pre-occupation would not last very long. He had seen a good deal of him in America, and was very well-disposed towards him, partly because Bertie was such an eminently likeable young man, but mainly because Amelie was so fond of him. For Lewis Palmer—a thing which most people would have been inclined to doubt—had a heart. His business, which occupied him, it is true, more than anything else in the world, was to him a thing quite apart from his human life and human affections. In it he was as relentless and as hard as it is possible for a man to be; as far as an affair was business, he was without pity or compassion, for business is as inhuman a science as algebra, and as unemotional, if properly conducted, as quadratic equations. A heart in such spheres would be anomalous—almost an impropriety. Had Bertie—a thing which he had no thought of doing—crossed Lewis Palmer's path in such a connection, he would have had not the slightest compunction in obliterating him, if he was of the nature of an obstacle, however minute. But as the affianced of Amelie, he was something of an object even of tenderness.

He had a few words with him after lunch.

'Arrived last night, Bertie?' he asked. 'Glad to see you. How are they all?'

Bertie pulled himself together, and smiled.

'All sorts of messages to you,' he said. 'They miss you awfully.'

'I guess I'm not missed most,' remarked Mr. Palmer. 'Can you wait here half an hour or so? I want to talk to you, but I've got other things that won't wait.'

Bertie looked at his watch.

'I can be back in an hour,' he said, 'if that will do.'

'Yes, an hour from now. Quarter to four, then,' and he nodded to him, shut up his heart again, and dismissed him from his thoughts as completely as he had left the room.

Bertie, as Mr. Palmer had supposed, had arrived in London only the evening before, and since Gallio was out of town, spending, in point of fact, a most

115

unremunerative fortnight at Monte Carlo, on a system which lost infallibly, though slowly, had at his invitation taken possession of his chambers in Jermyn Street. He had come down to breakfast in as happy and contented a frame of mind as any young man, gifted with good digestion and a charming girl to whom he was engaged, need hope ever to find himself, and had seen with some satisfaction that there was only one letter waiting for him. He had expected rather to find creditors clamouring round him, for he had a respectable number of them waiting for his leisure cash, and had supposed that they would very politely have notified him of their existence as soon as he arrived. But there was only one letter for him. He opened it; its purport was as simple as a statement of accounts, and type-written. It began:

'DEAR SIR,

'I have the honour to remind you of a document, from which I have extracted the following.'

Then in neat marks of quotation were appended certain sentences.

'Why did you bewitch me if it was not for this?'

'When I am with you I am tongue-tied. Even now my hand halts as I think of you.'

'You are the only woman in the world for me. I offer you all I am and have, and shall be and shall have.'

There was a decent space left after these and other quotations—a silence of good manners. Then the letter continued:

'Mrs. Emsworth has reason to believe that you are about to marry Miss Amelie Palmer. She therefore offers you the chance of regaining possession of the letter, from which we have given you extracts, for the sum of ten thousand pounds (£10,000). Should you decide to accept her offer, you are requested to draw a cheque for the above-mentioned sum to the account of her present manager, Mr. Harold Bilton, who, on receipt of it, will forward to you a sealed envelope containing the complete letter from which the above are extracts. Should this not reach you within twenty-four hours, you are at liberty to stop the cheque. If, however, such cheque does not reach Mr. Harold Bilton by the evening of January 7, he will post the sealed packet in his possession (of the contents of which he has no idea), containing the original letter from which the above are extracts, to Mr. Lewis S. Palmer, Carlton Hotel, London. He has been instructed to do this on behalf of Mrs. Emsworth without admitting any discussion or temporizing on your part.

> 'We are, sir,
>> 'Your respectful, obedient servants,
>>> 'A. B. C.'

The postmark on the envelope was London, W., and the envelope was type-written in purple ink.

Bertie's mouth, when he read this, got suddenly dry, and with a hand that he observed was quite steady, he poured himself out a cup of tea and sipped it, reading the letter through again. Also he had a horrible feeling of emptiness inside him, resembling great hunger, but of some sickly kind, for, so far from being hungry, he could not touch the eggs and bacon to which he had just helped himself. He could not yet even begin to think, but again he filled his cup with tea, again drank it, and again read the letter. Then he suddenly felt hot, stifled, and though the morning was of a brisk chilliness, he went to the window and leaned out. He was aware that a cold sweat had gathered on his forehead, and he wiped it away. Then all at once his feeling of physical faintness and thirst left him altogether, and he was back in his room, lighted a cigarette, and sat down squarely on his sofa to think the matter out.

His first impulse—namely, to go straight to Mr. Palmer with the letter—did not last long. He had told him, after Amelie had accepted him, in answer to questions which were very delicately put, that there were no pages in his past life which he feared. Mr. Palmer, with the tact and finesse which is inseparable from great ability, had indicated his meaning with absolute precision and clearness. He had not hinted that he wished Bertie to confess any liaisons he might ever have had, he only asked him with considerable solemnity to assure him that he had done nothing which, coming to light at a future time, could, humanly speaking, bring unhappiness to, and possibly rupture between, him and Amelie. He had not pressed him for an answer immediately.

'Think it all over,' he had said, 'and tell me to-morrow. Young men will be young men as long as women are women. I don't mean that. What I do mean is whether anyone can rake things up afterwards. If anyone can, I should like to know about it. I needn't ask you to be straight with me. I guess you are straight without being asked.'

Now, it had not occurred to Bertie to tell him about Mrs. Emsworth, for the very simple reason that he was quite innocent. That he had been foolish—mad, if you will—was perfectly true, but morally he was clean. And now, at this moment, she was on tour in America—where, he had no notion. Bilton, no doubt, knew, but Bilton had been instructed to admit no discussion of any kind. And to-morrow would be January 7.

His second impulse was also short-lived—namely, to go straight with the letter to Scotland Yard. But what did that mean? An action for blackmail against Mrs. Emsworth, a dragging into the public view all that had happened, a feast for the carrion-crows of London, and for him—well, celibacy. For Mrs. Emsworth, clever woman as she was, knew well what justice is done by the world to those who invoke the justice of the law. The verdict of the world is always the same: 'There must have been something in it;' and though every judge and jury in the land might testify to his innocence, the world would simply shrug its shoulders: 'There must have been something in it.' For it is not in the least necessary to touch pitch to be defiled; it is quite sufficient if somebody points a casual finger at you and merely says 'Pitch.'

Yes, it was on this that she, the blackmailer, counted; here lay her security—

namely, that his bringing her to justice meant that he must lay himself open to the justice of the world. And what justice in that case would Mr. Palmer give him? If he was to know at all, it must be Bertie who told him. And Bertie knew he could not, after the assurance he had given him.

For a moment his brain deserted the question of what to do, and put in as a parenthesis that the blackmail scheme had been brilliantly planned. It was excellently timed; it gave him quite long enough to think the matter over, and not rush, as he might possibly have done, in desperation to Mr. Palmer or Scotland Yard, if he had only been given an hour or so to decide, and, at the same time, it did not give him an opportunity of communicating with Mrs. Emsworth. The extracts, too, were cleverly chosen, their genuineness he could not doubt, and they gave him a very fair idea of the impression that the whole letter would make on an unbiassed mind. Then suddenly he sprang to his feet.

'But I am not guilty!' he cried. 'My God, I am not guilty!'

His fit of passion subsided as suddenly as it had sprung up, and his thoughts turned to Dorothy. He remembered with great distinctness his interview with her on the morning after her debut in New York, and the uneasiness with which what his sober self thought was mere chaff had inspired him. But afterwards, at their various meetings in New York and down at Long Island, he had been quite at his ease again, and ashamed of his momentary suspicions. She was a better actress than he knew, it appeared, for never did anything seem to him more genuine than her kindliness towards him. She had made friends with Amelie, too; for Amelie had told him of their meeting in the dewy gardens, of her entrancing way with children, which had quite won her heart. Then—this.

Then a third alternative struck him. What if he did nothing, just waited to see if anything would happen, if by to-morrow evening he had not paid this hideous sum to his blackmailer? But again he turned back daunted. The whole plot had been too elaborately, too neatly laid to allow him to think that the threat would not be carried out. If in a sudden passion Dorothy had threatened to send the letter to Mr. Palmer, he might, so he thought, have reasoned with her, appealed to her pity, appealed, above all, to her knowledge of his innocence. He might even have threatened, have coolly and seriously told her that he would lay information against her unless she gave up his letter to him. But he was not dealing, he felt, with a woman in a passion; he was dealing with a cold, well-planned plot, conceived perhaps in anger, but thought out by a very calm and calculating brain. There was not, he felt, even an outside chance that, having worked it out so carefully, she would hold her hand at the last moment. True, he held now in his own hand evidence against her for blackmail sufficient to secure her, if he chose, a severe sentence. Only he could not do it; he had not nerve enough to take that step. She had calculated on that, no doubt. She had calculated correctly.

Then this money must be raised somehow; there was no way out. In order to silence a false accusation against himself he had to pay £10,000. It was this question of how to get it that he carried about with him all the morning, and this that had sat beside him at lunch. Gallio might possibly lend it him, but it would entail telling Gallio the whole story, which he did not in the least wish to do. However, if no better means offered itself he determined to telegraph to him that evening. And so at a quarter to four, his brain still going its dreary rounds from point to point of his difficulties, he again presented himself at the Carlton.

He was shown by the noiseless valet through the noiseless door of Mr. Palmer's sitting-room. The latter had not heard him enter, and Bertie, in the strangeness of the sight that met his eye, forgot for a moment his own entanglements. For Lewis Palmer was seated in an easy-chair by the window, doing nothing. His arms hung limply by his side, his head was half sunk into his chest, and his whole attitude expressed a lassitude that was indescribable. But next minute he half turned his head languidly towards the door, and saw Bertie standing there.

'Ah, come in, come in,' he said. 'I was waiting for you. No, you are not late.'

He rose.

'Bertie, never be a very rich man,' he said. 'It is a damnable slavery. You can't stop; you have to go on. You can't rest; you are in the mill, and the mill keeps on turning.'

He stood silent a moment, then pulled himself together.

'I hope nobody overheard,' he said. 'They would think I was mad. Now and then, just now and then, I get like that, and then I would give all I have to get somebody to press out the wrinkles in my brain, and let it rest. I should be quite content to be poor, if I could forget all this fever in which my life has been spent. I might even do something as an art critic. There, it's all over. Sit down. There are the cigars by you.

'Now you talked to me straight enough once before,' he went on, 'and told me, I believe, the exact truth. I wanted you to start with Amelie with a clean sheet in that direction, and I want you to have a clean sheet in another. I want you to pay off all your debts. All, mind; don't come to me with more afterwards. I know it's difficult to state the whole. Please try to do so. Take time.'

Bertie sat quite still a moment, with a huge up-leap of relief in his mind.

'I can't tell you accurately,' he said. 'But I am afraid they are rather large.'

'Well, a million pounds,' suggested Mr. Palmer dryly. Bertie laughed; already he could laugh.

'No, not quite,' he said. 'But between ten thousand and twenty. About twelve I should say.'

'Confiding people, English tradesmen,' remarked Mr. Palmer. 'Been going to the Jews?'

'No.'

'Well, don't. My house doesn't charge so high. Now, I'm not going to give you the money. I shall deduct it from the settlement I am going to make, the amount of which I have already determined on. Only I shall give you that at once, and ask you to pay them at once.'

'You are most generous,' said Bertie. 'I can't thank you.'

'Don't, then. Are you sure thirteen thousand will cover them? Mind, it doesn't matter to me; it is all deducted.'

'I am sure it will.'

Mr. Palmer did not answer, but drew a chair to the table and wrote the cheque.

'Pay them at once, then,' he said. 'Now, you looked worried at lunch. Anything wrong?'

'It was,' said Bertie. 'It isn't now.'

Mr. Palmer looked at him a moment with strong approval.

'I like you,' he said. 'Now go away. The mill has to commence again.'

The relief was as profound as the oppression had been, and now that the strain was over Bertie was conscious of a luxurious relaxation; the tension and strain on his nerves had passed, and a feeling of happy weariness, as when a dreaded operation is well over, set in. He could scarcely yet find it in his mind to be bitter or angry even with Mrs. Emsworth; she had done a vile thing, but he would not any longer be in her power, and being free from it, he scarcely resented it, so strong was his relief. Mr. Palmer, he knew, had designed to make some settlement of money on him; what it was to be he did not yet know, but the fact that this had been deducted from it prevented his feeling that he had come by the money in any crooked fashion. As it was, a certain payment to be made to him had been partly anticipated, and he looked forward to paying his blackmail almost with eagerness.

He made an appointment by telegraph with Bilton for the next morning, and at the hour waited on him at his office in Pall Mall. He had always rather liked the man; his practical shrewdness, the entire absence of what might be called 'nonsense' about him, a certain hard, definite clearness about him and his ways, was somehow satisfactory to the mind. And this morning these characteristics were peculiarly developed.

He gave Bertie a blunt and genuine welcome.

'Delighted to see you,' he said. 'Just come over, haven't you? Smoke?'

Bertie took a cigarette.

'I've called about some business connected with Mrs. Emsworth,' he said. 'I am here to settle it.'

Bilton looked puzzled a moment.

'Mrs. Emsworth?' he said. 'Business with Mrs. Emsworth? Ah, I remember. She sent me certain instructions some time ago. Let's see; where did I put them?' He took down an alphabetical letter-case from a shelf, and after a short search drew out a packet.

'That's it,' he said. 'Ah, I see there is no discussion to pass between us. Curious love of mystery a woman has, especially when there is nothing to make a mystery about, as I dare say is the case here.'

'You don't know what the business is?' asked Bertie.

'I only know these instructions, and one of them, if you will pardon me reminding you, is that no discussion is to pass between us. You are to deliver to me a cheque, which I am to place to her account, and I am to deliver to you a sealed packet. This is it, is it not? Yes. You are also to deliver to me a certain letter which I am to verify, and then destroy in your presence.'

'I heard nothing of that,' said Bertie.

'It is in my instructions,' said Bilton.

'I can't give up that letter,' said Bertie. 'It——' He stopped.

Bilton got up.

'I am afraid I can do nothing, then,' he said, 'except fulfil the rest of Mrs. Emsworth's directions, and, if this is not done by the evening of January 7, to-day, give the packet to Mr. Palmer.'

He referred again to one of the papers he had taken out.

'Yes, give the packet to Mr. Palmer,' he repeated.

'Which you intend to do?' Bertie asked.

'Certainly. At the same time, I may tell you that I have written a very strong letter to Mrs. Emsworth, protesting against her making use of me in—in private matters of this kind. I am a busy man'—and he looked at his watch —'I have no taste for other people's intrigues.'

Bertie thought intently for a moment. If he gave up the letter, he would be powerless in the future to prove anything with regard to the blackmail. The fact that he had drawn a cheque for £10,000 to Bilton was in itself nothing to show that he had done so under threats, especially if, as it suddenly occurred to him, Bilton was, if not in league with Mrs. Emsworth, at any rate cognizant of her action. On the other hand, if he refused, he had to risk that letter of his being sent to Mr. Palmer. He had been unable to face that risk before, and it was as unfaceable now. But the idea that Bilton was concerned in this was interesting. It had been suggested by the slight over-emphasizing of the fact that he was busy, by the looking at his watch. That was, however vaguely, threatening; it implied time was short, or that he himself was concerned in Bertie's acceptation of the ultimatum.

Bilton sat down again and tapped with his fingers on the table.

'Excuse me, Lord Keynes,' he said, 'but no purpose is served by our sitting here like this. You will, of course, please yourself in this matter. Here is the packet for you if you decide one way; there is the letter-box if you decide the other.' The speech was well-chosen, and left no room for doubt in Bertie's mind that the letter-box would be used. He took the desired document from his pocket.

'Here is the cheque,' he said, 'and here is the letter. The latter, you say, you are going to verify. I, on my side, I suppose, may verify what you give me.'

Bilton appeared to consider this for a moment.

'There was nothing said about that,' he remarked, 'but I feel certain that the lady would be willing to let you receive proof of her honourable dealing with you.'

'Did you say honourable dealing?' asked Bertie in a tone which required no answer.

Bilton opened the letter Bertie gave him, referred to a paper out of the alphabetical case, looked at the cheque, and handed him the packet. Bertie glanced at it, saw enough, and put it in his pocket.

'That's correct, then,' said Bilton.

Bertie rose.

'Next time you see Mrs. Emsworth, pray congratulate her for me,' he said. 'She has missed her vocation by going on the stage.'

'I am inclined to disagree with you,' said Bilton. 'It has developed her sense of plot. Must you be going? Good-bye. I suppose you are off to America again in a month. You may meet her there.'

'That is not possible,' said Bertie.

Bilton's smile which sped the parting guest did not at once fade when the guest had gone. It remained, a smile of amusement, on his face for a considerable time.

'God, what a fool!' he permitted himself to remark as he settled down to his work again.

CHAPTER XIII

Some three weeks after this Ginger was occupying the whole of the most comfortable sofa in the rooms of his father occupied by Bertie, and was conversing to him in his usual amiable manner. The rooms wore the look of those belonging to a man shortly to take a journey; there were packets and parcels lying about, a bag gaped open-mouthed on a chair, and Bertie himself was sorting and tearing up papers at a desk, listening with half an ear to the equable flow of Ginger's conversation. He had a good deal to say, and a good deal to ask about, but, with the instinct of the skilled conversationalist, he did not bring out his news in spate, nor ask a succession of questions, but ambled easily, so to speak, up and down the lanes and byways of intercourse, only occasionally emerging on to the highroads.

'It may appear odd,' he was just saying, 'but I never was in these rooms before. Gallio has never asked me here. I am glad to see that he appears to make himself fairly comfortable. I suppose he is at Monte Carlo still. Heard from him, Bertie?'

'Yes, a letter of extreme approbation at my marriage, and a regret that he will be unable to visit America for it. Also a cheque for £500 as a wedding-present. Out of his hardly lost losings, he says.'

'Gallio's in funds now, or was till he went to Monte Carlo,' remarked Ginger. 'He got two hundred thousand for the sale of Molesworth. But he has to settle half of it on you, doesn't he? And where do I come in?'

'You don't, I'm afraid.'

'I think Gallio made a very good bargain,' said Ginger; 'but I think it remains to be seen whether Mr. Palmer didn't make a better.'

'How's that?'

'Whether, with his American spirit of enterprise, he won't begin digging for the fabulous coal which was supposed to exist.'

Bertie looked up.

'Turn Molesworth into a colliery? He won't find it very easy. You see, he has settled it on Amelie, or, rather, is going to on our marriage.'

'By Gad! he does things in style,' said Ginger. 'And you think Amelie would not allow it?'

'I think she would attach some weight to my wishes.'

'Do you feel strongly about it? I thought you were rather in favour of its being done when it was spoken of before.'

'I know; there was an awful need of money. It is a necessity before which sentiment must give way. But now there is not. And my sentiment is rather strong. After all, it has been ours a good long time; and now we can afford to keep the coal underfoot, if it is there at all. Besides, do you know for certain that he has any thought of it?'

'No; Bilton put it into my head,' said Ginger. 'He hinted that Mr. Palmer had made a good bargain. He seemed rather elated at something, so I did not question him further. I don't like elated people. I suppose he had made some good bargain, or done somebody in the eye; that is the American idea of humour. He went off to Davos the other day.'

Bertie again looked up.

'Hasn't he realized the fruitlessness of that yet?' he asked. 'Sybil refused him point-blank, I know; and really, when she follows that up by going out to Davos to coax Charlie back to life, you would have thought that a third party was not—well, exactly of the party.'

'Sybil is an enigma,' said Ginger. 'She went to America in the autumn with the avowed intention of getting married, with Bilton indicated. She comes back in a scurry, refuses him, and instantly constitutes herself life-preserver to Charlie, whom she had also refused. What is she playing at? That's what I want to know.'

Bertie took up a quantity of waste-papers, and thrust them down into the basket.

'She's not playing at anything just now,' he said. 'She's just being a human woman, trying to save the life of a friend. Judy talked to me about it. The only interest in life to Charlie was she, and she is trying to get him to take an interest in life that isn't her!'

'That will require some delicacy of touch,' remarked Ginger.

'It will. She has it—whether enough remains to be seen. Charlie had one foot in the grave when she came back, I'm told; she has taken that out, anyhow.'

'But does she mean to marry him?' asked Ginger. 'I can't believe she will succeed in getting him back to life without, anyhow, holding that out as a prospect.'

'It's really a delicate position,' said Bertie; 'and it is made more interesting by the fact that physically Charlie is so like Bilton. In other respects,' he added, 'they are remarkably dissimilar.'

'Do you like him?'

'No; I have got an awful distaste for him. Why I don't quite know. That rather accentuates it.'

Ginger sat up from his reclining attitude.

'Bertie, I'm awfully interested in one thing, and I haven't seen you since you came back,' he said. 'Was there any—well, any difficulty with Dorothy Emsworth?'

Bertie paused in his labours, divided in his mind as to whether he should tell Ginger or not. He had a great opinion of his shrewdness, but, having himself managed his crisis, paid up, and got back the letter, he did not consider that there was any need for advice or counsel from anybody. So he decided not to tell him.

'She was quite friendly in America,' he said; 'I saw her several times; she even stayed down at Port Washington.'

Ginger, as has been seen, was immensely interested in other people's affairs, having none, as he said, of his own which could possibly interest anybody. On this occasion he could not quite stifle his curiosity.

'I remember you telling me that you once wrote her a very—very friendly letter,' he said.

'Certainly. It is in my possession now. I keep it as an interesting memento.'

Ginger shuddered slightly.

'I should as soon think of keeping a corpse,' he said.

'Burn it. She's rather a brick to have given it you back, though. Sort of wedding-present?'

'Yes, a valuable one.'

'Does she still carry on with Bilton?' asked Ginger.

'I don't know.'

'Well, I hope she didn't show it him before she returned it,' said the other.

January in London, with few exceptions, had been a month of raw and foggy days—days that were bitter cold, with the coldness of a damp cloth, and stuffy with the airlessness of that which a damp cloth covers. Far otherwise was it at Davos, where morning after morning, after nights of still, intense cold, the sun rose over the snow-covered hills, and flamed like a golden giant, rejoicing in his strength, through the arc of crystalline blue. Much snow had fallen in December, but when the fall was past, the triumphant serenity of the brilliant climate reasserted itself. The pines above the long, one-streeted village had long ago shaken themselves clear of their covering, and stood out like large black holes burned in the hillside of white. Day after day the divine windlessness of the high Alpine valley had communicated something of its briskness to those fortunate enough to be there, and the exhilaration of the atmosphere seemed to percolate into minds of not more than ordinary vivacity.

The village itself lies on a gentle down gradient of road, some mile in length, where Alpine chalets jostle with huge modern hotels. Below lies the puffy little railway which climbs through the pinewoods above the town, and communicates in many loops and detours with the larger routes; and straight underneath the centre of the village is the skating-rink, where happy folk all day slide with set purpose on the elusive material, and with great content perform mystic evolutions of the most complicated order. Others, by the aid of the puffy railway, mount to the top of the hills above the town, and spend enraptured days in sliding down again on toboggans to the village of Klosters. Motion, in fact, of any other sort than that of walking is the aim and object of Davos life—an instinct dictated and rendered necessary by the keen exhilaration of the air. At no other place in the world, perhaps, is the sluggard so goaded to physical activity; at no other, perhaps, is the active brain so lulled or intoxicated into quiescence. It lies, in fact, basking and smiling, while the rejuvenated body, free from the low and cramping effects of thought, goes rejoicing on its way.

Charlie, by reason of his malady, had been debarred from taking either much or violent exercise; he had been told to be out always and to be idle usually. This he found extremely easy, for his mother was there to be idle with him, and Sybil was there to furnish entertainment for both. With her usual decision and eye for fitness, she had seen at once that for the present there was only one thing in the world worth doing—namely, skating. She skated extremely badly, but with an enjoyment that was almost pathetic, in consideration of the persistence of 'frequent fall.' Thus, morning after morning, she, setting out at earlier hours, would be followed down to the rink by Charlie and his mother, where they would lunch together, returning to the hotel before dark fell for the cosy brightness of the long winter evenings.

Mrs. Brancepeth was a widow, cultivated, intelligent, and gifted with a discernment that was at times really rather awkward to herself, though never to those to whom she applied it, since she never used what her intuition had enabled her to see, to their discomfort. This gift put her into very accurate possession of the state of affairs between Charlie and Sybil; it was clear to her, that is to say, that Sybil was wiling him back into the desire to live, waking his dormant interests, as if by oft-repeated little electric shocks of her own vitality, charming him back into life. She knew, of course, the state of her son's feelings towards Sybil, and did her the justice of allowing that, not byword or look, direct or indirect, did she ever hold herself out as the prize for which life was worth living. Indeed, Mrs. Brancepeth admired with all the highly-developed power of appreciation that was in her the constant effacement of herself which Sybil practised—effacement, that is, of the personal element, while by all healthy and impersonal channels she tried to rekindle his love for life. Whatever was—so Sybil's gospel appeared to run— was worth attention. Her own falls on the ice were matters for amused comment; the outside edge was *per se* a thing of beauty; the stately march of the sun was enough to turn one Parsee. Enthusiastic, vitally active as Sybil always had been, it required less penetration than Mrs. Brancepeth possessed to see that her amazing flood of vitality was deliberately outpoured for the sake of Charlie. This was the more evident to her by the fact that Sybil, when alone with her, subsided, sank into herself, and rested from an effort. At times, indeed, when Charlie was not there, she was almost peevish, which, in a woman of equable temper, is a sure sign of some overtaxed function. Such an instance occurred, so Mrs. Brancepeth thought, on an evening shortly before Bilton arrived at Davos. In the six weeks that they had now spent there, the elder woman had got to know the younger very well, to like her immensely, and to respect, with almost a sense of awe, the extreme cleverness with which she managed her affair. The 'affair' was briefly, to her mind, to make Charlie take a normal interest in life again, without exciting an abnormal interest in herself—to transfer his affection, in fact, from herself to life.

They had dined together that evening at their small table at the Beau Site, and

Sybil had traced loops on the tablecloth with a wineglass, and sketched threes and brackets to a centre with the prong of a fork.

'Yes, it sounds silly,' she said, 'but it is the most fascinating thing in the world to try to do anything which you at present believe yourself incapable of doing. I have no eye for colour at all, therefore two years ago I took violently, as Charlie remembers, to painting. I have no eye for balance, therefore now I spend my day in trying to execute complicated movements which depend entirely on it.'

Charlie's eye lit up.

'The quest of the impossible,' he said. 'How I sympathize!'

This 'was direct enough; with returning health he had got far greater directness. Mrs. Brancepeth waited for Sybil's reply; it came as direct as his.

'Oh, Charlie, you always confuse things,' she said. 'You do not mean the quest of the impossible, but the quest of the improbable. The quest of the improbable is the secret of our striving. Anyone can grasp the impossible; it is merely an affair of the imagination. I can amuse myself by planning out what my life would be if I were a man. What I cannot do is to plan out for myself a successful career as a woman.'

'Surely you have plans enough,' said Mrs. Brancepeth.

'No, no plans,' said Sybil—' desires merely. I have lots of desires. One is control of the outside edge; that is unrealized. Dear Charlie, you look so well this evening; that is another of my plans. It is getting on.'

'He gained two pounds last week,' said his mother.

'How nice! I lost a hundred, because I speculated on the Stock Exchange. It sounds rather grand to speculate, but it wasn't at all grand. What happened was that a pleasant young gentleman here, whose name I don't know, said two days ago to me, "Buy East Rands." I bought a hundred. They went down a point. I sold. But I bought many emotions with my hundred pounds. One was that one could get interested in anything, whether one knew what it was or not, as long as one put money into it. And if money interests you, surely anything else will.' This, too—so Mrs. Brancepeth interpreted it—was a successful red herring drawn across the path. Charlie appeared equally interested.

'Ah, you are wrong there, Sybil,' he said. 'Money *in excelsis* must be the most interesting thing in the world; there is nothing it cannot do.'

'Oh, it can do everything that is not worth doing,' interrupted Sybil; 'I grant that.'

'And most things that are,' he continued. 'For, except content, which it will not bring you, there is nothing which is not in its sphere.'

'Toothache,' said Sybil promptly. 'I had three minutes' toothache yesterday, and was miserable.'

'Painless extraction.'

'But not the courage for extraction,' said she. 'I always think that extraction is at the root of it. One can get along all right with what one has not got; what one cannot do is to part with something that one has which gives pain.'

Mrs. Brancepeth tapped with the handle of her fork on the table.

'This is irrelevant,' she said; 'the question before the house is the power of money.'

'Dear Mrs. Brancepeth,' said Sybil, 'please don't let us discuss; let us babble. "In a little while our lips are dumb," as some depressing poet says. Poets are so often depressing.'

'Sybil is the most prosaic poet I know,' said Charlie.

'She casts her thought really in the mould of poetry, and before it is cold she hammers it to prose. She is the only person I know who has the romantic temperament and is ashamed of it.'

'Not ashamed of it,' cried she; 'but it is not current coin. I hammer the metal into currency. And he calls me prosaic.' The ice was thin here, so thought Mrs. Brancepeth.

'Everyone has the same difficulty,' she said. 'One has either to hammer one's poetry into prose before it is current or trick out one's prose into poetry. The raw product of any of us—that is what it comes to—does not pass.'

'Ah, but what is the raw product?' said Charlie. 'If one knew, one would use it. But no one knows about himself. "Know thyself"—the first of mottoes, and, like all mottoes, impossible to act upon.'

'If you know other people, it is a good working basis about one's self,' said Sybil; 'one is very average—that is the important thing to remember.'

'But if everybody is average, why does A single out B?' asked Charlie. 'Why not C or D, up to Z?'

Sybil finished her pudding.

'I don't know,' she said. 'Probably because B comes first—is next to A. About money—of course it will not give you content. Content is a matter of temperament. But it will give you the power to gratify any taste; and, considering how many beautiful things there are in the world, it is a confession of idiocy or of want of taste, which is the same thing, not to be able to be absorbed in some one of them.'

'That is quite true,' said Mrs. Brancepeth; 'and it matters hardly at all what one is absorbed in so long as one is absorbed.

Charlie responded to this.

'And one's power of absorption depends almost entirely on health,' said he.

The evening post came in on this, and not long after Charlie went upstairs to answer certain letters which had come for him, leaving the other two together. Since the arrival of the post, Sybil had become very silent and preoccupied; one letter, in fact, she read three times over, with silent frownings between each perusal. At length she rose, took a turn or two up the room, and spoke.

'I have had disquieting news,' she said; 'and I want advice.'

'Do tell me, dear,' said Mrs. Brancepeth. 'I will do my best.'

'I don't know if you know Mr. Bilton,' she said. 'I have just heard from him; he is starting to-morrow for Davos.'

'Charlie has mentioned him,' said the other.

'You know who he is, then,' said Sybil. 'Shortly before I left England he proposed to me. I refused him. I don't want him to come here; but how is it possible for me to stop him?'

She faced about, and stood opposite the elder woman.

'What am I to do?' she asked. 'He is strong, masterful; I am afraid of him, and it will take a great deal of nervous force out of me. Now, I can't spare that.'

She paused a moment.

'Perhaps I had better say straight out what I mean,' she said. 'I am having rather a hard time as it is; that I take on myself very willingly. But every day leaves me more and more tired when the need for playing up is over. But it is worth it: I should be a very feeble creature if I did not feel that. Because he is getting better, is he not?'

Mrs. Brancepeth laid her hand on Sybil.

'Every day I thank God for what you are doing,' she said, 'and I thank you; but—but I suppose I have been more sanguine than I should. Is there no chance for Charlie?'

Sybil threw her arms out with a hopeless gesture.

'I don't know—literally I don't know. I like him so much that I can't offer him only liking; and I don't know that I have anything more to offer him. It is all very difficult. I don't suppose there is a woman in the world who knows herself so badly as I do. And I used to think I was so decisive, so clear cut. What is happening to me?'

Mrs. Brancepeth looked at her with a wonderful tenderness and pity. She had often noticed how completely she was in the clutch of her temperament, how the mood of the moment completely blotted out all other landmarks and guiding-posts which experience from without and her own character from within might have been supposed to be of some directing value in perplexities. But it was not so with her; in such things she was a child, ruled by the impulse—not led by the reason, nor steered by any formed character. With her the present moment so blotted out the past that all precedents, all warnings, all points which ninety-nine grown-up people out of a hundred have to help their decisions, were with her simply non-existent. If the present moment was pleasant, she abandoned herself to childish delight; if perplexing, she was the prey of in-soluble doubts. She had a passion for analysis, but her analysis, brilliant as it often was, was as fruitless as the Japanese cherry. It was the process of thought which she loved to dissect, and having dissected it, she threw it away. All this Mrs. Brancepeth saw—saw, too, that Sybil's was a nature to which it was no use to preach principles; the practical dealing with the concrete instance was all that could help her.

'Tell me more about Mr. Bilton,' she said.

'He is dominating,' said Sybil. 'I was greatly attracted by him. Then he did something disgusting, or so I thought it, and I was disillusioned. I even began to dislike him. But he has force, and it will need force on my part to fight him. What will the result be? I shall have less force to fight Charlie's microbes for him.'

'Yes, that is what you are doing,' said Mrs. Brancepeth softly.

'And even here, even when I see most clearly how much better he is getting, I ask myself whether I am doing wisely or not,' continued Sybil. 'What will the end be? Is he filled with certain hopes which I cannot say will ever be realized? And what if he is disappointed of them?'

There was no reply, and after a minute she went on.

'Mr. Bilton will arrive in two days,' she said; 'he will come to this hotel. It is impossible for me to cut him, not to recognise him. He is quite extraordinarily like Charlie, by the way. I must speak to him when he speaks to me. I must behave decently. And I know—oh, how well I know it!—he will interest me again. I shall be forced to be interested. There is that about him—some force, some relentless sort of machinery that goes grinding on, pulverizing what gets in its way.'

Mrs. Brancepeth rose.

'Now, dear, be quiet,' she said. 'You are working yourself up about it. Don't do that. Don't whip up your imagination on the subject. You take things too vividly.' Sybil smiled rather hopelessly.

'That does not help matters,' she said; 'some people take them not vividly enough. I am myself, you are yourself; the broad lines of each of us are inexorably laid down for us. All we can do is not to make a very shocking mess of them. We are all unsatisfactory. No, I don't think you are; you are very nice and restful. Now, what am I to do—not about Bilton, I mean, but now this minute. That is always so important.'

Mrs. Brancepeth laughed.

'And that is so like you,' she said. 'Go to bed, dear, and dream as vividly as you can of the outside edge.'

Bilton arrived two days afterwards, and, as was quite natural, paid a call on his friends before dinner in their sitting-room. As chance would have it, neither Charlie nor his mother were in, and he found Sybil alone. She rose and shook hands with him as he entered, but gave him no smile.

'I was surprised to get your letter,' she said; 'I thought you were too busy to come out to this very idle place.'

'I chose it for its idleness,' he said. 'I was very tired, and I have a busy time ahead of me again. It is economical to spend a fortnight in complete idleness rather than let your work suffer for a year.'

He paused a moment.

'That was my excuse,' he said; 'I had also a reason.' Sybil felt a sudden anger with him, which flared up and died down again as he went on.

'I am glad to find you alone,' he said, 'because I wanted to see you. I had to see you; I was thirsty for the sight of you. But do not be afraid; I shall not make myself importunate; I shall say nothing to offend you; I shall not entreat you by word or look. I just wanted—wanted to see you: that is all.'

He spoke rather low, and rather more slowly than his wont; but next moment he resumed the ordinary tone of his speech.

'I came here a couple of years ago,' said he; 'and I carried away with me an extraordinary sense of coolness and rest. I think one's brain goes to sleep here. We Americans need that; we have awful insomnia of the brain. I want to go sliding on a silly sledge down a steep place; I want to fall about on skates, and not read the paper.'

Sybil laughed; there had been a certain modesty and good taste in his first speech that had rather touched her, and from that he had gone straight to ordinary converse. The assurance of the harmlessness of his intentions seemed to her very genuine. As a matter of fact, it was profoundly calculated, and produced just the effect he wanted; for he particularly desired to be admitted without embarrassment or delay into the others' party.

To Charlie's mind, this addition—for though Bilton never seemed to intrude himself, yet he usually was there—was nothing more at first than a slight nuisance. More than that, it could not be called, since he knew of Sybil's complete and final rejection of Bilton as a lover, and it was not consonant with the sweetness of his own nature to be rendered jealous and exacting about her friends. But by degrees—so gradual that he could not notice the growth of the feeling, but only register the fact that it had grown—he became aware of uneasiness of mind, which, as it increased, diminished from the great content in which he had passed the earlier weeks of their stay at Davos. Also he began to realize that in the shade of his mind there had grown up unconsciously a hope—or, if not a hope, the possibility of the hope—that he himself might find in her some day more than a friend. He had often asked himself before whether he still cherished and watered the tender seedling, and as often he had honestly told himself that he did not. But Bilton's coming, and the terms he was on with Sybil, cast a light into his own dark places, and he knew that that hops was still not rooted up from his mind. And, realizing this, he realized how vital such a hope was to him.

Sybil, too, during the ten days following Bilton's arrival, had insensibly changed in her attitude towards him. Having definitely decided that he should not be her lover, she speedily began to find in him excellences as a friend which she had scarcely realized before. As a lover, she had found him wanting; a certain coarseness of nature in him prevented her from receiving him on that footing. But once off that ground, this coarseness almost ceased to offend her; at any rate, transferred on to the less intimate plane, it ranked a 'minus' of the same calibre as one of his numerous 'pluses.' Among these, his practical qualities greatly appealed to her—his quickness at grasping the salient points of any question; his very firm hold on concrete affairs, from the quickest and securest way of tying a bootlace to his lucid exposition of American finance, as typified in that Napoleon, Lewis Palmer, or his knowledge in his own business of what constituted a play that would draw. On a hundred occasions every day she had some exhibition of this brought to her notice; in whatever he did or said he showed efficiency. That quality, as she had settled, was not one to be loved, but socially she delighted in it. Moreover, the force she had feared seemed to be in abeyance. He made no demands on her nervous energies that she recognised as demands.

Now, love, though proverbially blind, is often very prone to see something which has no existence whatever, and before long Charlie began to conjure up a very complete phantom, which would have done credit to a much finer imagination than he really possessed, had not he viewed the situation through the eyes of a lover, to whose vision all is intensified. He saw, what was true, that Sybil listened with very genuine interest to what Bilton had to say; he saw her an eager pupil of that excellent skater; he saw, if some expedition was projected, that she left all the arrangements of sleighs and food in his hands. To the unbiassed observer nothing could have been more natural, for he talked well on subjects that interested her, he gave her valuable aid towards accomplishing the elusive outside back edge, and his arrangements in expeditions were admirable; for sleighs were punctual, and nothing was forgotten out of the luncheon-basket. But Charlie was not unbiassed, and the conclusions that slowly and silently formed themselves in his mind were both untrue in the abstract and in the concrete unjust to her. He was still sufficiently young to have an attack of childishness, and he was quite sufficiently in love with her to be a prey to jealousy.

The second week of Bilton's stay had passed, and still he dropped no hint about his imminent return, and on this particular morning, after a rather worried week, rendered not more easy because he kept his worries strictly to himself, Charlie had just returned rather gloomily from a visit to his doctor.

During the last ten days he had gone down a little in weight, and, though the doctor would have preferred it otherwise, he reminded him that he must have ups and downs; no cure was uninterrupted progress. But this, piled on the top of his other cares, which were rendered harder to bear by a couple of days of south wind, instead of the cold purity of windlessness, unduly depressed him, and Sybil, coming out of the hotel to the sheltered corner of the veranda which he usually occupied in the morning, found him somewhat listless and dejected. But, with tact which had often succeeded before, she affected not to notice it, and discoursed on indifferent subjects.

'Such a bore!' she said. 'The road down the valley is too soft for sleighing, and the rink is too sloppy for skating.'

Charlie brightened up a little; he seemed to have seen much less of her lately.

'So you're going to have an idle day,' he said. 'Sit and talk to me.'

'Well, we are going out almost immediately,' she said, 'just to go down the Schwester toboggan-run, which they say is still possible. I wish you could come, Charlie, but there's no way of getting up except walking.'

Charlie instantly froze into himself.

'I'm afraid that's quite impossible,' he said. 'You're going with Bilton, I suppose.'

'Yes; I rather think he's waiting for me.'

Charlie registered to himself the fact that she had not asked for the doctor's report of him, though Monday was his regular day for being overhauled.

'Never keep people waiting,' he said, and opened a book. Then his better disposition came to his aid.

'I hope it will be possible for you to get a good run,' he said cordially. 'It is horrid, this weather, is it not?'

'Horrid—quite horrid!' she said. 'Well, good-bye; your mother will be out directly.'

He sat there after she had left him, with book open, but not reading. A pale, watery sun, instead of the golden monarch enthroned in cloudless blue, peered like a white plate through the clouds blown up by the south wind, and, instead of a dry and vivifying air, the atmosphere was loaded with moisture, the eaves dripped with the melting snow, and every now and then, with a whisper and a thud, some sheet would detach itself form a house-roof and plunge into the roadway below. Instead of presenting an expanse of crystalline whiteness, the snow-fields were stained and yellowish to the eye; hideous corners of corrugated roofs showed where the coverlet of white had slipped; all the raw discomfort of a thaw was in the air. To Charlie, both owing to his physical condition and his unspoken trouble, the heavy chilliness of the day was peculiarly oppressive; his mother also was detained indoors, and for an hour he was prey to the gloomiest reflections. It was all no use, so lie told himself; since October he had heartily tried with all his power both to get better and to recapture the normal joy of living. But now, as so often happened, he had begun to slip back again; next week no doubt would tell a further tale of hardly-earned ground lost, and week would follow week, and he would slip back and back. Even if he pulled through, even if he became strong again, what was there in life for him worth recovering for? He had thought— deluded himself into thinking—that perhaps Sybil might come to care for him, but with sudden bitter intuition he guessed that he was really no nearer winning her love than he had been before he had been taken ill. Great compassion, the divine womanly instinct to help a man, had brought her out here; the improvement in his health, the successful combating of his disease, was due to that. But it was but a bitter gift she had brought him; it was as if she had brought him through some illness only to give him over to the hangman at the last. And she had not asked about the doctor's report. That seemed to him in his dis-ordered frame of mind to clinch the matter. Instead she had gone off tobogganing with Bilton. True, she had refused him in the autumn, but how many marriages have been prefaced by that?

Charlie shivered slightly, and looked about him for a rug, for the damp of the day made a man chilly, where the dryness of far greater cold would have been but warming and invigorating. But he had not brought one out, and, saying to himself that he would go in to fetch one in a minute, he still sat on, looking for a break in the clouds that encompassed him. But he could not find one; the taste had gone out of the world again.

The Schwester run had been in unexpectedly good order, and Sybil did not get back to the hotel till late in the afternoon. The weather had cleared since noon, and about twilight the curtain of clouds had been dispersed, the south wind had ceased, and the splendid frosty stars again hung embroidered on the velvet of the night. Instead of plunging through the snow, before they reached the hotel their footsteps went crisply on the crackly crust, and the steel runners of their trailing toboggans sang like tea-kettles as they slid over the re-frozen surface. Already her spirits had been high, and, with the increased exhilaration of the air, they rose to nonsense point.

'Climate, climate,' she was saying—'how is it that people worship money and brains and beauty, and never worship climate, which is the one thing in the world that matters? Of course, you don't think that, because you live in New York, which is unbearable three-quarters of the year and intolerable the rest—isn't that it?—and get accustomed to doing without climate, just as you train oysters to live out of water until you are ready to eat them. But to me nothing but climate is really of any importance. I am so much better than when I came here; and I was quite well when I came,' she added.

'It seems to have suited Charlie Brancepeth very well,' said Bilton.

'Yes, he's much better; soon he'll be quite well. He gets more like you, Mr. Bilton, as he regains his health, every day. It really is very odd, because I don't suppose two people were ever so unlike in character. But the climate here has been good for your character as well as Charlie's lungs.'

'Have I improved? I'm delighted to hear it. I thought I was a hopeless case.'

'Not at all—no more hopeless than Charlie. You have developed a side your character which I hardly suspected you of having, and are beginning to take perfectly frivolous pursuits with great seriousness. You were much more annoyed at losing ten seconds to-day in that spill than you were at losing your cigarette-case.'

'I have been a pupil, that's all,' he said; 'I have been well taught since I have been here.'

'*Tanti complimenti,*' said she. 'Really, when you came I was afraid you would be absorbed in telegrams and bargains and bulls and bears. But you have not; you have played very nicely. How much longer do you stop?'

They had come to the hotel, and were passing the big squares of light cast by the hall windows. He dropped the rope of his toboggan as she asked this, and stopped to pick it up, looking her full in the face.

'I shall go when I am told,' he said—' not a day before.' She looked at him, and understood. It was the first personal word he had said to her since the little interview on her arrival, but it was so modest again, so self-obliterating, that it did not offend her with a sense that he had broken his word when he promised not to speak to her again on intimate subjects. It was sufficient to remind him of it very gently, just to cool him off, so to speak.

'We should all miss you, I am sure,' she said.

Charlie did not appear at dinner that evening. He had caught a little chill, it appeared, in the morning, and had gone to bed in a good deal of discomfort, with a somewhat high temperature. Mrs. Brancepeth, though she would not confess to any anxiety, yet felt anxious, and as soon as dinner was over went off to see how he was. She came back before many minutes were over, and signalled to Sybil across the salon, who got up at once and followed her.

'Is there anything wrong?' she asked.

'Yes; I have asked Dr. Thaxter to come and see him. His temperature has risen again. But he asked me if he could see you for a moment; I wish you would go. He is very restless, and I think you might quiet him; for you know,' she said, looking at her, 'I think you can do more for him than any doctor.'

Sybil stood there a minute, biting her lip. She had a physical repulsion to illness, which, though it shocked her that she should feel it, yet dominated her. Since she had taken Charlie in hand, she had had daily to wrestle with it, and though, owing to his very satisfactory progress, it had become easier to overcome, yet it was always there. But she decided almost immediately.

'Yes, I will go,' she said, then paused. 'Does he look terrible? Will it shock me?' she asked.

Mrs. Brancepeth's eyes lit up with a momentary indignation.

'Ah, what does that matter?' she exclaimed involuntarily. 'No, dear, I did not mean to say that. I know your horror of illness. But go to him; it will not shock you. He is looking rather flushed; his eyes are very bright.'

She took Sybil's hands in hers.

'Oh, make him better, make him better!' she said; 'make him want to live!'

Entreaty vibrated in her voice, and her hands trembled. Sybil felt immensely sorry for her, and her sorrow overcame her repugnance at what lay before her. Her horror for illness was of the same character as a child's fear of the dark— unreasonable, but overmastering. But in the presence of this mother's anxiety it was conquered for the moment.

'I will do what I can,' she said—' I will do what I honestly can. Are you coming with me?'

'No; he wants to see you alone.' And, as she spoke, a sudden pang of jealousy and rebellion struck her. Why should she who would give her life for him with thankful willingness be powerless to help him, while half that love from another woman might prove so efficacious, could she but exert its strength? But next moment that was gone; no other thought but the mother's yearning for her son was there.

Sybil went from her up the passage to Charlie's room, and entered softly. At that moment, hearing perhaps the rustle of her dress, he turned his head on his pillow, and looked towards the door, and in dead silence for a moment their eyes met. His face was very much flushed; his eyes, as his mother had said, were very bright, but bright with the burning of fever; and the indescribable sharpness and hardness of feature that comes with illness was there. But as Sybil looked, no horror was hers, and no shrinking. All she knew was that a man, suffering and ill, lay there—a man to whom she was the reason of living and the sun of life; a man whom she had known long, liked always, loved never. In his eyes there burned not only fever, but, as he saw her, the unquenchable light of love in all its dumb faithfulness. She had seen it often before, and had rejected it, but now it smote upon her heart. Something within her melted; and as a butterfly cracks its chrysalis, and emerges weak, hardly yet conscious of the new life, of the iridescence of its own wings, of the sunlight which till now has been hidden from it by that sheath of its shell, so something new trembled on the threshold of her heart—pity—which knew not yet that with which it was entwined. And with the waking of herself within her came the knowledge of what to do and say intuitively, because she was at last a woman.

She came quickly across the room, smiling at him.

'Charlie, Charlie, this will never do,' she said. 'I leave you alone for one day, and you instantly behave naughtily like this. I am ashamed of you.'

'Sybil, it is good of you to come and see me,' he said; 'I wanted to see you so much.'

Then the inevitable querulousness of illness mastered him.

'Oh, I am so uncomfortable,' he said—' so hot and feverish.' And he flung-his arm outside the bedclothes.

'Poor old Charlie!' she said; 'poor old fellow! It is a bore. Now, put that arm back at once. There. Now, you are not going to talk to me now, but I am going to make you ever so much more comfortable, put the pillow for you so, and you are going to see the doctor, and then you are going to sleep. Headache? Poor old boy! And I shall sit here and talk to you till the doctor comes.'

She drew a chair to the bedside, and he turned more over in bed so that he looked directly at her.

'Oh, I'm ill, I'm ill,' he said; 'and it was quite my own fault. I sat outside this morning without a rug, and I knew I was catching a chill. And I didn't care. You see, you didn't care. You never asked me what the doctor's report was this morning, and I—I determined not to care either. I am sorry; I shouldn't have said that.'

Sybil's hand trembled as she arranged the bedclothes, which he had thrown off.

'I was a brute,' said she, 'and——' She paused. 'Charlie, you must get well,' she cried suddenly.

He lay quite still a moment, with breath coming quickly.

'You said that as if you cared,' he said.

CHAPTER XIV

The marriage of Bertie Keynes and Amelie was to be celebrated at New York towards the end of February, and bade fair to be the *comble* up to date (not even excepting the famous pearl fishery) of Mrs. Palmer's social successes. It was to take place in St. Luke's Church, Fifth Avenue, and for days beforehand the ordinary services had been altogether suspended, because the church had to be made fit to be the theatre of the ceremony, and a perfect army of furniture-men, upholsterers, carpenters, and plumbers occupied it. The ordinary square-backed wooden pews were removed from the body of the church, which was carpeted from wall to wall with purple felt, and rows of *fauteuils* in scarlet morocco, like the stalls of an opera-house, occupied their places. To complete the resemblance, each chair was marked with its particular number in its own row, and the occupants, who gave up their tickets at the church door, retaining only the tallies, were shown to their places, where they found in each chair a copy of the service printed on vellum and bound by Riviere, by scarlet-coated footmen. Similarly, the free seats in the gallery were cleared out in order to make room for the very magnificent orchestra, which beguiled the hours of waiting for the guests with inspiriting and purely secular pieces, and during the choral part of the service accompanied the choir.

In front of the altar, where the actual ceremony would take place, there had been constructed, hanging from the roof, an immense bell-shaped frame made of wood and canvas, which was completely covered inside and out with white flowers, and reached from side to side of what the reporters called the sacred edifice. It had been quite impossible, even for Mrs. Palmer, to procure at this time of year sufficient real flowers, and, as a matter of fact, they were largely artificial, like everything else. Round the edge of this large bell, suspended by invisible wires, but appearing to float in the air, were life-size baby figures of *amorini*, made of wood and beautifully tinted, winged, and almost completely nude, who discharged gilded arrows from their gilded bows towards the pair who were to stand in the centre of the bell. Numbers of others peeped from the banks of flowers that lined the walls, all aiming in the same direction, so that the bridegroom, one would have thought, might reasonably compare himself to a modern St. Sebastian. Framed in these banks of flowers also were several pictures belonging to Lewis Palmer, all bearing on what might be called classical matrimony: a Titian of Europa and the Bull, a Veronese of Bacchus and Ariadne, and a more than doubtful Rubens of Leda and the Swan. Gilded harps twined with flowers leaned about in odd corners, and the general impression was that one had come, not into a church, but, by some deplorable mistake, into the Venusberg as depicted in the first act of 'Tannhauser.'

The ceremony, of course, had been many times rehearsed, and for days beforehand the dummy bridegroom's procession had crossed Fifth Avenue (the house exactly opposite was to be Bertie's domicile for the night preceding the marriage), and taken up its position, chalked out, at the church door. That event was signalled to the *chef d'orchestre* in the gallery, who was thereupon to begin the Mendelssohn wedding-march, and to the bride's procession, which was to start at the same moment from Mr. Lewis Palmer's house four blocks off. This, proceeding at walking speed, should reach the church door exactly at the conclusion of the wedding-march, whereupon the two processions, dummy-Bertie attended by his usher, dummy-Amelie by her bridesmaids, moved up the church to right and left of the bell, at such a pace that the voice which breathed o'er Eden ceased breathing as they reached their places. Then—this was a startling innovation—Mr. and Mrs. Palmer, arm in arm, were to have an unattended progress up the aisle to two very suitable golden chairs, which at this moment would be the only unoccupied places in the church, while the choir in their honour were to sing a short hymn specially written for the occasion, and addressed to them, beginning:

> 'Blessed parents here who see
> This bright hour arriving.'

Then the bride and bridegroom took their places under the bell, and the service proceeded in the usual manner. One rehearsal was rudely interrupted by the fall of one of the wooden *amorini* at this point, which narrowly missed the dummy-bridegroom's head, and fell with a loud crash, splintering itself into match-wood on, the floor of the chancel. So another one was procured, and they were all more securely wired. Immense baskets of white flowers were to be carried by the bridesmaids, which they were to strew in the path of the bride both as she entered and left the church with her husband; and from the belfry outside, as they emerged, a shower of sham satin slippers with little parachute wings, so that they should float in the air and sink very gradually on to the heads of the amazed crowd, was to be discharged. These had been tested privately, and were not used in the rehearsals.

Bertie had arrived in New York some fortnight before the marriage, leaving Mr. Palmer, who was very much occupied, in England, to follow a week later. Wedding-presents for both of them had begun arriving, and were still doing so in shoals, and every day he was occupied for several hours in writing letters of gratitude. He soon got a certain facility at this, but one morning there arrived for him a present which astonished him. The present itself was a charming dressing-bag (there was nothing surprising in this, for it was the eleventh he had received), and the donor was Mrs. Emsworth. She wrote with it a characteristic little note, saying that she was unable to come to the ceremony, as she was at Chicago, and begging him to forget her and not acknowledge the gift. She was making a great success with her tour, and was getting quite rich. Considering what had happened, this seemed to him one of the most superb pieces of impertinence ever perpetrated. 'She was getting quite rich!' Quite so; she had made a considerable sum lately apart from her theatrical business; she could well afford to give him a dressing-bag.

But the impertinence of it, the irresistible impertinence! How like the *gamin* who puts his tongue in his cheek and says 'Yah!' He almost laughed when he thought of it. But the laughter died at the memory of those sickening hours in London on the day he had received the blackmailing letter, and in a sudden spasm of anger against her, not pausing to consider whether it was wise or not, he gave orders that the bag should be packed up again and sent back to her at Chicago, without word of any kind. She would understand quite well.

This incident, small though it was in itself, served to increase a certain depression and uneasiness that beset him during this fortnight. The appalling apparatus and dis-play which was to be made over the wedding was intolerable to him; never before, as he read and re-read the instructions which had been sent him as to the timing of his own movements in what he mentally termed 'the show,' had the huge, preposterous vulgarity of the American mind fully struck him. The thought of what his wedding-day would be like was unfaceable, and the unextinguishable mirth of Ginger, who had come over as his best man, was not consoling.

'Here the bridegroom, crowned with garlands and ribands, shall be led underneath the largest *amorino*, which at a given signal shall descend upon his head, while the orchestra plays the Dead March from "Saul,"' had been his comment when the accident in rehearsal happened, and Bertie, though he laughed, groaned inwardly.

All this, however, was, as he recognised, but a temporary worry, and did not seriously affect him. More intimately disquieting was the perpetual sense of his nerves being jarred by the voices, manners, aims, mode of looking at life of the society into which he was to marry. Not for a moment did he even hint to himself that his manner of living and conducting himself, traditional to him, English, was in the smallest degree better or wiser than the manner of living and conducting themselves practised by these people, traditional (though less so) to them, American. Only there was an enormous difference, which had been seen by him in the autumn and dismissed as unessential, since it concerned only their manners, and had nothing to do with their immense kindliness of heart, which he never doubted or questioned for a moment. What he questioned now was whether manners did not spring, after all, from something which might be essential, something, the lack of which in one case, the presence of it in another, might make you find a man or a woman tolerable or intolerable if brought into continuous contact. He was going to marry this charming American girl, whose friends, interests, companions, pursuits, were American. It was reasonable and natural for her—indeed, it would have shown a certain heartlessness had it not been so—that she should wish to continue to be in touch with her friends and interests. For no human being can be plucked up, like a plant, and have its roots buried in an alien soil; transplant it without a lump of its own earth, and it will infallibly wither. Nor had Bertie the least intention of making the attempt to transplant her like that. All along he had known that the American invasion would come to his house; he no more expected Amelie to give up her American *milieu* than she would have expected him to give up his English *milieu*. Indeed, when Mr. Palmer had presented him with a charming little *bijou* flat in New York, he had accepted the implication that he would pay from time to time a visit there with the same unquestioning acquiescence.

But now in his second visit he found to his dismay that, so far from ceasing to mind or notice the difference between the two peoples, the difference was accentuated as far as notice went, and doubled as far as minding went. His nerves, no doubt, were a little out of order, and what would have scarcely affected him in a serener frame of mind was in his present mood like the squeak of a slate pencil.

Yet behind all this, even as the sky extends for millions of miles behind a stormy and cloudy foreground, lay his feeling for Amelie herself. True, once in his life the passion for a woman had burned in him with so absorbing and fierce a flame that for more than two years afterwards he had soberly believed that he never again could feel any touch of passion for another. His adoration for Dorothy Emsworth had been his first *grande passion*; it was therefore probably his last, for such a thing does not come twice. Men whose lives are morally unedifying might doubt it, so he said to himself, but merely because they have never experienced it at all. To them has come a succession of strong desires, but this never. And though he did not give, nor did he make pretence of giving, to Amelie that which Mrs. Emsworth could find no use for, yet he gave her very honestly another way of love: he gave her very strong and honest affection; he gave her immense admiration; lie gave her as much, for he was of ardent nature, as many men have ever felt. All the chords of his lyre sounded for her. But once there had been another chord; that he could not give her, for it was gone.

Consequently, when he wondered whether continuous contact with American *milieu* might not prove absolutely intolerable, he did not include in his misgivings his continuous contact with Amelie. He had deliberately set out in the quest of a wealthy wife, and he had found one in all ways so charming, so lovable, that the mercenary side of his quest was out of sight. That quest, he admitted to himself, was not a very exalted one; but as his father had pointed out, he could not, practically speaking, marry a poor girl—at least, without marrying a great deal of discomfort—and it was therefore more sensible to look for his wife among wealth. He had been quite prepared, in fact, for marrying a girl who 'would do,' provided she saw the matter in the same light. Amelie did much more than 'do.'

Two nights before his marriage he had been to a very ingenious party, the author and inventor of which had been Reggie Armstrong. It was called a 'Noah's Ark' party, for he had caused his stable-yard to be flooded, and erected in the centre of it a huge wooden building in shape and form exactly like the Noah's arks which children play with. It had false painted windows on it, the whole was in crude and glaring colours, and it was approached up a gang-plank across the stable-yard. At the door stood Reggie Armstrong on a little wooden stand, dressed like Noah in a brown ulster, with a stiff wide-awake hat and a false black beard, and by him the four other people who were the joint hosts. Mrs. Palmer was one, representing Mrs. Noah, and three young New York bachelors were Shem, Ham, and Japheth. A confused noise came from within the ark, and as the astonished guests entered they saw that all round the walls were cages containing real live animals. A pair of elephants occupied the top end, a snarling tiger was in the next cage; there were giraffes, lions, pumas, antelopes, all sorts of birds in diminishing order of size, and at the tail a small glass-covered box containing fleas. Shrill cries of excited admiration greeted this striking piece of genius, and in the rather pungent menagerie atmosphere, to the snarling of the tiger, the growling of lions, the mewing of cats, the barking of dogs, and the neighing of the equine species, the banquet, at which each guest sat on a wooden stool, and ate off wooden plates, in order to accentuate the primitive nature of the surroundings, ran its appointed course, and took rank among the brilliant entertainments of the world.

After dinner, bridge and normality followed, and it was natural that Bertie should find a corner as quiet as possible to have a talk with Amelie. They had wandered together round the cages, had tried to make themselves heard at the lion's end, but that monarch of the forest roared so continuously that it was impossible to catch a word anyone else was saying unless he shouted. And as their conversation was not naturally adapted to shouting, they sought the comparative quiet of the end which harboured the meaner insects

Amelie had looked at the last case of all, and turned to Bertie.

'It's very complete,' she said.

'Very,' said he, and their eyes met, and both laughed.

'Now, tell me exactly what you think of it,' she went on, turning her back on the fleas and sitting down. 'I really want to know what you think of it, Bertie.'

Bertie looked round to see that they were alone.

'It appears to me absolutely idiotic,' he said.

She did not reply at once.

'Mamma—ah, you like me to say mother—mother was one of the hosts,' she observed.

'I know. But you asked me what I thought.'

'Reggie's very rich,' she said. 'It doesn't make any difference to him. I suppose a beggar would think me idiotic to wear jewels, which might be converted into cash. At least, I suppose it is that you mean—the senseless expenditure.'

'No; one can't say any expenditure is senseless,' said he, 'since it is a matter of degree, a matter of how much you have to spend. If a man spent all his capital on such an entertainment, or indeed on any, it would be senseless, but, as you say, Armstrong is very rich.'

'What do you mean, then?'

'I mean that it is idiotic, because it doesn't give one any real pleasure. It gives one real pleasure to see those pearls lying on your neck.'

'Oh, but it does give pleasure, though perhaps not to you,' she said. 'Lots of people here think it's just exquisite. I suppose that means they are idiots.'

She paused a moment.

'You've been very frank,' she said; 'I will be, too. When I see you here, when I see that darling Ginger here, I think it is idiotic. But I don't otherwise. You see, I've been brought up in it all. You have been brought up differently. All my life I have been in the middle of this -this senseless expenditure. You have been in gray old houses, and big green parks, and quiet places, among people with low voices.'

He made a gesture to stop her. It was no use saying these things.

'No, I want to say this,' she said; 'I have meant to say it often, and I haven't been able. I have chosen, you see—I have chosen you. And I have seen often that we have grated on you; I have seen you thinking how senseless this all is. But, Bertie, I can't give up my friends, and I don't suppose I can change my nature. I can't promise to become English. I can't promise even to try. But I love you.'

She looked up at him with those great gray eyes, and for a moment something rose in his breast, till he almost thought that the intolerable joy of a passion he had once felt was about to burn again within him. But it rose, stayed short of the point, and sank again.

'I don't ask you to, Amelie,' he said. 'I am not so unreasonable or unfair as to ask you to change. And you left to say last what was best of all.'

Suddenly he felt an impulse almost overwhelming to tell her all, to tell her that, tender and strong as was his affection for her, he had known once a love that was different in kind from this, a love which he thought a man can only feel once, and when he felt it, it was not for her. Yet how could he do it? How define a moonbeam? And what good would it be when done? It might perhaps vaguely distress and disquiet her, but it could serve no other purpose, except that it would satisfy a certain demand for honesty felt by himself. The impulse, he dimly felt, was of a momentous nature; it involved principle which lies behind expediency, but though for a space it was very strong, it soon passed, and the want of practical purpose in telling her took its place. To minimize pain and to multiply pleasure was one of Bertie's maxims; suffering of any sort was repugnant to him, whether he or another was the sufferer. Such a desire is part always of a kindly nature, but when, as in his case, it is a dominant factor, one of the dominant lords of conduct, it is the sign of a nature not only kindly, but emphatically lazy—one which will always drift as long as possible, one which in a moral sense will never go to the dentist before its teeth ache, and will then not try to have them saved, but take gas and part with them.

His last words to Amelie made the girl's cheek glow and her eye brighten. She loved her lover's lack of effusiveness, for to her it indicated the depth of still waters. In everything she found him as she would have him, and when he said 'you left till last the best of all,' she felt that no torrent of words, no battery of impassioned looks, could have been so convincingly genuine as the dry simplicity of his words. Like every other woman or man who has ever loved, she had imagined for herself the ideal lover, and enshrined it in some human tabernacle. To her Bertie was the one and only tabernacle wherein her love could dwell. He had told her with a limpid directness in the early days of their engagement that when he came a-wooing he had come, of set purpose, to a wealthy house, and this declaration, which would in a nature less sweet and generous than hers have prompted, in case of a lover's quarrel, the stifled whisper 'you wished to marry me for my money,' had not the most shadowy existence in her. She knew otherwise; the fortunate accident of her wealth had been no more, so she believed, than the mere master of the ceremonies who had introduced them.

The completeness of his reply so satisfied her that, after a short pause, she spoke at once of other things.

'Father has settled Molesworth on me,' she said. 'He has made it my own.'

'Will you ask me there sometimes?' said Bertie.

'Yes, perhaps. Are you very fond of it?'

'Yes, somehow right inside me I am. I think one gets a very strong, though not at all a violent, feeling for a place where one has been brought up. One's father was brought up there, too, you see, and one's grandfather. The feeling isn't worth much; we have tried to sell it for years, and whistled for a buyer in vain.'

She sighed.

'We Americans have no sense of home at all,' she said. 'Really, we all live in hotels for preference. I don't suppose I shall ever get it, or even understand it. Is it—is it worth having, that sense of home?'

'I don't know that it is. It is a comfortable feeling, that is all. "My own fireside"; it is a domestic sort of joy, which rather reminds one of Cowper's poems.'

'I shall read them,' remarked Amelie with decision. Bertie laughed.

'You will certainly go to sleep over them,' he said.

'That will be domestic too. Come, Bertie, I'm going to jabber like the others.'

'Jabber to me.'

'I can't jabber to you. You are not jabberable. Look at me once; that must be our good-night.'

Mr. Palmer had arrived in New York some week or so before, and had occupied himself for a whole day over the matter of settlements. Molesworth he had given to Amelie, had settled a million pounds sterling on her, and on Bertie two hundred and thirty-seven thousand, the curious exactitude of this sum being due to the fact that he had intended to settle a quarter of a million on him, of which he had already received thirteen thousand. He also recommended him a few suitable investments for it, while Mrs. Palmer, after getting rid of the first high pressure of satisfaction by sending to Amelie a perfect packing-case of diamonds, directed a torrent of different objects, chiefly mounted in gold, at both of them.

Bertie went home that night in a more settled and buoyant frame of mind than had been his since his arrival in America. Never before had he felt so certain of a happy and harmonious future. What Amelie's feeling for him was he dimly guessed from his knowledge of what once had been his for another, while for his part he gave her all he had to give—admiration, affection, desire. Only—and this, as far as he knew, was no longer among the capabilities of his nature—he did not give her their fusion into one white flame; he only offered, as it were, packets of the separate ingredients. But, as Sybil Massington had said, there are many ways of love; he took the best he knew. The knowledge of this, and the straight and honest acceptation of it by himself, was tranquillizing, and possibly a sedative to his conscience, for his thoughts as he strolled down Fifth Avenue on that night, strangely warm for the earliness of the month, strayed slowly, like his footsteps, to past years, and it would have surprised anyone who looked on his extraordinarily youthful and untroubled face to know how very old he was feeling as his mind drifted with the quiet strength of some ocean-tide back, *via* wedding-presents, to Dorothy. How absolutely she had dominated his every thought and feeling, how completely for those months he had ceased to have any independent will of his own, being absorbed and melted into her. He remembered one June in particular; they had both been in London, and day after day he had gone to see her in her house in Curzon Street. The weather was very hot, and she had a craze for living in nearly empty rooms; all her carpets had been taken up, and all her floors polished—everything not essential to comfort had been stacked in garrets, and the rooms were empty except for flowers. Lilacs had been magnificent that year—they were her favourite flowers—and the smell of lilac to him now meant that he lived once again, in the flash of a moment, that month of beautiful days when he had been so exquisitely unhappy with the unsatisfied yearning of his first passion. All that month she had kept him in a sort of rapturous agony of suspense, which kept ever growing nearer to certainty. Then, at the end, to bring matters to a crisis, he had written her that letter, and not gone near her for two days. Then, having no answer, he went, and she laughed at him and sent him away. Well, he had paid dearly for that letter, both in the desolating inability to care for anything in the months that followed, and also in other ways. What it cost him in hard cash did not trouble him. After all, he was infinitely her debtor; it was she who had let him see (though she had plucked the vision away again) to what height of ecstasy his own average human nature could rise.

What must a woman of that kind be made of? he wondered to himself. Was she so grossly stupid that she never had a glimpse of what she meant to him, or was she so utterly hard that, having seen that, she had not the decency anyhow to go into mourning, as it were, for him just for a little? Stupidity he could not accuse her of; there was no one of such lightning-like power of intuition to divine the mood of a man. No; she must have seen it and known it, and brushed it from her, as one brushes a fly off one's coat. For not a month after that she had left London with Bilton, whom she never professed to care for. But he was rich, and certainly he had done a great deal for her, for he had taken her from her position of 'pretty woman' actress, seen her capability of dramatic impersonation, and got her play after play where she had to behave like herself, till now, in a certain sort of rôle, there was no woman who touched her. Also, he had somehow made her the fashion; he had gauged his age correctly, and given it what it wanted. He had seen the trend of society both in England and America—seen its hardness, its heartlessness, its imperative need of being amused, its passion for money, and for its stage he had given it Mrs. Emsworth, an incarnation of itself.

Yes; she was hard, hard, hard as her own diamonds, and as brilliant, as many-faceted. Sometimes out of her, as out of them, a divinely soft light would shine, but if you tried to warm yourself in that mellow blaze there was no heat there; if in the excellent splendour and softness of the light you would think for a moment that there was a heart there, you would find only the cold, clear-cut edges. Had she not proved it—she who, not satisfied with leading him on, with letting him fall passionately in love with her, only to divert herself a little in watching that storm of passion which she observed from behind her shut window, only to draw the blind down when she had looked enough, had even used the letter he wrote her to make money out of it? How well she knew him, his weakness, his ineradicable instinct to save trouble, avoid disturbances, so that, when she wrote, or caused to be written, the letter of blackmail, she did it probably without the least fear that she was putting herself in a dangerous position. Nor was she—secure in the knowledge of Bertie's engagement, she was certain to get her money. And, as no doubt she also knew well, against her he could not have taken legal steps, for the memory of the love he once bore her. No; she was safe, quite safe.

He let himself into his flat with his latch-key, and saw several letters lying on the table. The English mail had come in, and Ginger, who had got home before him, was busy with his own correspondence, and only looked up and nodded at Bertie as he entered. For Bertie himself there were several English letters, chiefly congratulatory, a parcel from Tiffany's, 'by order of Mrs. Palmer,' containing a gold sapphire-starred cigarette-case, and two or three letters from America, one of which was type-written. For some reason, which he hardly formulated to himself, he took it up, and examined on front and back before opening it. Then he laid it down again, mixed a whisky and soda, and, returning to it, tore it open. It contained one square sheet, and ran as follows:

'Hearing that you are about to be married to Miss Amelie Palmer, it may interest you to learn that we are in possession of an autograph letter of yours to Mrs. Emsworth. The following phrases may recall it to your mind:

'"I loved you more than ever last night, though I thought I could not have loved you more than I really did."

'"Lilac, lilac; it reminds me of you more than any picture of you could."

'"You know my devotion to you. For me there is no other in the world."'

(Then, as before, followed a space.)

'Should you care to possess yourself of this, we will let you have it for £5,000. The money should be sent to Mr. Harold Bilton at his business office, 1,324a, Broadway, for Mrs. Emsworth's account, by to-morrow (Tuesday) evening. In the event of its not being to hand, we shall presume that you do not wish to have the letter, which we shall thereupon forward by special messenger that evening to Mr. Lewis S. Palmer.

'Mr. Bilton, who has lately arrived in New York, is authorized to receive the above-mentioned sum from you, should you settle to adopt this course, but to permit no discussion of any kind referring to the matter in hand.

'We are, dear Sir,
'Your faithful, obedient servants,
'A. B. C.'

Bertie read it through, folded it neatly up, replaced it in its envelope, and walked across to where Ginger was sitting absorbed in a letter.

'Any news?' he asked.

'Yes, a good deal.'

Ginger finished the sheet he was reading, got up briskly, and helped himself to whisky.

'Noah's Ark,' he observed. 'Great and merciful God!'

'You seemed to be enjoying yourself,' said his brother.

'I was, enormously. But it's great and merciful, all the same. That's all. Oh no, one thing more. Bertie, I think your girl is worth the rest of this continent. News? Yes, news from Davos. Charlie is better, ever so much better, and his nurse throughout has been Sybil. In fact, there is going to be love in a cottage, I think. Charlie writes. He seems to like the idea of a cottage.'

'She's going to marry him?' asked Bertie.

Ginger smiled.

'Now I come to think of it, he doesn't mention the word,' he observed.

'You're rather coarse,' remarked Bertie.

'I am. I thought it might cheer you up. You look rather down. Anything wrong?'

'Nothing whatever.'

Ginger strolled back to his chair, put his whisky on one arm, a little heap of cigarettes on the other, and curled himself up between them.

'The young folk are all growing up and being married,' he said. 'It makes me feel extremely old, and it is a little uncomfortable. I've done nothing—but that might happen to anybody—and I've felt nothing. What is it like to feel things, Bertie?'

'Depends what they are.'

'No, I mean independently of what they are. I don't know what strong emotion is. I don't know what it is to be carried off one's feet. I am much interested in many things, but impersonally. Now, you—you have adored, and you have been adored. I have sat and looked on. Does it leave you duller, do you think, to feel a thing, and then cease to feel it, than you would have been if you never felt it at all?'

Bertie considered this a moment.

'You never cease to feel things,' he said. 'A thing that has been exquisitely sweet becomes bitter, and continues bitter. You taste the jam first, and the powder afterwards.'

He turned to the mantelpiece, took up a cigarette, and then, with a sudden trembling hand, threw it into the grate.

'And you pay for it all,' he said—' you pay over and over again. Good-night, Ginger.'

CHAPTER XV

It was a glorious blue and golden morning in early June, and the soft brilliant sunshine of English summer weather flooded the glades of the park at Molesworth, where Amelie, intent on the finishing of a water-colour sketch, sat on a fallen tree-trunk, and Bertie lay on the grass by her side reading at intervals to her from a volume of Tennyson he had brought out with him. She was almost too busy with her painting to follow very clearly what he read, but the sound of his voice thrilled her with a big, quiet happiness, and when he was silent, the consciousness of his presence by her was hardly less vivid. All the same, she was attending very closely to what she was doing, and her brush industriously recorded what the upward sweep of her gray eyes had noted before she bent them again with bowed head on her sketch.

Indeed, that which lay before her was very well worth her attention. In front of them lay a sward of fine-woven turf, and from under the shade of the huge oak which spread its living canopies of green above them they looked through aisles of noble trees into the open, heathery ground of the far distance. The cool greenness, dim and subaqueous in tone, stretched to right and left of them in all shades of colour; here underneath the oak it was dark and almost sombre; there, where a clean-limbed, slender beech foamed up in the freshness of its pale foliage into the blue cup of heaven, the colour was enchantingly vivid and delicate, as if to match, even as the rose-colour of youthful cheeks matches the slender litheness of the frame, the girlish grace of the tree itself. Flecks of sunlight lay like spangles on the grass below the trees, and in spaces between them the blue blaze of the June day poured down on to the flower-decked grass. The last of the bluebells still lingered in shady places, as if pieces of sky had fallen there; tall fox-gloves rose in spires of blossoms through thickets of bramble; buttercups made a sunlight of their own, and in the shelter of scattered coppices the pale wind-flowers still dreamed in whiteness.

Not far in front of them, the centre point of Amelie's sketch, rose a huge thorn, covered with clusters of crimson blossom, standing in full sunlight, so throbbing and bursting with colour that she almost fancied she could see on the pale green of the slender-fingered birches that grew near some red reflection of that glorious blaze. To the right of it one could see through the tree-trunks the gray palings of an enclosed cover, where the ground tumbled upwards under pines, and the velvet of the turf was riddled and sandy with rabbit-holes. A fringe of elders, with the white umbrella of their flowers, grew there, and tawny honeysuckle added one more note to the great symphony of delicate woodland smell.

And even more entrancing than the woodland smell, more subtly mingled than that bouquet of coolness and greenness, of the aroma of pines, the drowsiness of the honeysuckle, the languor of the elders, was the symphony of woodland sound, the forest murmur that filled the ear even as the greenness filled and refreshed the eye. The hum of insects, of bees at their fragrant labour, was the bourdon note that pervaded everything; a light breeze stirred in the trees, calling out of each its own distinctive note—from the pines the sound of waves very far off, from the birches a thin, sibilant murmur, from the beech something a little lower in the scale, and from the tall grasses a whisper and a sigh. A late cuckoo chimed, still mellow-throated, doves moaned softly, thrushes fluted their repeated notes from bush to bush, calling to one another in the joy of the great vigorous life that filled these enchanted glades, and out in the open larks, black specks against the blue, hung over the nests of their mates, and towered in the triumph of their song. But best of all, pervasive even as the hum of bees, was the ripple and gurgle and chuckle and pouring of water, that one note more liquid than the nightingale's.

Right down the centre of the glade came the stream, brimmed with the rains of spring, and filling its bed from edge to edge. Here its course lay over gravel-beds, and the pebbles glanced and glimmered with the living light that the sun poured down through the pellucid transparency of the water. Then came a sharp elbow in its course, and it fretted its way, with sound of melodious outpouring, through the tangled roots of some tree that stood bare in the angle of the turning. Then for a space the ground was more clayey, and a carpet of green water-weeds were combed and waved by the woven ropes of water. Deeper pools lay here, and under the protection of the banks, where some promontory of rocky stuff made a breakwater, the broad fans of water-lilies and the golden crown of their blossoms found anchorage for their sappy stems. Dragon-flies, as if revisiting the scenes of their childhood, where they had nosed in the mud, or lain, blind, pupre, till the spring of their awakening, hovered iridescent and flashed like jewels flying through the air over the sunlit shallows; white-throated swallows skimmed up-stream, and companies of swifts chided together. Rushes waded knee-deep into the water, loose-strife stepped gingerly to the brink, and to all the stream prattled and sang and went on its sweet way.

Amelie laid down her brushes, and held out her sketch to Bertie.

'Criticise,' she said.

He looked at it a moment in silence.

'It's very good,' he said; 'but you still want the—the big softness of it all. It is still a little hard.'

She sighed.

'I knew you would say that,' she said, 'and it's perfectly true. Perhaps I shall get to be able to do it in time. It's all very well to say that a sketch is merely a matter of line and colour, but it isn't; there is a "feeling" which is beyond either.'

She took it back from him.

'Anyone could see it was painted by an American,' she observed.

Bertie laughed.

'That's where you are wrong,' he said; 'most Americans would say it was done by an Englishwoman.'

She smiled to herself with a secret pleasure, laid her sketch by her to dry, slid off the trunk where she had been sitting, and sat down on the grass by her husband.

'Read to me again,' she said. 'Read that song that ends:

> '"The moan of doves in immemorial elms,
> And murmur of innumerable bees."'

She leaned her head on his shoulder, and sat with eyes half-closed, as in his low, gentle voice he read through the exquisite passage.

'It is English,' she said, when he had finished; 'and, oh, Bertie, that means a lot to me. Bertie, are you happy?'

He closed the book, and sat thinking a moment before he answered her. It was true that he had never supposed that he was capable of being so happy as he had been in these last three months. It was true also that his affection for his wife had grown with every day they had passed together, yet the question was a difficult one to answer. A few months ago, had she asked him in his present mood the same question, he would instantly have said 'Yes'; but with the growth of his capacity for happiness and for loving her had grown the demand for happiness and love which his nature made. Instead of acquiescing in the conclusion that he never again could possibly love as he had once loved, he had begun to want that again; he was no longer content with this limitation.

'Ah, my dearest,' he said, 'happiness is not in your power or mine. No, I am not quite happy; I want something more.'

He sat up as her eyes questioned him.

'I want the impossible, I suppose,' he said; 'I want to be fire. You have made me want that.'

For a moment some shadow of vague trouble crossed her eyes.

'I don't think I understand,' she said.

Bertie plucked a long feather of grass, and chewed the juicy end of it. He had not meant to say quite so much.

'I'm not sure that I understand either,' he said. 'It is quite easy to understand complicated things, but when one gets to the plain, simple things like love and death, then one realizes how little one understands. Is it not so?'

The trouble grew.

'I never ask for confidences,' she said, 'so you mustn't think I am doing so; but, Bertie, sometimes I feel that there is a piece of you which I do not know —some locked room, or—or it is like that haunted house we went to the other day, where there is a space unaccounted for. One goes into all the rooms, but by the measurements there is yet another room which one cannot find.'

The intuition of this rather startled and shocked him.

'So you credit me with a Bluebeard's chamber?' he asked. 'It is far more likely to be a cupboard for lumber.'

'Have you some lumber, then?' she asked quickly.

The bitter taste of that which had been exquisitely sweet was at this moment very present to him—more bitter, perhaps, than it had ever been. For he regretted now, not that which was past, but its absence from the present; and the curious persistence of Amelie rather vexed him.

'Ah, we all must have a little lumber,' he said, with an unconscious touch of impatience in his voice. 'In this rough and tumble of a world we all get some bits of things broken—ideas, ideals, desires, what you will. They are our lumber; and it is wiser to turn the key on them—not bring them out and try to mend them.'

Amelie noticed the impatience of which he was unconscious.

'Cannot I help you to mend them, Bertie?' she asked, with a wonderful wistfulness in her voice. 'And have I vexed you?'

He threw the grass spearwise down the wind.

'I think you could not really vex me,' he said. 'But you can't help me to mend them; nobody can—not even you.'

She picked up her sketching things in silence, washed out her brushes, and closed her sketch-book.

'Let us forget it all, then,' she said briskly. 'Let us put the hands of the clock back ten minutes, and go on from then. "The murmur of innumerable bees." All June is in that line, is it not? Bertie, what a beautiful June we have had!'

'And it is not over yet,' said he.

'No; but people come to us this evening, you know, and on Monday we go up to town. Come, we must go back to the house; it is lunch-time, and the post will be in.'

But for both of them the huge blue of the day was flecked with a little cloud.

After lunch Amelie had a few calls to make, and some little business to transact in the village, and Bertie, who sturdily refused to accompany her, ordered his horse, and went for a rambling ride through the park. Somehow the vague conversation of that ten minutes in the morning had dimly but rather deeply upset him. In any case, it had the effect, so to speak, of smashing open his lumber-room door, on which he had so carefully turned the key. Twice before had it been rudely opened—on those occasions by Mrs. Emsworth herself, when she had got from him first ten thousand pounds for what was only a copy of his letter, and, secondly, five thousand more, two evenings before his marriage. It was with a sense of shame that even now made his cheeks burn when he thought of it, that he recalled his own utter weakness, his dread of possible exposure. Even at the time he knew that the wise thing to do would have been to have gone straight to Mr. Palmer with the letter for which he had paid ten thousand pounds and the second blackmailing letter, and have, with these proofs in his hand of the vileness of the scheme, told him the whole truth. But his nerves could no more face it than they could have allowed him to pull out a tooth or a nail of his own, and next day he had gone, cursing his own flabbiness, to Bilton's office, and obediently paid the second levy. Bilton himself was not there, but a young and rather insolently-mannered clerk, who addressed him as 'Earl Keynes,' had been authorized to receive his cheque and the type-written letter in exchange for a small packet which contained, as he satisfied himself, a couple of sheets in his own handwriting, torn half across. He had, of course, kept the first letter which he had bought back, and, comparing the two, he came to the conclusion that the first was a very careful forgery, the second the genuine letter.

But this afternoon it was not so much his own weakness in having been so easy a prey to the blackmailer, and in having been incapable of forcing himself to tell the whole thing to Mr. Palmer, that lay like a shadow on him, as his present inability to feel as he once felt. He had unlocked the despatch-box where he kept the letters on his return this morning with Amelie, and read one through again. Passion vibrated there—a passion which had once been his; he could recall it perfectly; he could remember with the most vivid distinctness the rapture of desire in which he had written those sheets of adoration. It had seemed to him then that life was *this*: that the whole world, and whatever it contained that was lovely and worth the worship of man, found in her its completion. The best and the worst of him—for it was all of him that wrote thus—was hers, in the passionate self-abandonment of love. For that gift she had in return called him a pretty boy, and told him not to talk nonsense; but for the faculty of feeling that nonsense again for his wife he would have given everything he had. He saw and fully recognised the exquisite quality of Amelie's beauty, and the beautiful and generous soul that dwelt therein. Day by day he saw the sweet unfolding of her nature—an unfolding as silent and as perfect as the blossoming of a rose. He admired her, he felt passion for her, but a passion that never was lost and blinded by itself, as his passion for Dorothy had been. Often in that June of lilacs he had come home from seeing her, and sat for hours, as if intoxicated or stupefied, unable to speak or think even, only lie with mind open under the eye of his sun. It was that power he would have given the world to recapture.

His ramblings had led him into an outlying piece of the park which he seldom visited—a somewhat bleak, heathery upland, not more than a mile or so from the house, but away from the beauty of the wooded glades where he and Amelie had spent the morning. He was about to turn, when, at some little distance off, he saw a couple of men standing by a tall red rod planted in the ground, one of whom apparently was taking observations through some sort of telescopic instrument. About a couple of hundred yards further on was another rod, and, following the line with his eye, he saw that between them and the park paling was yet another. He rode up to them, and, with a certain resentment, inquired what they were doing, and got for answer that they were under orders to survey this piece of country for the projected railway. They further explained that the line, when it reached the ridge over which he had ridden, would probably enter a tunnel, and emerge again only outside the park. Her ladyship, one of the men remarked in a rather insolent tone, had given permission for the survey.

Bertie turned his horse round, and rode back homewards, doing his honest best not to think what he thought. In his heart he was very much hurt that Amelie had not told him, and somehow the idea that the park was apparently to be invaded and cut up by a railway-line was extraordinarily repugnant to him. A couple of years ago, it is true, both he and his father would have welcomed any scheme which should turn that white elephant, the Molesworth property, into cash, at whatever violation of its forest glades; yet now, when only the bare, outlying portions were to be given to the invader, he intensely disliked the thought of it. Money was no longer needful; the railroad might go hang.

He found Amelie in the garden when he got back, and, instead of giving her the little caress which was still usual between them after only an hour or two's separation, he began abruptly.

'I found some men surveying on the far warrens,' he said. 'They told me they had your permission.'

Amelie frowned slightly, as if puzzled.

'Yes, I believe the agent did say something about it two days ago,' she said. 'It is only a survey they are making; there is nothing settled.'

'I think you might have told me,' said he. 'But of course the place is yours; you will please yourself.'

This hurt her; he had rather intended it should. But she answered with admirable gentleness.

'I am sorry,' she said; 'I quite forgot to tell you. The thing seemed to me immaterial. Of course, I should have consulted you before settling anything.'

Bertie felt rather ashamed of his ill-temper, and, remembering the omission of their usual little ceremony, he picked up her hand as it lay on the arm of her chair, and pressed it.

'Yes, dear, I am stupid to have made anything of it,' he said. 'But tell me, Amelie, what is the proposed line?'

'A branch line from Cardiff, joining the Liverpool and Southampton. It is only a preliminary survey, I believe. Of course, I meant to talk to you about it as soon as they opened negotiations with us; I may as well now. It will cross the far warren for about a mile, I believe, and then tunnel under the ridge. It will not interfere with us in any way. It is completely cut off from the house and the woods. And I suppose they would pay something substantial. I had meant to give you that.'

Bertie's feeling of shame grew a little hotter.

'I am a cross-grained brute,' he said. 'Am I forgiven?' She smiled at him.

'Do you ask that?' she said. 'But oh, Bertie, don't hurt me even ever so little. A little hurt from you hurts so much.'

So another cloud flecked the blue of June.

That afternoon their guests began to arrive for the week-end party. It was the first they had given, and Amelie somehow felt a little nervous, for it was her debut as hostess. Lord Bolton was coming, and, in a way, it seemed to her hardly decent that she should be receiving him in this house. She had met him once or twice before, and was vaguely terrified at him. Sybil Massington was coming too, with Charlie, to whom she was to be married in July. Ginger was accompanying his father; other friends of Bertie's raised their numbers to a dozen, and both her own parents, with Reggie Armstrong as gentleman-in-waiting to Mrs. Palmer, were to make a sort of family party. This consciousness that she was on trial made her the least bit in the world self-conscious, and deep down in her mind, tucked away in its darkest corner, but still there, was a sort of haunting anxiety about her mother. Again and again she tried to picture to herself Mrs. Palmer and Gallio engaged in friendly desultory conversation, but as often she abandoned this projected situation as unthinkable. She even hoped—hoped in a whisper, that is to say—that for some reason her mother would be prevented from coming. That whisper she stifled as often as it sounded, thoroughly ashamed of it; but it was there.

But Providence declined to have any special dealings on this point, and Mrs. Palmer's entry into the house was clearly audible to her as she sat in the garden with those of her guests who had arrived. Gallio was already there, his thin but fresh-coloured face and flossy white hair, his general air of great distinction and complete imperturtability, seeming admirably suited to the dignified stability of the gray house and the spaciousness of the ancestral lawns. He had been most affectionate and gentle to her, had called her 'his dear daughter,' had kissed her hand with a courtly grace, and made her feel intensely ill at ease. Then came the sound of screamings from the house, and if the simile of a substantial butterfly with a shrill voice discharged from a catapult conveys anything to the reader, it was in such manner that Mrs. Palmer came through the open French windows of the drawing-room, and with outstretched arms swooped swiftly across the lawn to Amelie.

'My dearest, sweetest angel child,' she cried—screams of emotion mingled with kissing—' why, if I haven't been just dreaming day and night of seeing you again!'—more screams—' Why, you look so well; you look just too lovely for words. I've been just crazy to see you!'

Lord Bolton had in the previous year firmly declined the honour of Mrs. Palmer's acquaintance, saying he did not wish to be deaf for the remainder of a misspent life; and Amelie introduced her to him.

'Very pleased to make your acquaintance, Lord Bolton,' she said; 'and to have the pleasure of meeting you here makes it just too complete.'

Gallio shook hands.

'I have looked forward to this,' he said with his best paternal air. 'Bertie, dear Amelie, you, and my unworthy self—the family group in the family frame.' And his eye wandered over the great gray façade of the house.

'Well, I think that's too beautifully put,' said Mrs. Palmer; 'that's a real

160

poetical thought. Lewis,' she called to her husband, 'Lord Bolton's been too poetical for words. Well, I'm sure!'

Gallio's thin lips tightened a little.

'How are you, Mr. Palmer?' he said. 'I am most fortunate to have been able to come down to-day. I was afraid I should not be able to, but when my dear daughter said you were both coming, I could not let anything stand in the way.'

'Why, that was just lovely of you,' said Mrs. Palmer, as she moved to Amelie's side at the tea-table, and went on in a loud aside, as Gallio engaged Mr. Palmer in conversation. 'Dearest child,' she said, 'you look simply too sweet. And I've lost my heart to Lord Bolton. I think he's just lovely, with his white hair and all—just the old nobleman I used to dream about before I married Lewis. Now, give me some tea, poured out with your own hands at your own house, you darling Countess of Keynes. Well, I'm sure, I'm just crazy with pleasure!'

Mrs. Palmer flowed on in a shrill and equable torrent of conversation. Her particular timbre of voice made talking in her vicinity as difficult as talking in a rail way-tunnel, for it echoed and reverberated in a manner which rendered all else inaudible.

'I read all about your presentation in the *New York Herald*,' she went on —'"the new American beauty, the young and charming Countess of Keynes"; and you'll laugh, Amelie, but I ordered a special edition with all about you printed in gilt letters, and just flooded Newport with the copies. I guess Newport will find it as hard to beat you as it did to beat the pearl-party. Newport will just curl up and die; I guess you've done for Newport. And there's one thing I want to ask: Do I, Lord Bolton, take any rank as mother of a countess? I could find nothing about it in your Debrett.'

Gallio turned to her with his most courtly air.

'Ah, Mrs. Palmer,' he said, 'we have no rank in England to equal that which a charming and beautiful woman enjoys in her own right.'

The famous cry resounded over the lawns, and beat in echo against the house.

'Why, if that isn't just too sweet of you!' she cried. 'Lewis, here's Lord Bolton saying such things to me as you never thought of saying. And where's Reggie Armstrong? Reggie, did you hear what Lord Bolton said? You did, though you pretend you didn't. You're just green with jealousy. I can see the greenness reflected on your strawberries. Well, I never!'

Sybil Massington and others had arrived already, and the assembled party, some fifteen or sixteen, were now all gathered on the lawn, drinking tea and eating strawberries with a slight air of constraint, as if social thunder of some kind was in the air. Bertie, who had been receiving his guests indoors and bringing them out, was in a low chair just opposite Mrs. Palmer, listening with rather less than half an ear to what Sybil was saying to him. Quite involuntarily, at this speech he raised a deprecating eyebrow, looked up, and caught Amelie's eye. She flushed slightly, and looked away again. Some rather heavy rejoinder on the part of Reggie Armstrong followed, and Gallio sat down opposite Bertie and Sybil.

'Charming woman,' he said in his very low, gentle voice; 'she has all the brightness of the Western civilization.'

Bertie could not help smiling, and, looking up again, caught Amelie's glance, and felt guilty. The resounding voice went on:

'It's just my idea of the English country house,' she said; 'it's just ancestral. Why, Lewis might go and establish his office right here under these trees, and give Vanderbilt fits, as he did last year, and the trees wouldn't care. That's what I've just lain awake and coveted till three in the morning. Why, I was at Windsor last week, and I assure you Windsor looks like a mushroom beside this. It's just English. Lord Bolton, however you could let Lewis have it I can't think. Come and sit by me, and pay me some more compliments. Why, it tickles me to death to sit here and talk to you. I think you're just lovely.'

Gallio rose obediently.

'Tact, too,' he observed to Mrs. Massington, as he turned to comply with Mrs. Palmer's frank and direct request.

In fact, for the time things could not have been worse, and Mrs. Palmer's voluble shrillness, bawling all sorts of things which were neither wicked nor stupid nor anything objectionable, except that they were simply impossible, at Gallio, who sat beside her, and encouraged her by his exquisite courtliness of manner into imagining that she was being the most brilliant success, was too much for the nerves of some of the English section, who strolled away about the lawn with fine deliberation, and carefully abstained from any comment. But in process of time Amelie took her mother away to see her room, and Gallio, suave to the last, made her his best bow, as she declared for the twentieth time that she considered him the loveliest man she had ever met. Bertie had strolled away with Charlie and Sybil Massington, feeling that in its small way the situation was unbearable. It was one of the hideous, bitter little comedies of life, where everyone is ridiculous, yet it is impossible to laugh for fear of crying. He knew so well how Mrs. Palmer felt, how Gallio felt, how he himself felt, and he was afraid he knew how Amelie felt.

Sybil had much to say.

'It is quite like a fairy-story, Bertie. Here are Charlie and I—the poor young man who proposed to drop into an early grave, and who proposed to me instead, who has now no more idea of dropping into a grave than I have—and here are you and Amelie, with Molesworth once more your home. Bertie, if you hadn't fallen in love with Amelie, you would have argued yourself the most obtuse young man in the world. Why she fell in love with you is harder to say. She has got extraordinary charm; I felt it as soon as I saw her. You were in luck when you went a-wooing. So were you, Charlie—why didn't you say that?'

'You really didn't give me much time,' said Charlie in self-justification.

'No, that's true. Bertie, what fun we had in Long Island! Really, that time was most amusing. And we all meet again here—all but Mrs. Emsworth, that is to say. By the way, she has come back; she is staying somewhere in the neighbourhood. Did her tour end as successfully as it began?'

'She wrote to me just before my marriage saying she was getting quite rich,' said Bertie, wincing a little.

'How nice! I wish I was. Charlie, they are all rich except you and me. Never mind; we will stay with them all a great deal, which will be charming for them. And the Palmers' house in London—have you seen it? Really, it is magnificent. Who did it? Mrs. Palmer or her husband? It can't have been done by a firm; the taste is too individual, too certain.'

'Mr. Palmer did it,' said Bertie. 'I fancy he ordered every individual thing, down to the smallest details.'

'I fancied it must be he; Mrs. Palmer is a little more *voulu*—more bird of Paradise.'

She laughed.

'I can't help laughing,' she said. 'To anyone with any eye for human comedy the scene at tea was delicious. She is a great dear, and I am very fond of her; but, frankly, she and Gallio together were extraordinarily funny. I love contrasts—notes of jarring colour.'

Bertie did not laugh.

'I was furious with Gallio,' he said; 'he tried to make a fool of her.'

'Assuredly he did not succeed,' said Sybil. 'Mrs. Palmer was delighted with him. Anyhow, he had to be polite or rude; he chose to be extremely polite.'

'Amelie saw,' said Bertie briefly, and the subject dropped.

They strolled back in the enveloping light of the sunset, which flooded and pervaded the air with level rays. The glades where he had sat with his wife that morning were full of the soft luminousness of the sun, which entered below the leafy boughs of the thick trees and lit them from end to end with a wonderful glory. Birds were busy with their evensong in the bushes, and, as at noonday, the countless hum of insects was still in the air. Bertie, still rather disturbed for Amelie's sake at the little tea-time comedy, felt soothed by the leisurely tranquillity of the hour, and the two others, a little apart, passed from time to time some whispered confidence. But the mellow call of the bell from the Elizabethan turret warned them that the minutes to dinner-time were numbered, and they briskened their steps back to the house. The other two went upstairs, but Bertie turned for a moment to his sitting-room in quest of evening news, and found Amelie there waiting for him. Her face was a little flushed, and some shadow of trouble clouded it.

'I wanted to see you a moment before dinner,' she said. 'I——' And she stopped.

'What is it, dear?' said he gently.

'You know. He, your father, was laughing at her; he made other people laugh at her; he made you laugh. I don't think it was a good joke. There are many sorts of bad breeding; I think he showed one of the worst.'

'I am sorry you take it like that, Amelie,' said he. 'It is true I laughed, but I did not laugh at your mother; I laughed at the comedy of the situation.'

'He made a fool of her,' continued Amelie; 'but I think he made a cad of himself.'

'That is rather strong language,' said Bertie.

'I think it is suitable language. I think you ought to ask him to behave with courtesy to my guests—not with exaggerated courtesy.'

Bertie thought for a moment.

'I will tell him that he hurt your feelings, if you wish,' said he at length.

'That is not the point,' said she.

'For me it is.'

She turned on him a long, luminous look.

'Then you don't understand,' she said. 'My meaning is that I will not have my mother insulted in my house.'

He frowned.

'You make too much of it,' he said.

'You won't do as I ask, then?' she said.

'If you think it over, you will see that it would serve no good purpose.'

She left the window where she was standing, and began to move towards the door.

'I never ask twice,' she said. 'By the way, Mrs. Emsworth has telegraphed to know whether she may come over to lunch to-morrow. She is staying at Midhurst.'

'Please make some excuse,' said Bertie quickly; 'I do not wish her to come here.'

'Why not?'

'I desire you to make her some excuse,' he repeated.

She looked up, started at the quiet peremptoriness of his tone, and again there flashed into her mind the thought that had been there this morning, when she told him that there was a piece of him she did not know. At this moment she felt she localized it.

'What reason do you give me?' she asked. 'You used to be quite friendly with her last autumn.'

'Quite true; but I am not now.'

'Have you seen her since?' asked Amelie, not quite recognising from what that question really sprang.

'No, I have not.'

He paused.

'Why did you ask that?' he said quietly.

'It was a reasonable question,' she said. 'Mrs. Emsworth is a friend of mine too; I have every right to ask her to the house, unless you give me good reason.'

'I ask you not to exercise that right,' said Bertie.

Suddenly, and almost audibly in its distinctness, Amelie's mind said to her, 'We are quarrelling.' Her love for him, frightened, ran, as it were, towards him, but stumbled over her pride. She did not answer him, but left the room, feeling sick at heart.

CHAPTER XVI

The construction of the intermediate pieces of line which were to connect Liverpool with Southampton by a direct route were finished by July, and, running powers over the lines of other existing companies having been acquired, the new service was open for traffic by the beginning of August. As Mr. Palmer had foreseen, the immense saving of time and convenience of transport effected by this direct linking together of the two ports had been, as soon as the Bill for the projected line had passed the Houses of Parliament, instantly recognised by the various fleets that used these ports, and its success was assured long before its completion. Added to this, the economical and businesslike methods of running trains which were adopted by him, based on American systems, enabled the line to cut down rates, while it secured for its customers far more rapid transport, so that it obtained from the first practically a monopoly of the goods traffic between the ports. A quantity of gentlemen, who in some vague sort of manner considered that they were acting in the sacred name of patriotism, wrote hundreds of violent letters to the papers, protesting against this fresh American invasion; while others, equally vaguely, in the sacred name of Art, ranted themselves hoarse over the steel-girder budges that desecrated the most lovely spots in the rural fortresses of England, and the black, squat, but eminently efficient, engines that drew the trains of unlovely merchandise. But this *vox, et præterea nihil*, soon died away, and the only influence it had on traffic was perhaps to call added attention to the eminent advantages enjoyed by the customers of Mr. Palmer's line. Consequently, neither he nor they had any quarrel with it.

'All this he had foreseen, and more. It became practically necessary, as he had known all along, for Swansea and Cardiff to put themselves into communication with this system, and as early as June, as we have seen, surveyors were busy on the Molesworth estate over the route. The winter before Mr. Palmer had purchased both it and the adjoining Wyfold estate, knowing that the line of direct communication must pass through one or the other; and when towards the end of July the experts pronounced very strongly in favour of the Molesworth route, he forwarded their recommendation to Amelie, with the request that she would come and talk matters over with him before she left town.

The last month had not passed very happily for her; it lacked, at least, that wonderful edge of happiness which May and June had given her. The little rift which had opened between her and Bertie had not closed again, and, if anything, it had become rather wider. She had obeyed his request, and not asked Mrs. Emsworth to lunch, but she had done so unwillingly, rebelling in her mind against this arbitrariness which expected to be obeyed and yet would give no reason for what it wished done. In consequence—for her protest, though mute, was very obvious—the spirit of her compliance was almost as irritating to him as her disobedience would have been. Furthermore, at that interview she had had with him suspicion, vague and darkling, she knew lurked in the shadow of her mind; the piece of him she did not know irresistibly connected itself with Mrs. Emsworth. There it had grown like some mushroom, and, though she did not officially, so to speak, recognise its existence, it was there. Other things, too, had tended to separate them, and in particular the treatment (or so she called it) of her mother by the world of London. She had expected to see and saw that London in general flocked to Mrs. Palmer's new house, where the entertainments, if not quite so wildly improbable as those which awoke the echoes in the glades of Long Island, were on the most lavish and exuberant scale. Consequently London, with its keen eye for the buttered side of the bread, went there in its crowds, drank Mrs. Palmer's champagne, danced to her fiddles, won her money at bridge, and enjoyed the performances of all the most notable singers and pianists in the world with the greatest contentment. But what Amelie saw also was the half-shrugged shoulders, the instantaneous glance of the eye, the raised eyebrow, the just-not-genuine smile of those who were the most constant *habitués* there. Mrs. Palmer, in fact, was in London, not of London. This Amelie resented, and, by way of retaliation, she had, as was perfectly natural, her mother constantly in her own house, and filled it with Americans perhaps rather more than was perfectly natural. For the rest, there had been nothing the least resembling an open breach between her and Bertie; he accepted the continual presence of her countrymen without the slightest protest, and never, even by the smallest inflection of voice or manner, was other than absolutely civil to everyone she asked. Indeed, the perfect evenness of his manner added its quota to the constraint that lay between them; in her heart of hearts she knew that he often found neither interest nor entertainment in her guests, and the chilled perfection of his mode of conducting himself towards them but served as a barrier the more.

But what most stood between them was her undefinable suspicion about Mrs. Emsworth. On that day the cankerworm had entered, and since then she had again and again asked herself whether Bertie's affection for her had ever been of the same quality as the love she had felt for him. She remembered with horrible distinctness his words, 'I want to be fire,' and they, which at the moment had seemed to her but an expression of the ever unsatisfied yearning of love, which always, however perfect, still desires to go yet deeper, now wore a more sinister interpretation, and were to her the kindling of a secret heart-burning. What if this natural and simplest interpretation was true? What If he had never really felt fire for her?

Such was the abbreviated reading of her spiritual diary down to the day when she drove to see her father. Though he had been in London all this last month, she had scarcely set eyes on him, so immersed had he been in the railroad business, and it was with a childish eagerness that she looked forward to having a long talk with him. In the trouble of her mind she felt great longing for that kind, unwearied affection which he ever had for her—an affection not very demonstrative, but extraordinarily real and solid. The effusiveness of her mother's love just now was less satisfying to her, for Mrs. Palmer had been for the last six weeks a mere whirling atom in the mill of social success; and while one hand, so to speak, was entwined round Amelie's neck in a maternal embrace, the other would be scribbling notes of invitation and regret to the flower of England's nobility.

She got to the house rather late for lunch, and was struck by the resemblance which the moral atmosphere of the dining-room bore to that of Basle railway-station. There was the same sense that everybody was just going to catch a train; that they were exchanging last words as they took their hurried meal. Her father, next whom she sat, was an exception, for he ate his thin slices of toasted Hovis bread and drank his milk with the deliberateness which his digestion demanded; but everyone else seemed to be unable to attend to what was going on at this moment, because they all were thinking of what they would be doing the next. Even her father, too, seemed rather preoccupied, and from time to time she saw that his eyes were fixed on herself with a certain anxious look, which was removed as soon as he saw she observed it.

With regard to the railroad scheme, his explanation after lunch was very short. A big ordnance map showed her where the line would enter the park, where it would enter the tunnel, not to appear again till it had passed outside the precinct. Its whole course would be quite remote from the house—remote also from the wooded side of the park; they would be as unconscious of its presence there as if it was in the next county. The Wyfold route, on the other hand, which perhaps might be adopted if Amelie put serious obstacles in the company's way, would actually be very much closer to the house and the forested piece of the park than the other.

Mr. Palmer made these explanations as if he anticipated some opposition on Amelie's part, and he was pleased to find none.

'It seems to me much the most sensible plan,' she said; 'and, as you say, the railway will really interfere with us less if it is in Molesworth than if it was in Wyfold. I must just tell Bertie about it, and I will send you my formal consent this evening. I will leave everything connected with the sale in your hands.'

She pushed the maps away from her with rather a weary air.

'And how are you, papá,' she said, falling into her old habit of addressing him. 'I haven't set eyes on you for weeks.'

Mr. Palmer gave a moment's consideration to how he was before he answered.

'Well, I guess I'm a bit out of condition in the brain,' he said. 'From the business point of view, England is the most enervating place I ever came to. These directors and business men here are about as much use as nursery-maids. They go down to their offices round about eleven, and sit there till one. Then they eat a heavy lunch, and stroll back about two to see if anything has happened. Of course it hasn't; things don't happen unless you make them happen. So they light a big cigar, and go down to Woking for an evening round of golf after the fatigues of the day. Saturdays they don't put in an appearance at all. That's their idea of business. And it tells on me rather; it's difficult to keep up ordinary high pressure when you're surrounded by so many flabby bits of chewed string. I guess I'll go back to America in the fall, and get braced up.' 'It don't affect mamma,' said Amelie, falling more and more into her native vernacular. 'She just flies around same as ever. She's having a real daisy of a time, she says.' Mr. Palmer did not listen to this; he was pursuing his own melancholy reflections on English business methods.

'It reminds me of a poultry-yard,' he said. 'An Englishman, on the rare occasions when he lays an egg, has to flap his wings and crow over it, instead of sitting down to hatch it. Why, I suppose they've given fifty lunches to boards of the directors over this twopenny-halfpenny line of mine already. There was a luncheon on the formation of the board; there was a luncheon to celebrate their determination to set to work at once; there was a luncheon to celebrate their doing so. There was a dinner on the occasion of the cutting of the first sod of earth; they brought down some fool-sort of Highness to do it. They had a week at the seaside when the Bill passed through the House, and when the first train runs next month, they'll all go and have a rest-cure on the completion of their labours. What they want is something to cure them of their habit of always resting.' He got up from his chair in some impatience, folded up the maps, and stood looking at his daughter in silence for a moment.

'Say, Amelie,' he said, 'and what kind of time have you been having? All going serene and domestically? Bertie been behaving himself? Do either of you want anything? You look a bit down, somehow—kind of tired about the eyes.'

Amelie looked up at him; the 'tired about the eyes' seemed to be a wonderfully true interpretation of how she felt.

'Oh, we trot along,' she said. 'I suppose everyone has their bits of worries. Mamma has when she accepts three dinner invitations for the same evening. You have when your directors give luncheon-parties instead of doing business. We all have.'

'Can't see why you should,' he said. 'I don't like you to worry, Amelie. What's it all about?'

He paused a moment.

'Have you heard anything about Bertie which bothers you?' he asked; 'or hasn't he been good to you?'

She did not answer at once, for, in her rather super-sensitized frame of mind, it seemed to her that her father's first question was not vague or general, but that he had some special, definite reason for asking. From that it was but the shortest of links necessary to couple the question with that which grew mushroom-like in the shadow of her mind.

'No; he has been perfectly good to me, and I have heard nothing that bothers me,' she said.

She looked up at her father as she spoke. He was standing close to her—a short, gray-whiskered man, insignificant in face and features except for those wonderful eyes. In his hand, the hand which by a stroke of the pen, a signing of the name, could set in motion the force of millions, was a little silver paper-knife which she had once given him. Even now, as she knew—for he had said he could only give her five minutes after lunch—there were waiting for him a hundred schemes to be considered, a hundred more levers to move the world 'as he chose. But he stood there, waiting with a woman's infinite patience for any impulse towards confidence she-might feel—just a tender, solicitous father, grasping in his hand a daughter's insignificant gift.

'We have always been chums, Amelie,' he said, with a sort of appealing wistfulness. 'When you were quite little, you always used to bring me your little worries for us to smooth out together. I used to be pretty smart at it; I used to be devilish proud of the way I could take the frown out of your little forehead.'

She held out her hand to him.

'You are an old darling,' she said, with unshed tears springing to her eyes. 'But I tell you this truth: it is only I who have been worrying. I have been imagining all sorts of things, so that I have got to believe them. That is the matter with me.'

'You have heard nothing specific?' he asked.

Again that question arrested her, awoke her imaginings, and she made up her mind on what had long been a pondered idea.

She got up at once.

'Nothing whatever,' she said, with a resumption of her usual manner. 'Now I am going. Take care of yourself, papa darling, and wake this sleepy old county up. I adore its sleepiness myself, and I know you can never rouse it, otherwise I should not suggest it.'

The carriage was waiting for her, and she got briskly in.

'Mrs. Emsworth's,' she said to the footman.

As she drove there, she tried to stifle thought, for she knew that her design was to confirm or dispel a suspicion that should never have been hers. She was doing a thing which was based on a wrong done to her husband in thought. That she knew, but she combated it by saying to herself.

'What if it is true?'

She found Mrs. Emsworth at home and delighted to see her, and for a little they just interchanged the generalities which, between two people who have not seen each other for some time, are the necessary ushers to real talk. The day was very hot, and Dorothy, catlike, basked and purred in it. There was something rather *décolleté* about her appearance, and something in her general atmosphere was equally so. She was, in fact, very different, so she struck Amelie, from the woman who told the gardener's son the fairy-story on the dewy lawn at Long Island.

'I am charmed to see you,' she said for the second time, when Amelie was seated; 'and I was furious the other day when you put me off coming to see you at Molesworth. Had you a prim party? If so, it was kind of you. Priggish, prim, and prudish—those are the qualities I dislike—probably,' she added with admirable candour, 'because I do not happen to be fortunate enough to possess them.' She paused a moment; then an idea seemed to strike her. 'And where and how is Bertie?' she asked. 'I haven't set eyes on him for months— not since the party in Long Island, in fact.'

'He said he hadn't seen you since then the other day,' said Amelie.

'No; I'm rather hurt, because at one time, you know, we were the greatest friends. I used to see him every day nearly. Then—'

She got up with her slow, catlike movements, and stretched herself luxuriously, and laughed a lazy laugh of somewhat animal enjoyment. Something about Amelie's attitude—her reserve, her stiffness, which was altogether unlike what she remembered of her in Long Island—rather irritated her, and woke in her that *gamin* spirit of mischief which was a very sensible ingredient in her nature. Amelie was putting her nose in the air, giving herself airs, and if there was one thing in the world Dorothy could not stand, it was that. Then, to fortify the mischievous spirit, she remembered the unexplained return of her present to Bertie. He, too, was giving himself airs; his nose was in the air. And when Dorothy saw a nose in the air, it was her habit to very rudely lay hold of it, so to speak, and rub it in the mud. Then, as a coping-stone to her nose-in-air theory, had come Amelie's refusal to let her come over to Molesworth. Decidedly this was a case for treatment. Also her love of making mischief—an occupation, we are led to infer, specially designed by Satan—was rather strong in her. So she laughed her laugh, and continued.

'Then he dropped me,' she said—' just opened his fingers and let me drop. I suppose I ought to have been broken, but I wasn't.'

She had sat down again in a very long, low chair opposite Amelie, and noticed, with great inward amusement, the tense interest with which Amelie listened to her.

'I suppose Bertie's been playing about again,' she thought to herself. 'An amorous young man, but it isn't playing the game now he's married.' And, with only three-quarters of her mind bent on mischief, she went on:

'Yes, I suppose I ought to have been broken, but one gets tough, you know. But when I sent him a really charming wedding-present, and had it sent back without a word, I thought it was rather strong. That was being dropped with a vengeance.'

'Did Bertie do that?' asked Amelie.

'Yes, dear, unless you did. Back it came, anyhow. Now, if I had not been the sweetest-tempered, meekest little Moses that ever lived, I should have—well, made it unpleasant.'

Amelie flushed; her manner was still far from pleasing Dorothy, for she sat as upright in her chair as if the plague lurked in the back or arms of it.

'I don't understand you,' she said; 'how could you make it unpleasant for Bertie?'

Mrs. Emsworth laughed; Amelie really was too stately for words.

'My dear, you are new to London, of course, but I wonder that no candid friend has ever told you. Bertie was once just madly in love with me. It was a great bore though I liked him well enough. But such classical ardour was beyond me. His letter—has he never confessed to you about the letter he wrote me? It was quite a lyrical letter, and it made me scream. I was just *the* only thing on God's earth.'

'Can you show it me?' asked Amelie very quietly. 'I should think it must be amusing.'

She made a rather pitiful attempt to laugh.

'I wish I could,' said the other, still maliciously; 'I am sure you would shriek over it. But I tore it up ages ago—last autumn, to be accurate, the first time I saw Bertie in America. It was rather kind of me—rather excessively kind, I have sometimes thought; I might have had some fun over it.'

She glanced carelessly across to Amelie. The girl had grown quite pale, even to the lips, and her hands were trembling. Instantly a compunction as quick as all her emotions seized the other.

'Ah! you mustn't mind my nonsense, dear Amelie,' she cried, jumping up. 'I have been talking very foolishly; I did not think it would make you mind like that.'

She took the girl's hand, but Amelie withdrew it.

'But there was this letter,' she said. 'And Bertie did make love to you?'

'Yes; why not? Show me the man, the most respectable married man, who says he has never kissed another girl in his life, and I will show you a liar. What does it matter?'

'A lyrical letter?' said Amelie.

'Yes, I wish I had kept it; I would show it you.'

Suddenly a wave almost of physical nausea swept over Amelie. She had all the stainless purity of thought of a girl who has been married young to the first man she has ever loved, and in the first moment of her knowing definitely that Bertie at one time had made love to this woman she felt sick— simply sick. She rose from her chair, and put on her gloves, while Dorothy

173

watched her, conscious that some emotion which she herself had so long forgotten, had she ever experienced it, that she no longer comprehended it, mastered her. And, with the best intentions in the world, not recognising that any further allusion to her own friend-ship with Bertie would only further disgust and sicken his wife, she said:

'That was all. There was never anything more—anything wrong.'

Amelie turned on her a marble face.

'How am I to know?' she asked. 'What prevented it? His morals, the lyrical letter-writer, or yours?'

Dorothy felt a strong though momentary impulse to box her ears. It would probably have been a good thing if she had yielded to it. She herself had felt for Amelie a sort of wondering pity that a matter so long dead could possibly be bitter still, and, acting under that, she had done her best to reassure her. But Amelie had slapped that generous impulse in the face; she had also chosen to express doubt as to the truth of what she had been told; and a rather more pronounced felinity awoke in Dorothy's face.

'You had better go and talk it out with Bertie,' she said.

'Ask him to repeat what he remembers of that letter. He is sure to have some recollection of it even now that he is so happily married. You can then draw your own conclusions, and, as far as I am concerned, you are perfectly free to do so. Oh yes, and tell him that I constantly use the dressing-bag he so kindly returned, and think of him.'

Amelie went out, feeling as if her world had fallen in ruins about her head. Possibilities which she had been ashamed of harbouring in her mind suddenly leapt out into flaring certainties, and they enveloped her. She could not think as yet coherently or connectedly; wherever she turned her thoughts, a flame flashed in her eyes. All her secret doubts were justified: Bertie had loved this woman; it was she who had called out the notes of his lyre, while she herself was given the shillings and pence—all the small change of the dower of love which he had once showered on Mrs. Emsworth. She could get no further than this; in this circle her thoughts ran round and round, like a squirrel in a revolving cage. Wherever she tried to go, she was still pawing round that one circle; she could get no further; the range of her mental processes was limited to that. And she now knew at once that she had to go on her way, whatever it was, unattended, uncomforted; and even in the exaggerated desolation of these first moments she could make the one resolve that no one, not even her father, should ever know. This her pride imperatively demanded: whatever she had to bear, she would bear in silence. And she could bear anything except pity.

174

'I want to be fire'—that was explained now, and that he should want that seemed to her an added insult.

'My dear Amelie,' he seemed to say, 'you are a charming girl, but you don't interest me—like that. I wish you did; I really wish you did.'

She bit her under-lip till it was white with the pressure of her teeth, and clasped her hands so tightly in her lap that the sharp facets of the stones in her rings dinted her fingers. The future spelt impossibility. There were hours daily to be gone through with Bertie; what of them? What of the little lover-like caresses that were still constant between them? What, indeed, of the whole tissue of his simulated love—of his wish to be fire? For the moment, whether it was true or not that the acme of his relationship with Mrs. Emsworth culminated actually in that 'lyrical letter' or not, she hardly cared; it was there, in any case, that his fire had burned—had burned itself out.

For a moment the spinning cage of her thoughts paused, and she moved forward in a straight and horrible line. Since her engagement to Bertie those two had not met. Bertie had returned her wedding-present; he had refused to have her at the house. Why? Because he was afraid of seeing her, lest The fire had burned for her; what if it had *not* yet burned itself out?

CHAPTER XVII

The London season was over, and with most admirable industry, now that that garden was empty of flowers, the bees of the world flew in all directions to other gardens, where the autumn flowers bloomed. Cowes was crammed, Carlsbad—this was a medicinal flower—was crammed also. Scotland was beginning to echo with the buzzing, and in a hundred country houses all over the kingdom other bees were resting a moment, cleaning the pollen from their legs, as it were, before they went forth again.

One hot August afternoon a small company of bees were pollen-cleaning at Haworth, talking over, that is to say, the events of the last few months— London's little adventures and ironies. With the exception of Bertie, who was in Scotland with his wife, the party was much the same as that which had sat there just a year ago, before the departure of him and Sybil Massington to America. In fact, the only other change was that the latter was Mrs. Massington no longer. But, just as before, she sat in an extremely comfortable chair on the lawn, with Charlie by her side, and Ginger, his hat over his face, lying on the grass in front of them. As before, also, he was employed in editing the history of the world, and making parenthetical prophecies for the future.

'Oh, we are certainly getting on,' he was saying, 'and the last year, I am happy to inform you, shows great progress. The Palmerization of England is perhaps the most significant sign of the times. England, in fact, consists of men, women and Palmers, chiefly the latter. If you want to go by trains anywhere, the money you pay for your ticket goes into the pockets of Palmers. If you want——'

'You shouldn't complain, then,' interrupted Sybil.

'I don't; I like it. At least, I like most of it. But not all. I went down to Molesworth the other day. There were gangs of navvies busy on the construction of the line. That I don't mind; it was remote from the house.'

'But until Mr. Palmer bought it, you were all remote from the house, too,' said Sybil. 'You none of you ever went near it.'

'Quite true. Reverberating throbs shook the air where they were blasting the tunnel. That also I don't mind, but on the lawn, in the glades, in the garden, they were sinking bore-holes to find the extent and direction of the new coalfield.'

'Have they found coal?' asked Charlie.

'Yes; they found it in the tunnel. They found it also on the Wyfold estate, between which and the tunnel lie the house and gardens. Therefore, I suppose, in a year's time the whole place will be a colliery. I don't like that.'

'I didn't think Amelie would do that,' said Sybil. 'Nor did Bertie. I remember talking to him about it. He said he thought that his wish would have influence with her. One can't blame her, any more than one blames a truffle-hound for finding truffles. It is in the blood, that scent and search for wealth. Of course, the borings are only exploratory, but what is the point of exploring if you do not mean to utilize what you find?'

'I thought she was so fond of Molesworth,' said Sybil.

'She was at first, but she has taken an extraordinary dislike to it. She——' and he stopped.

There was silence a moment.

'But they haven't quarrelled?' asked Sybil at length.

'Oh dear no. They are staying about together in Scotland now. But something has happened. What has happened, I suppose she knows. Bertie doesn't.'

'Since when was this?' asked Charlie.

'About six weeks ago, towards the middle of July—and quite suddenly. Bertie says she had been lunching with her father one day, to talk over the railway matters, and when she came back she was quite a different person. Quite polite, you understand, quite courteous and considerate, but as far away as the Antipodes.'

Sybil got out of her chair with a sudden quick movement.

'Mrs. Emsworth,' she said.

'But there was nothing to know,' said Ginger. 'There were no revelations possible, because there was nothing to reveal.'

'Mrs. Emsworth,' said Sybil again emphatically. 'I remember seeing her about that time, and she told me that Amelie had been to call on her. She said she had been rather prim, rather priggish, and in that connection made remarks about the refining influence of married life. I asked what she meant, and she said that Bertie had cut her, dropped her. She was rather incisive over it, and tried to laugh about it. But she didn't like it, all the same. I can recommend her remarks about Puritans to the attention of—of Puritans.'

Ginger sat up.

'Amelie's an awfully good sort,' he said—'and so is Bertie. But to dine with them as I did just before they went North was like dining with a piece of ice at one end of the table, and a lump of snow at the other. Now, what has happened? I reconstruct this: that Mrs. Emsworth, being annoyed with Bertie, told Amelie what friends they had been. There's a working hypothesis, anyhow.'

'But platonically,' said Charlie.

'Bertie's Platonism was—was Aristotelian in its intensity,' said Ginger. 'He once wrote a letter to her, I believe, which might have been open to misconstruction.'

'And she told Amelie about it, do you think?' asked Sybil.

'That occurs to one. There's Judy taking her Sunday walk. It's just like last year. She is coming here, and she shall give us advice.'

They called to her, but to hurry Judy when she was taking her exercise was an impossible task. However, she arrived at last, and the case was laid before her. She heard in silence, and turned to Ginger.

'Do you mind interfering?' she asked.

'No, I like it. What, then?'

'Write to Bertie. Tell him that Amelie called on Mrs. Emsworth that day.'

'Dear oracle,' observed Sybil.

Judy put down her sunshade, for here under the trees the shade was deep and the air cool.

'I hate seeing two excellent people making such a mess of their lives,' she said. 'They are both proud, they are both reticent, and neither will speak unless the other speaks first. I have a great belief in having things out. If only Amelie would pull Bertie's hair or scratch his face, and say "What are you behaving like sour milk for?" or if only he would do that to her, something must happen. But they go 011 freezing and freezing—every day the ice gets thicker. Soon it will be frozen into a solid block. That is why I advise Ginger to throw a stone at it; so to speak, without delay.'

'I don't know that Bertie will thank me,' said Ginger. 'I don't think he takes the same pleasure in being interfered with as I take in interfering.'

'Probably not. But no situation can be worse than that which at present exists. I remember I was there when she told Bertie that she had given orders to make half a dozen boring-holes for coal in the park. She announced it in the same tone as she might have announced that she had given orders for the carriage to be round at half-past two. And Bertie hardly looked up from his book, and merely said: "The diamond drill is generally used, I believe, in making bore-holes."'

'That is Bertie at his worst,' said Ginger.

'It seemed to me tolerably bad. I looked at Amelie to see how she took it. Her face was like frozen marble. But as she turned away her lip quivered a moment. It made me feel ill. Then soon afterwards I looked at Bertie. He was not reading, but staring straight in front of him. He looked as if his face was made of wood. So I say: "Stir them up at any price."'

Ginger sighed heavily.

'Vanity of vanities,' he said. 'A year ago Bertie thought that nothing would be intolerable if he had money. We most of us think the same until we have got it. Then we find that nothing, on the whole, matters less. That one sees in America. We are supposed to take our pleasures sadly. But in America they take them seriously as well. All the gold of the Indies cannot make a man gay. And all the Palmerization that is going on does not add one jot to anybody's happiness.'

'I hate it,' said Judy suddenly. 'I look on America as some awful cuttlefish. Its tentacles are reaching over the world. It grips hold of some place, and no power on earth can detach those suckers. You cannot see it coming, because it clouds the whole of the atmosphere with the thick opacity of its juice, wealth.

Thus, before you know, it is there, and you are powerless. It has come to England. It laid hold first on the newline from Liverpool to Southampton. That is spreading in all directions. It is in London in every sense of the word. What woman was the central figure there this year? The Queen? Not at all. Mrs. Palmer at Seaton House. It laid hold of Worcestershire. The huge new coalfield on the Wyfold estate is theirs. Molesworth is to be a coalfield. Then there is your admirer, Sybil. Half the theatres in London belong to Mr. Bilton. And the worst of it is that, from all practical points of view, America is our benefactor. Theatres are better ventilated and better lighted. Coal will be cheaper; one will get about the country more expeditiously. Only very soon it will not be our country. That is the only drawback, and it is a purely sentimental one.'

Sybil shivered slightly.

'Charlie,' she said, 'I look upon you as my life-preserver. A tentacle touched —just touched me. The juice of wealth, as Judy says, had prevented my seeing what was coming. But one night you were ill, do you remember?' She smiled at him, the complete smile of happiness.

'Life-preserver?' said he. 'And what were you?'

Judy turned to Ginger.

'These slight connubialities are rather embarrassing,' she said. 'Will you walk with me while I finish my exercise for the day?'

Sybil laughed.

'Don't go just yet, Judy,' she said. 'Charlie and I will send you away when we want to be alone.'

Judy rose with some dignity.

'My self-respect cannot *quite* stand that,' she said. 'Come, Ginger. You shall walk back with me to the house, and I will hold the pen when you write to Bertie.'

'I shall put that in the postscript,' he said. 'The vials of wrath shall descend on both of us.'

The two strolled away out of the shadow of the trees into the yellow flood of sunshine that hung over the lawn. The air was very windless, and the flower-beds below the house basked in full summer luxuriance of colour. Far away in a misty hollow the town of Winchester sunned itself under a blue haze of heat, and languid, dim-sounding church bells clanged distantly. Sybil turned towards her husband.

'A year ago—just a year ago,' she said, 'we sat here like this. I always remember that day as a day of pause before I started on adventures. Oh, Charlie, on what tiny things life and happiness depend! Just as a bullet may pass within an inch of your head, and not touch you, when another inch would have killed you, so the smallest incident may turn the whole course of things. For, do you know, if I had not been in Mrs. Emsworth's room when Mr. Bilton came in, I believe I should have married him.'

'Well, then you see that had just got to happen,' said Charlie, smiling at her.

'I suppose so. Do you know I am very happy to-day.'

'Why particularly?'

'Ah, one never knows the reason for happiness. If one knows the reason, one is only pleased. Ah! there is the train coming out of the cutting. What was it we settled it said?'

'You thought "Utility"; I thought "Brutalité." They sound very much alike.'

There was a pause; the train rumbled itself away into the distance, and its diminuendo grew overscored again with the sounds of summer.

'I met Mr. Bilton again the other night,' said Sybil. 'He wished me every happiness. I felt rather inclined to send the wish back, like Bertie with Mrs. Emsworth's wedding-present. He didn't please me, somehow. I don't trust him. Charlie, he is extraordinarily like you.'

'Many thanks.'

'You old darling! Do you know, I believe it was that which made me first— first cast a favourable eye on him.'

'And what made you firmly remove that favourable eye?'

'I have told you. Then I came back to England and found you ill, and I embarked on a career of most futile diplomacy. I wanted to win you back to life, you see, without permitting or harbouring any sentiment. You proposed to die because you were bored. That seemed to me feeble, futile.'

Charlie laughed.

'It was rather. But under the same circumstances I should do the same again.'

'Ah, the same circumstances can't occur.'

He turned to her with the love-light shining brightly in his eyes.

'Let us "lean and love it over again,"' he said. 'How did it happen? What change came to you? Tell me.'

'And to you?'

'There never came a change to me. I have always loved you.'

'It was your illness first of all,' she said, 'and that made me want to help. I am very practical; the futility of your dying seemed to me so stupid. And as my handiwork, the attachment of you to life, grew, I got rather proud of it. It was like taking a plant that was lying all draggled in the mud and training it upright.'

She paused a moment.

'That grew,' she went on, 'till one night you were taken suddenly ill at Davos. I came up to see you, do you remember? And at that moment—this is the only way I can explain it—I began to become a woman. So that, if you or I could owe each other anything, dear, the debt I owe you is infinitely greater than what you owe me. I gave you perhaps a few years of life, you gave me life itself and love.'

She bent her head, took up his hand where it lay on the arm of her chair, and kissed it.

'Ah, not that, Sybil,' said he.

'Yes, just that,' she answered.

The letter which the joint wits of Judy and Ginger concocted that afternoon went northwards, and reached its destination next morning. It told Bertie merely the fact that on the day on which Amelie had lunched with her father she had been to see Mrs. Emsworth afterwards, and suggested that it would be worth while finding out, if possible, what took place there. Of late the estrangement between him and Amelie, though it had in no ways healed, had been, since they were staying in other houses, where there was less opportunity for intimacy and thus less sense of its absence, less intolerably and constantly present to his consciousness. Every now and then, as on the occasion when she told him that they were going to bore for coal, there had been bitter and stinging moments, but such were rare, and their intercourse, which was rare also, was distinguished by cool if not frigid courtesy.

On this particular morning they were leaving the house they had been staying in near Inverness, and were coming South again to visit other friends in the North of England. It was perfectly natural, therefore, that Bertie should travel some part of the way, at any rate, in a smoking-carriage, but, the train being an express, he never omitted to visit her carriage when it stopped, and inquired whether she wanted anything. Once she was thirsty, and he got her some lemonade from the refreshment-room, bought her papers, and opened for her a window which was stiff to move. These little attentions were accepted by her with the same courtesy as that with which they were offered, and he would stand on the platform chatting to her through the window, or seating himself for a few minutes in her carriage, till it was time for him to go back to his own. They lunched together in her carriage, and it was at her suggestion that at the next stopping-place he went back to the other to smoke after lunch. It was then that he opened the letters which had reached him that morning, having in the hurry of departure forgotten to do so, and found Ginger's communication.

At first his impulse was to do nothing whatever, and treat the letter as if it had never been received, and, following the dictation of his *laisser aller* nature, make no further effort to investigate any possible source of his domestic estrangement. In a way (the freezing process had already gone far) he had got used to his aloofness from his wife; the acuteness of it had got dulled with time, the intolerable had become bearable. He was tired with conjecturing what had happened, and the pride which at first had prevented him straightforwardly going to her and saying 'What have I done?' had become habit. Not having done so before, he could not now, and until she voluntarily told him the matter must remain in silence. Disgust, fastidiousness, and a bitter sense of having been cheated, had at first stood in her way, where pride stood in his, and she, like him, having lost her first opportunity, waited for him to be the first to speak. But as he watched through the window the giddy scudding by of the brown wind-scoured moors, his indifference began to fade, and curiosity (at first it was no more than that) took its place. Having successfully blackmailed him, had Dorothy, in order to emphasize his own weakness, told his wife that which he had already paid so much to keep secret? To have blackmailed him at all was so utterly unlike what he knew of her that he told himself he knew nothing at all, and if this conjecture was right, she became something monstrous, something portentous. He would really very much like to know if she was stupendous enough to do that.

A rather bitter smile crossed his face, and he took out of his despatch-box a small packet containing the two letters for which he had paid so highly, and a copy of the second blackmailing letter, which he had made before he delivered his cheque and the original at Bilton's office in New York. His own letter he read through again, wondering at himself. Those words of wild adoration—even now he felt a faint internal thrill at the recollection of the mood they conjured up again—were written to a woman who had done this. It seemed to him incredible that no inkling of her real nature had ever crossed his mind. It seemed impossible that he could have loved one to whom this was possible. For mere interest in a phenomenon like this he must find out what had passed between her and Amelie. It was impossible to ask Amelie, therefore he would ask her.

He wrote to her that night asking whether he might come and see her as soon as he got to town. Their northern visits were nearly at an end, and he would be passing through in about a week's time. The matter, he added, was one which might be of great importance to him and his future happiness, and no one in the world could help him but her.

The answer he got was thoroughly characteristic—characteristic, that is, of the Dorothy Emsworth whom he knew, thoroughly uncharacteristic of the Dorothy who had blackmailed and then mocked at him by telling his wife what he had paid so heavily for her not to know.

'Charmed to see you' (it ran), 'though you have behaved so very badly. Yes, perhaps I can help you. I don't know. I am rather afraid I made mischief with your wife; but she annoyed me, and I have, as you well know, the temper of Beelzebub. Really, I am very fond of Amelie, but she is not very fond of me. Deeply pathetic, but I shall get over it.

'Yours ever,
'D. E.'

'P.S.—Thank you so much for the charming dressing-bag you sent me. I use it constantly. It has your crest and initials on it, so that I am constantly reminded of you. By the way, I shall give it you hot when we meet, so it is only fair you should be warned.'

Bertie read this and re-read it, and for the first time a doubt stood by him, dim and shadowy, but apparent, visible to the senses. This last letter was so like her; it threw into brighter light the unlikeness to her of the affair of the blackmail. Yet there was no other explanation the least plausible.

A week later they were both in London. The Palmers were there also, on the eve of their departure to America—Mrs. Palmer having spent August very pleasantly in about thirty different houses, her husband having spent it very profitably in one. In other words, he had remained the whole month in London, and devoted himself to the consolidation and extension of his English interests. He had been able to go ahead more completely on his own lines, and with his own rapidity, owing to the absence of other directors on their holidays, and, octopus-like, had spread his tentacles far and wide. But now affairs in America demanded his presence, and he was leaving his English business in the hands of Bilton, who appeared to him, the better he knew him, to be extraordinarily efficient. He was almost as rapid, and quite as indefatigable, as Mr. Palmer himself, and had the faculty of being able to absorb himself in one branch of his work from ten to eleven, and to pass without pause into a similar state of absorption over another. Since, then,

Seaton House was open, and to open their own house just for a couple of days was unnecessary, Bertie and Amelie took up their quarters there.

Mrs. Emsworth, under Bilton's direction, was to make another American tour this autumn, and was, in fact, in London only for a day or two before she left by the same boat by which the Palmers were also going. She had made an appointment with Bertie for the afternoon of the day after his arrival in London, and since she had warned him that he might expect a hot time, he took with him, in order to equalize the temperature on both sides, the contents of the packet that lived under lock and key in his despatch-box. He had himself no wish to indulge in recrimination; as he had told her, he wanted and entreated her help, but if she was proposing to hurl, so to speak, the returned dressing-bag at his head, the letter seemed to him of the nature of a gun that wanted a great deal of silencing.

She was at home when he arrived, and he was at once shown up into the room he knew so well. The outside blinds were down to keep out the stress of the August heat, and the air was thick with the scent of flowers. Then there came the rustle of a dress on the landing outside, and she entered.

'Are you there, Bertie?' she asked. 'It is so dark one can see nothing.'

She drew up one of the blinds.

'That is better,' she said. 'Now, what do you want?' She gave him no other greeting of hand-shake, but sat down on the sofa opposite the chair where he had been sitting. At the sight of her all his pent-up anger and indignation rushed to the surface; he had not known before how vile what she had done seemed to him.

'What have I done to you that you should treat me like this?' he broke out. 'Once I gave you my heart, myself, all I was, and you laughed at me. Then— oh my God! it is too much.'

She looked at him in blank surprise.

'You got over it,' she said. 'You married somebody else. I think I behaved rather well. If I had chosen I might have made things unpleasant for you. But I am not that sort of woman.'

Bertie heard himself laugh, though he was unconscious of any amusement.

'I paid you a high price, and you cheated me,' he said.

'I paid you again. That was not enough, but you must needs tell her. That is the sort of woman you are.'

Dorothy sat up.

'Either you are mad or I,' she said. 'I think it is you. As I told you, your wife annoyed me. She was prim, priggish, Puritan. I thought it would do her good to know that once you were foolish enough to write me a letter. I wished I had kept it, I remember. I should have liked to have seen her face when I showed it her. I can't bear prigs. But you paying me, and I cheating you? If you will excuse the expression, I wish the devil you would tell me what you mean.'

Bertie leant forward.

'You are inimitable,' he said. 'I never much respected your power as an actress till to-day. But I see I was wrong. You told me you were getting rich. So rich, perhaps, that ten thousand pounds for a forgery, and then five thousand more, escape your memory.'

He got up; the mere statement of what she had done, now that he was face to face with her, infuriated him to a sort of madness of rage.

'If you will excuse the expression, you' devil,' he said.

He came a step nearer, and saw her shrink from him, and look round as if to see where the bell was.

'No, no; I am not going to touch you,' he said. 'You needn't be frightened.'

He took from his pocket the letters, and unfolded them.

'Do you remember this, and this?' he said. 'And this, a copy of the instructions you gave? All that I think I could have forgiven you. But on the top of it, you tell Amelie. By your own confession you tell her that, and anything more, I suppose, that occurred to you. No doubt you told her that you had gratified my passion for you. That is the only thing that can account for the change that came over her from the time she saw you.'

Dorothy's frightened look had passed completely off.

'Give me those, Bertie,' she said quietly. 'Before God, I swear to give you them back. You can trust me. I don't use that name unless I mean it.'

His anger had so transported him that his errand to her had been forgotten. He had come to ask for her help, to learn anyhow, if she would tell him, exactly what she had said to Amelie. But the sight of her had somehow driven him to frenzy, to a pitch of passionate anger which he had not known he was capable of. But her words, the quietness of them, the sobriety with which she spoke, sobered him. There was something, too, in her tone that convinced him. So in silence he handed them all to her.

She read through them all without once raising her eyes. Then she gave them back to him, and sat still with eyes downcast. When she raised them, he saw that they were full of tears.

185

'I know nothing whatever of the whole affair,' she said.

'The torn letter, I think, is yours. I remember tearing it up myself on the day on which you came to see me in New York. The other two I know nothing of. And you thought—you, Bertie, who knew me—thought I had done that.'

'I thought you had done that!' he repeated mockingly.

Then his doubt stood beside him again, a little clearer, a little more precise in outline, and his tone changed.

'You didn't do it?' he said.

She looked at him, half in scorn, half in pity.

'I!' she said in a tone indescribable, and no more. She was far too deeply hurt to reproach him; no words could meet the situation. But, looking at him, she saw the anger die out of his face, and knew that he believed her.

'I am sorry, I am sorry,' he stammered.

She made a gesture of impatience.

'Tell me all about it from the beginning,' she said; and she heard him in silence.

'And you thought I had done that,' she said. 'Certainly it looked like it, but you ought to have known it was impossible. You did not. Now listen.'

She paused a moment.

'Bertie, for many months you saw me almost daily, and guessed nothing. Of all the men I have known—I have known several—I loved one. You. That was why I always refused you. It was my one decent impulse. It was not easy for me. Nor was it easy for me to see you marry Amelie. But I loved you, and liked her. And in a very dim and vague sort of way I realized that there was such a thing as keeping good, as being clean. Even I realized that. So I kept you by me as long as I could, because your passion for me made you lead a proper life. You did not know that other women even existed while you could see me. Then you wrote that letter, and I knew that I could resist no longer if I continued to see you. So I sent you away. I have done a good many horrible things in my life, but I have done just that one decent one. One thing more. You have never known me do a mean thing. I wonder you dared think it was I who blackmailed you. Now, that is absolutely all. I have no other word to say about myself.'

'I have one,' he said. 'Can you forgive me?'

'I have no idea,' she answered.

She got up and walked once or twice up and down the room, he sitting where he was, not looking at her, but hearing only the *frou-frou* of her dress. Then he heard the sprit of a lighted match, and a moment afterwards she blew a great cloud of smoke into his face.

'You disgusting, horrible pig!' she said. 'My fingers simply tingle to box your ears. Now, what is to be done? It is perfectly clear who blackmailed you, and if you like you can have him in the hollow of your hand.'

'Bilton,' said Bertie.

'Of course. He really is rather a charming character. He had a grudge against me, because I told Sybil Brancepeth of—of past events. He has made a good attempt to pay it off. Now, what will you do? Personally, I should like you to prosecute him, and I will come to the trial. You could get him years and years for that. But you must not do it except with your wife's permission. England is the home of linen-washing in public; it is the one industry that remains to us. But you must ask her first. Tell me, what terms are you on?'

'Polite speaking terms.'

Dorothy laughed.

'What fools husbands and wives are!' she remarked. 'Why don't you have it out with her? Why don't you explode, boil over, beat her, or something? It is partly my fault, too. I saw she thought there was more to be told, and I did not trouble to convince her, for she did behave so primly. Nose in the air, as if I was a bad smell.'

She paused a moment.

'Go to her now at once,' she said, 'before you have time to think it over. Show her the letter; tell her the whole story. Off with you. Ah! wait a minute.'

She left the room quickly, and came back again with the dressing-bag in her hand.

'Will you take it now?' she said, with her enchanting smile.

He could not speak; there was a pathos about her gaiety that gripped his throat.

'All happiness to you and her, dear Bertie,' she said. 'Now go away.'

It was between eleven and twelve that night when Bertie left the smoking-room and went upstairs. His wife had gone some quarter of an hour before, but Mr. Palmer had detained him talking. He tapped at her bedroom door; her maid opened it, and after a moment he was admitted. She was sitting before her glass in a blue silk and lace dressing gown, and her hair, a rippling sheet of molten gold, was streaming down her back.

'You want to speak to me?' she asked.

'If I may.'

'You can go,' she said to the maid. 'I will send for you if I want you.'

Amelie got up, smoothing her hair back behind her ears. If she had been the most finished coquette, she would have done exactly that; art would have imitated the complete naturalness of the movement. Her face was very pale, and looked infinitely weary, but its beauty, the beauty of that falling river of gold, the beauty of her bare arm, and the gentle swell of her bosom, half seen through the low opening of the neck of her dressing-gown, had never been more dazzling. But her eyes were lustreless; they looked on him as on a stranger.

'What is it?' she asked.

He tried to school his tongue to begin, but for the moment it would not.

'Would to-morrow do as well?' asked Amelie. 'I am rather tired.'

'No; I want to tell you to-night,' said he. 'It is about Mrs. Emsworth.'

She flushed, and turned her head a little away.

'I do not care to hear,' she said.

'I must tell you, all the same,' he said.

She shrugged her shoulders ever so slightly.

'I cannot prevent you,' she said.

She sat down by her toilet-table, turning only a shoulder to him, and with her cool white hands idly arranged the things that stood there, and he began his tale. He told her everything from the beginning: of his wild infatuation for Mrs. Emsworth, of the absolute innocence of that attachment, and of the letter he had written. She interrupted him here.

'I do not see why you tell me this,' she said. 'I knew all you have told me.'

'You did not know it from me,' he said. 'That makes a difference.'

For the first time her face softened a little.

'Yes,' she said, 'I see that.'

'Do you believe what I tell you?'

She turned now and faced him.

'No, Bertie, I am afraid not,' she said. 'It is not reasonable. We all know what sort of a woman Mrs. Emsworth is. You say you were madly in love with her. We know also what a man's code of morality usually is. Is it reasonable?'

'There is a reason,' he said.

'Tell it me, then.'

'It is hard to tell you,' he said. 'But it is this: She loved me. For that reason she wished me not—not to act unworthily. So she laughed at me. She sent me away.'

Amelie got up and stood in front of him, with head downcast. Instinctively and completely she knew this to be the truth, and was humbled. She touched his arm gently with her finger-tips.

'Yes, that is a very good reason,' she said. 'Bertie, I am sorry. All these awful weeks I have believed the other. It has made everything black and bitter to me.'

'Have you minded so much?' he asked.

'I have minded more than I can possibly tell you,' she said. 'But I believe you now. And I am sorry.'

Bertie took her hand and kissed it. There was more to tell yet.

'I want to tell you first about the letter,' he said, 'and then there is just one word more. Mrs. Emsworth destroyed it, or believed she did, but it fell into the hands of a man, whom I will name if you wish. At least, she regards it as certain it was he. He blackmailed me twice over it, sending me once a copy of the letter, the second time the letter itself. I paid him both times.'

'Who was it?' asked she.

'Harold Bilton. Now, what do you wish me to do?'

'It will mean publicity if you prosecute him?' she asked. 'All those horrors of a court?'

'Yes.'

'I don't think I could bear it about you,' she said. 'Threaten him if you like. Get back your money if you can. But not that, Bertie.'

'It shall be as you wish.'

'Do you want to very much?'

'I see red when I think of him,' said he.

'Ah, don't, don't!' she said.

She was silent a moment.

'One thing more, then,' he said. 'I want to show you the letter. I want you to know all. I have brought it here. Will you read it?'

'Yes, if you wish,' she said.

She took it from him, and went over to the brighter light of the dressing-table to read it by. It was long, and it took her some minutes, and in those minutes she learned for the first time what a man's love could be, and she envied with a sense of passionate longing the woman to whom it was written. That was the fire he had spoken of. When she had finished she gave it back to him.

'I have read it all,' she said. 'Poor Bertie! You suffered.'

She paused, and suddenly her jealousy and her desire flamed high.

'You never spoke to me like that,' she said.

His white face looked down on her.

'No, dear. Since then, until weeks after we were married, I thought all power of feeling like that was dead in me. I had forgotten what it meant. I could not imagine ever wanting to care like that again. Then by degrees you and your sweetness and your love and your beauty awoke the desire again. That desire grew, and my power to feel it grew with it, till it trembled on the verge of passion. It was growing every day when things began to come between us, till in these last weeks we have been worse than strangers.'

Something woke in her eyes that he had not seen there for months.

'And will it grow again now?' she asked. 'Or have I spoiled it all?'

He drew her to him.

'Amelie, forgive me,' he said. 'Whether you can or not, I don't know, but if you still care for me at all, try, try to help me.'

The light in her eyes grew more wonderful.

'If I care for you?' she asked. 'If I care for you?'

He kissed her on her beautiful eyes and on her mouth.

'So it is all told, dear,' said he, 'and you will help me. You look very tired. I have been keeping you up.'

'I am not tired now,' she said. 'And, Bertie, Bertie, there is one thing yet. Before very many months I shall be the mother of your child.'

And the long pent-up tempest of her love for him broke, overwhelming and flooding her. Her arms were pressed round his neck, and from his shoulder she raised her face to his.

'Your child,' she whispered again.

CHAPTER XVIII

On the second morning after this Bilton was seated at breakfast, with his confidential secretary by him, who was engaged in opening and reading his letters to him, and taking shorthand notes of his replies. Bilton himself glanced at the envelopes and directions first, and reserved for his own opening anything that carried a superscription of privacy, or was in the hand of anyone with whom he was on terms of intimacy. There were never many of these; the bulk of his daily correspondence was of a purely business character, which was, on the whole, infinitely more to his mind than the effusions of friends. Of late his mail-bag had put on weight enormously, the English affairs of Mr. Palmer and the swelling trade of his own personal enterprises having almost doubled it in the last few months; but this increase was wholly welcome to him, since every letter received and answered meant business.

On this particular morning there was nothing, as far as he could see, designed for his private eye, and the quiet, smooth-voiced young American who sat by him had the field to himself. Some letters required but a monosyllabic reply from his master, which he jotted down in a corner of the page; others were longer, and demanded some half-page of cabalistic notes; others, again, were set aside to be dealt with by Bilton himself. There were to-day several of them dealing with the subject of a threatened strike at the railway works which were in process of establishment at the junction where the Cardiff line, now in process of construction, would join the existing Liverpool and Southampton. The business was an annoying one; bricklayers employed on repairs on a tunnel there were already out, and now a demand came from platelayers on the same section. Another letter was from the engineer in charge of that section of the line. The entrance to the tunnel, on the work of which the bricklayers had been employed, was, of course, perfectly safe with its wooden casing and strutting, but in case of heavy or continuous rain the ground might get soft, and the struts sink in the ground, thus rendering the passage unsafe for trains. He suggested that labour should be brought from elsewhere at once, unless the men could be induced to go back to work.

The letters dealing with this Bilton had caused to be put on one side; towards the end of his breakfast he asked for a second reading of them. Some of the matters appeared to him to be rather urgent; in addition to that, Mr. Palmer was leaving for Liverpool and America the next morning, and would thus be out of touch for the next eight days. So, after a little consideration, he dictated a telegram to say that he would go down there himself that afternoon.

There were but few letters remaining, and, during Bilton's pause for consideration, the secretary had opened the rest, and had them ready to read. The next was from Amelie.

'DEAR SIR,

'Kindly order all work of coal-boring on the Molesworth property to be stopped until further instructions from me.

'Faithfully yours,
'
AMELIE KEYNES.'

Bilton frowned, and held out his hand for this.

'I'll answer that,' he said. 'Go on.'

The smooth-voiced secretary proceeded:

'We are instructed by our client the Earl Keynes to apply to you for the prompt payment of the sum of fifteen thousand pounds. Should your cheque for this not reach us by the evening of Tuesday, September 3, his lordship will place the matter in other hands. He desires me to admit no discussion either from you or your representatives.

'We are, dear sir,
'Faithfully yours,
'HOBARTS & HOWARD.'

Bilton did not ask for this; he plucked it out of the young man's hand.

'Anything more?' he asked.

'No, sir; that is all.'

'Very good. I shall leave by the two o'clock train for Molesworth. I shall spend the night there, and get back to-morrow. If by the evening's post to-day or by to-morrow morning's post there is anything further from Messrs. Hobarts and Howard, telegraph it to me.'

Bilton did not at once move from the breakfast-table after his secretary had left him, but remained seated there, his elbow on the table, his lips caressing an unlit cigar. Adept as he was at seeing combinations, and supplying from his imagination factors which alone would account for certain combinations presented to him as problems, he could not at once see his way through this. More than that, he could not determine with any internal satisfaction on his next move. That move might, of course, be merely a negative move—mere inaction on his part; but, turn the matter over in what way he might, he could not see how to say 'check' in answer to this 'check.' He was threatened— threatened, too, by a firm of eminently reputable solicitors who presumably would not undertake business of any but the securest nature. Fifteen thousand pounds, it is true, did not mean anything very particular to him, but he saw further than that. Should he pay it, the very fact of his payment was equivalent, to his shrewd American brain, to a confession of his guilt. What if he paid only to find that he had clinched the proof against himself? And if he did not pay, if he shrugged his shoulders at the whole matter, what if the 'other hands' were entrusted with it?'

He rose from the table, biting his cigar through.

'The blackmailer blackmailed,' he muttered. 'New sensational novel. Guess I'll think it over.'

He glanced again at the letter, and saw that he had till the evening of the next day in which to commit himself definitely to one or the other course of action. He would be back in London in the course of the next afternoon; there would be time then, and to-day he was really too busy to give the matter the attention which he was afraid it deserved. But by mid-day to-morrow the affair of the strike in any case would be off his mind; he would devote the whole of the hours occupied by his journey back to London, if necessary, to the consideration of this matter. Then there was the note from Amelie stopping the coal-boring.... In a moment a possible reconstruction of what had happened suggested itself to him. She knew.

He went down to the scene of the strike that afternoon, and found things rather more serious than he had anticipated. The bricklayers had already gone out, the platelayers had sent in demands which he did not feel himself justified in accepting without consultation with Mr. Palmer, and, what was much more serious, in spite of their indentures, there was a hint of trouble with the signalmen. It took him, indeed, some two or three hours to find out the full extent of that with which the line was threatened, and in the back of his mind all the time was the consciousness of that with which he himself was threatened. He had, in fact, to leave the inspection of the tunnel till the next morning. He left also till the next morning, in case the result of his negotiations with the strikers might prove to be nugatory, the despatch of a telegram to Mr. Palmer, asking him to have the express in which he would travel to Liverpool stopped at the Wyfold junction, so that he himself might get in there, and during the journey to Liverpool talk over the situation. In that case it would be necessary also perhaps to get an extra day for himself in his own private matter; and after dinner he telegraphed to Messrs. Hobarts and Howard saying that he would reply to them by the evening of September 4. Extremely urgent business, he said, engaged his attention, and, being at a loss to understand their communication, he asked for this extension.

He went up to bed in the rather dingy hotel in which he was forced to stay, conscious of extreme weariness, but unhappily conscious of an inability to obtain the refreshment of sleep. Often before now he had suffered from insomnia, and he was aware when he got into bed that the worst form of insomnia—namely, the utter absence of the slightest drowsiness, which to some extent compensates for the absence of sleep—was likely to be his. He knew that there lay before him a seemingly infinite period of intensely active thought, inharmoniously linked with an intensely active desire for sleep. A mill-race of coherent images foamed through his brain, all tinged with failure. He cursed himself for all he had done: he had made a mess of his courtship of Sybil; he had made a mess over the wretched fifteen thousand pounds. Knowing Bertie, he thought he had known how safe this small transaction was. True, it was scarcely worth while, but the man who makes his million makes it by consideration of very much smaller sums, and it was not in his nature to have neglected any chance. The chance seemed certain: his money was paid; his letters were returned; never had blackmail gone on smoother wheels. But in his wakefulness, and in his agitation about the strike, which involved larger issues to him than the mere payment of this sum, the latter assumed nightmare proportions; it swelled and encompassed him. If he paid, there was his confession; if he did not pay, there were the 'other hands' ready to undertake the business. 'I did not think the young man had so much blood in him,' he thought, as he tossed in his abominable feather-bed.

During the last forty-eight hours the plans of the Palmer family had somewhat altered. Mrs. Palmer, for instance, had discovered that it was necessary to start at ten in the morning in order to join the Liverpool and Southampton line, by which her husband wished to travel. That was clearly out of the question, and the matter resolved itself into a decision whether they should go by Euston or spend the night at Molesworth, stopping the Liverpool express there. The latter counsel prevailed, and a couple of hours after Bilton had left London they also left, four of them; for Bertie was of the party. His plans, too, had changed. He was going to America now instead of following a fortnight later.

The inn at which Bilton passed the night was close to the railway-station at Frampton, near which on the south lay the tunnel where there was trouble with the strikers. Frampton itself was originally a small village, but was now extending huge suckers of jerry-built houses into the country; for it lay on the junction between the Liverpool and Southampton line, and the new communication with South Wales. It was on the junction, too, of the Molesworth and Wyfold estates, Molesworth lying on the north, Wyfold to the south. Consequently, the Palmer party had passed through it the afternoon before, and had got out at the station of Molesworth, some five miles further on. This, of course, was unknown to Bilton, who imagined they were still in London.

He rose from his bed the next morning feeling tired and unrefreshed, dressed, and sent a telegram to Mr. Palmer at Seaton House, asking him to have the train stopped at Wyfold, where he himself would get in, as he wanted to consult with him over the situation. It should reach him in London in plenty of time before he started, and he himself would have the greater part of the morning at Frampton, and would get over to Wyfold in time to take the train there. He wished also to see for himself the condition of the unfinished and abandoned work in the tunnel, and get an estimate, if possible, from the engineer of the shortest time in which it would be possible to finish the work without interrupting traffic, in case he decided to import labour at once. His work in connection with other matters, however, took him rather longer than he had anticipated, and he set off down the mile of line which lay between Frampton and the tunnel to meet the engineer who was appointed to be waiting for him there rather short of time. He had expected to be obliged to go over to Wyfold in the course of the morning, and he had therefore telegraphed to have the train stopped there. This had proved, however, to be unnecessary, but it was too late now to alter the rendezvous to Frampton.

The tunnel in question was a very deep burrow under some mile of hill that rose steeply above it, and its completion—or so close an approach to completion that it could be used—had been the great triumph of speed in the construction of the line. He found that the work remaining to be done was easily compassable within a week or two, if sufficient numbers of men could be brought to the spot, while there was also at the Wyfold end of the tunnel another unfinished piece of less extent, if anything, than this. The report of the engineer also put matters in rather a less serious light: the great beams and timber which supported the wooden arch over which the bricks had to be laid were at present absolutely secure; it would take weeks of rain before danger was even threatened, but would it not be well, if possible, to finish so small a job at once, and have it off their minds? Bilton was decidedly of this opinion, and gave orders that steps should be taken to get outside labour without delay. This concluded his morning's work.

He looked at his watch; it was later than he had known, and to walk back a mile to Frampton, where he could get a trap, and then drive over the huge ridge of the tunnel down into Wyfold, might mean missing the train, which would stop for him there, but would assuredly not wait if he was not on the platform. But the engineer had an easy solution. Why not walk through the tunnel, which would take very little longer than going back to Frampton? He would thus find himself within a mile of the Wyfold Station? He could get there in very little over half an hour, going briskly, and would easily be in time to step into the stopped express. No train was due on either line for the next half-hour; in fact, the next train that would pass would be the Southampton to Liverpool express, in which at the moment he would himself be travelling. The engineer would provide him with a lantern, which he could leave at the signal-box at the other end of the tunnel.

This seemed an admirable arrangement, and in a couple of minutes he had set off. The light cast by the lantern was excellent; it shone brightly to guide his path, and gleamed on the rails of the four tracks as they pointed in narrowing perspective up the black cavern that lay before him until they were lost in the darkness. He walked on the right-hand side of the tunnel; immediately on his left, was the main line from Southampton to Liverpool, along which he would soon return at a brisker pace than that which was his now. For some hundreds of yards the gray glimmer from the end of the tunnel where he had entered also cast a diffused light into the darkness, but as he proceeded the light faded and grew dim, and when he was now some third of the way through, the slight continuous bend in the tunnel, which had been necessary in order to avoid a belt of unstable and shifty strata, obscured it altogether, and he walked, but for the light from his lantern, in absolute darkness. His own footsteps echoed queerly from the curved vault, but there was otherwise dead silence save for some occasional drip of water; all outside noises of the world were entirely cut off from him.

He was stepping along thus when he saw, with a sudden start of horror, that there was something dark lying between the second and third pair of rails a little way ahead of him. From the fact that he started, he was conscious that his nerves were not working with their accustomed smoothness and coolness, and he heard his heart hammering in his throat. Then he pulled himself together, crossed the two rails which lay between him and it, turned the lantern on it, and saw next moment, with a spasm of relief, that it was only a coat, left there and forgotten, no doubt, by some workman. With a cheap impulse of kindness, he picked it up, meaning to leave it with his lantern at the signal-box at the far end. But as he picked it up and stepped on again to regain the side path where he had been walking, his foot tripped in it, or on the corner of some sleeper, and he fell forward, the lantern flying from his hand, and smashing itself to atoms on the hard metal of the road, and his head struck full on the temple against the steel of the track. The blow completely stunned him.

About the same time the party left Molesworth to drive to the station, where the Liverpool express would be stopped for them. It was a distance of not more than three miles, but they stopped in the village close to the station in case there was anything at the post-office which had come by the second post, and would thus miss them. There was only one thing—a telegram from Bilton, re-directed from Seaton House, asking that the train might be stopped at Wyfold. So they drove on to the station, and there learned that the express had already passed through Wyfold without stopping, and would reach Molesworth in six or seven minutes. So Mr. Palmer, who never wasted regrets on the inevitable, shrugged his shoulders and inspected the book-stall, while Mrs. Palmer inundated the telegraph-office with despatches, and Bertie and Amelie strolled up and down the platform.

Bilton came to himself with a blank unconsciousness of where he was. It was quite dark, and he first realized that he was not in bed by the feel of his clothes. Then he put his hand to his head, and drew it away with a start of horror, for it was warm and wet. Then he felt with his hand the metal of the roadway, and, following that, encountered one of the rails. At that the broken ends of memory joined themselves, and he knew where he was. Simultaneously he heard the dead silence broken by a distant roar and rumble.

At this he started to his feet, wavered, and nearly fell again. All his senses were suddenly electrified, vivified, by that noise, and he remembered all— how he had started to walk through the tunnel, how he had picked up the coat, how he had fallen, how the engineer had told him that the next train through would be that to Liverpool. But where was he? On which line had he fallen? There were four tracks; he thought he ought to move to the right across the rails—no, to the left. Hell! was it to the right or to the left that that train would pass?

The roar got louder; it echoed with an infernal clangour from the curved sides of the tunnel; it prevented him thinking, and he felt sure that if it would only stop for one second his head would be clear, and he could take two steps to safety. But that noise must stop a moment, and in a frenzy, no longer master of himself, he shouted hoarsely, and impotently waved his hand in the darkness. From which way did it come? From in front of him or behind him? If he could only settle that, he would know what to do.

The roaring grew unbearable: it drove him mad; and, with his fingers in his ears, he began to run he did not know where, and he again tripped on some rail and fell. On the sides of the tunnel there shone a red, gloomy light, but he did not see it; above the roar and rattle of the racing wheels there sounded the hot, quick panting of some monster, but he did not hear it. He knew one moment of awful shock, of the sense of being torn and battered in pieces; then the roar sank down, as the train passed on, and diminished into silence as it emerged from the darkness of the tunnel into the pure and glorious sunlight of that September morning. And to him who had been pitiless and relentless in life had come death as swift and relentless as himself.

Amelie and Bertie were at the fore-end of the platform when the express drew up, and they turned back. Just as they got opposite the engine, Bertie gave one short gasp of horror, and grasped his wife's arm.

'Bertie, what is it?' she said.

'Go on, Amelie,' he said quickly. 'Don't look to right or left, but walk straight on.'

She obeyed him, and he went to the engine-driver.

'There is something on your engine,' he said.

EPILOGUE

It was a March day of glorious windy brightness, and all down the glades of Molesworth, where Bertie and Amelie had sat one hot morning in June last year, innumerable companies of daffodils danced and flickered in the sun. The great trees were yet for the most part bare of leaves, but round the birches a green mist hovered, and the red buds on the limes were ready to burst. Boisterous, but warm and fruitful, and teeming with the promise of the opening year, the wind shouted through the branches, and bowled, as a child bowls a hoop, great fleecy clouds across the blue of the sky. Movement, light, fruitfulness of the warm earth, were all triumphant; the strength of all that lived was renewed; spring was there.

To-day Amelie was pacing alone up and down the glade near the fallen tree-trunk where she had sketched before. She walked briskly, for it was not yet a day to loiter in; and as she came to the end of her beat within sight of the house, she looked eagerly towards it as if expecting someone. But the brilliance of her face and of the smile that every now and then hovered round her lips was in no way diminished when she turned again without seeing him whom she waited for. It seemed she was content to wait, and, though eager, did not fear disappointment.

The grass where she walked was all bright with the springing shoots of young growth, and the daffodils nodded and tossed their heads all round her. Not yet was the full note of woodland summer sounding, but the great orchestra of nature, as it were, was tuning up for the concert. Somehow the fragmentary broken sounds and scraps of summer melody strangely pleased her; often she stopped in her walk, and looked with her brilliant smile to right and left. Once she threw her arms wide, so that her red cloak stood away from her bosom, as if to take the world to it.

At last he came, and her heart embraced him ere yet he reached her. He was hatless, and the yellow gold of his hair was tossed by the wind. At the sight of him her whole being leaped towards him with stronger ecstasy than she had known yet, for the love between them seemed perfect; and she, woman-like, and loving her task, knew that a little word of comfort and sympathy was demanded of her.

'Dear one,' she said, and 'Dear one' again. 'Poor Bertie! you look tired. You should have waited the night in London, and come down this evening.'

'Should I, when you were waiting?' he asked. 'Oh, what a morning from God! And you, Amelie, among the daffodils.'

She put her arm into his.

'Tell me,' she said, 'did you get there in time? Did your father know you?'

Bertie shook his head.

'No; he knew no one from the time of his seizure. But I am glad I went. He will be buried here on Friday.'

She pressed his arm; that sympathy of touch was more eloquent to him than words.

'And the baby?' he asked.

'Oh, Bertie, so wonderful! Nurse says he will speak in no time at all if he goes on like this. She says she never saw such a clever baby.'

Bertie laughed.

'That is a remark I never heard before,' he said.

'Then you will hear it lots of times in future,' said Amelie with some dignity; 'nurse says it nearly every day.'

They had passed out of the shade of the trees on to the lawn near the house. Just in front of them was an ugly patch of black-looking earth, on which, however, the new growth of grass was beginning to show. Amelie stopped when they came to it.

'Ah, Bertie, those weeks!' she said—'those weeks when we were strangers!

This black patch, where the bore-hole was begun, makes them more vivid to me than my memory of them. It is like them—a black patch.'

'Yet the grass springs again,' said he.

She took both his hands in hers.

'Yes, Bertie,' she said, 'the grass springs again, for the winter is past; I read it this morning only. It says beautiful things. "The flowers appear on the earth, and the time of the singing of birds is come." That is now, is it not? Then, further on, "My beloved is mine, and I am his."'

'And that is the best of all,' said he.

THE END